"I T[...] a Certai[...] Toward You.

"By what right?" Diana snapped.

"Last night," he whispered. "I believe that gives a man some rights, don't you?"

"Really, Beau, I hardly think that—"

"I do think that. I think it was special, and you're special, and you owe it to me to behave in a certain way."

"In what certain way? Like your mistress? Like your chattel? Like a southern belle?"

"Like a woman who's made a commitment."

"Do you know what I'm committed to, Beau?"

Beau sighed wearily. "To your job. To your story. To the truth. But what I want to know," he went on softly, "is when you're going to commit yourself to the other part of you. The woman. The lover."

Dear Reader:

There is an electricity between two people in love that makes everything they do magic, larger than life. This is what we bring you in SILHOUETTE INTIMATE MOMENTS.

SILHOUETTE INTIMATE MOMENTS are longer, more sensuous romance novels filled with adventure, suspense, glamor or melodrama. These books have an element no one else has tapped: excitement.

We are proud to present the very best romance has to offer from the very best romance writers. In the coming months look for some of your favorite authors such as Elizabeth Lowell, Nora Roberts, Erin St. Claire and Brooke Hastings.

These books are for the woman who wants more than she has ever had before. These books are for you. As always, we look forward to your comments and suggestions. You can write to me at the address below:

Karen Solem
Editor-in-Chief
Silhouette Books
P. O. Box 769
New York, N.Y. 10019

Diana's Folly

Jillian Blake

Silhouette Intimate Moments

Published by Silhouette Books New York

America's Publisher of Contemporary Romance

SILHOUETTE BOOKS, a Division of Simon & Schuster, Inc.
1230 Avenue of the Americas, New York, N.Y. 10020

Copyright © 1983 by Jillian Blake

Distributed by Pocket Books

ISBN: 0-671-49243-8

First Silhouette Books printing November, 1983

10 9 8 7 6 5 4 3 2 1

America's Publisher of Contemporary Romance

Printed in the U.S.A.

For Cindy and Betsy,
who helped me spin a yarn

Chapter 1

"RIGHT THIS WAY, MA'AM. ROOM 406." THE BELLHOP LED the way smartly into the room. "Looks to me like your friend's already come and gone."

"My friend? Come and gone where?" Diana Jennings looked at the young man, not knowing what he meant. The bellhop laid her two canvas suitcases heavily across a double bed and nodded toward the open suitcase strewn across the other bed a few feet away.

"I'd lay odds the lady high-tailed herself down to the Poolsider Bar," the bellhop informed her sagely. "That's where most of the print people hang out." He pursed his lips. "On the other hand, if you was TV folks instead of newspaper folks, I'd guess she was over at the Gazebo—that's our outdoor bar. But seeing as y'all are from the New York *Chronicle* . . ." He let the sentence trail off unfinished, and pleased with the wealth of inside information he had displayed, a grin spread across his freckled face like a slow drawl.

"Ah. You must be talking about Alison." Diana

nodded, making a small clicking sound with her tongue against the inside of her teeth to hide her exasperation. She had completely forgotten that she would be sharing the hotel room with Alison Chase, a feature writer for the *Chronicle*. Forgotten, most likely, because sharing a room was a minor annoyance and there had been some less than minor annoyances to deal with in the past few days. A late-breaking story to finish up in New York had meant arriving later than planned in Louisville, not to mention having to endure a grasshopper flight that seemed to stop on every available runway south of Virginia. And then there was the added strain of having to pretend she didn't care that someone else had been assigned the Red Sox while she was sent down here to . . .

Diana sighed heavily and laid her briefcase and typewriter on the bureau. "Yes," she said, as much to herself as to the bellhop, "I expect that's exactly where the lady high-tailed herself."

She had not intended to imitate the man's broad southern accent. Now, noticing that he blinked and recoiled his chin slightly at her words, Diana realized the man thought he was being ridiculed. To soften the effect, she smiled swiftly and winked. "Then I guess the Poolsider's the place to be, huh?"

The bellhop's grin popped back onto his face. "You bet!" he exclaimed. "It's a regular city-room circus down there this afternoon!"

"City-room circus—That's cute; that really is." Diana smiled appreciatively.

"Oh, that's not my own original personal idea, ma'am," the bellhop said quickly. "That's just what Beau Gatling calls it. A regular old three-ring city-room circus, that's what ol' Beau says."

"I see." Diana cocked her head, cucumber-green eyes wide with polite interest. "And who is this ol' Beau Gatling?"

"You don't know Beau?" The bellhop glanced automatically at the press pass pinned to Diana's straw-colored linen jacket as if he suddenly suspected the validity of her credentials. "Beauregard Gatling? Of the *Louisville Times-Union?* The ace word jockey?"

He seemed so distressed by the mere possibility that Diana didn't have the heart to admit her ignorance. "Ohhhh. *That* Beau Gatling!" She turned away so he wouldn't see her smile at the look of pure relief that passed over his face. "Yes," she mused dryly to her reflection in the mirror over the bureau, "that does sound like something ol' Beau would say, now that you mention it."

The bellhop nodded briskly. "Anyway," he confided, his confidence restored, "I can tell you the party just goes on and on down there, all the way through Derby Week. The Gazebo's just the same. Right through the race, too." He shook his head, awed at the idea of such fortitude. "I don't mind telling you, ma'am, I sometimes wonder if those guys even leave the bar to watch the race!"

Diana laughed so heartily at this that the bellhop began to swagger, although he was careful not to move out of range when he saw her rummaging through her purse for a tip.

"Still, they do write their stories, so I guess someone's on the job, right?" He leaned against the wall by the bureau, obviously in the mood for more cozy chatting. "Anyway, you'll probably be spending a lot of time down there too, huh, just like your friend." He gazed at Diana with new interest. "Not a bad place to hang out, I guess, with all those guys and all."

Still smiling, Diana met his admiring eyes as she handed him a dollar bill. She had recognized the all-too-familiar change of tone, but the bellhop ignored her dismissive silence and chattered on.

"Nice-looking lady like yourself, in the middle of all that excitement—you' darned lucky to have that press pass, I can tell you that." He didn't seem to notice that Diana had risen to her full height so that he had to look slightly upward in order to gaze meaningfully into her eyes. "You write fashions or something for that New York paper?" He shook his head. "Mighty lucky to be down here for the Derby," he repeated.

"I don't write fashion." Diana glanced obliquely at the kid, but his eyes were lingering in the vicinity of her press badge, so he didn't see the warning on her face.

"Down here for the female angle, then," he replied promptly. "It's a good idea, especially with that filly running so hot. That Diana's Folly—a cute angle, yeah, I see." His eyes gleamed at his own cleverness.

Diana turned back to the mirror. The bellhop's obstinate presence was beginning to wear on her already-weary nerves. She would have to get him out of her room fast. Idly, she began to puff out her shoulder-length dark hair, making an effort to keep her voice even. "Good guess," she admitted, "but not quite right."

"I'm close, though, huh? I can guess these things pretty good." Delighted to be holding what he thought was a sophisticated conversation with an older woman, the bellhop leaned back more comfortably against the wall, staring at Diana's long back and flared hips with ill-concealed admiration. "What are you here to write about, then? Social stuff?"

The serene half smile never left Diana's face. She ran her fingers through the thick waves at the nape of her neck several times before turning around slowly to reply.

"Actually," she said sweetly, "I'm here from New York to deliver illicit drugs for the trainers to give their horses. For the jockeys, too, of course. And for the guys at the Poolsider. Come to think of it, ol' Beaure-gard Gatling is my best customer!"

Throughout this outrageous speech, the bellhop had been edging backward along the wall toward the door. The mixture of horror and confusion on his reddened

face was amusing, but Diana had the grace to wait until
the door had closed behind him with a sharp retort
before laughing out loud.

For several reasons, Diana did not go immediately to
join her colleagues at the Poolsider Bar. She wanted to
get settled first, unpack her typewriter and get her
bearings, both professionally and personally. Traveling
was part of her job, and she did a lot of it. But she had
found that unless she allotted time to breathe before
plunging in to whatever event she had been sent to
cover, she never quite felt caught up.

The feeling of having missed out on a crucial moment, of having forgotten to do something important
right from the start, was sure to show up in her work.
And Diana, as the only full-time female sportswriter
for the New York *Chronicle*, could not afford that. It
was her seamless flow of words, prose that an editor
had once described as "picking up the exact rhythm of
the game," that had gained her both attention and
respect in the male-dominated world of sports reporting. And, she suspected, some editors would seize upon
the slightest flaw in that seamless style to accuse her of
incompetency. It wasn't that she had to do better as a
woman—it was just that she had to constantly prove
she could do as well.

There was another reason—besides Alison, but Alison came under a different category just now—for her
reluctance to join her male peers at the Poolsider. All
during the flight she had been trying to talk herself out
of a serious beef against Cameron Davis, her editor at
the *Chronicle*, for having sent her to the Derby in the
first place. Her semimalicious behavior toward the poor
bellhop was evidence to Diana that she had not been
successful in putting the issue aside.

Of course, she had been pleased at getting the Derby
assignment. Of course, she had taken it as a mark of
Cam's special faith in her ability to turn it into a

"world-class story"—his words, not hers. Naturally, she was aware of the honor such an assignment bestowed; usually, only national press and senior staff were given plums like the Derby.

But Cam knew Diana was up to the task. He was counting, he said, on her seamless prose—that compliment had *not* originally been his—to win some national recognition for the sports desk at the *Chronicle*.

There had, of course, been something left unspoken between them during that meeting, something behind Cam's hearty praise and Diana's measured gratitude in return. Neither of them had cared to acknowledge it aloud, and that was why it still rankled Diana after three days and almost a thousand miles.

Diana had wanted another plum. She had hoped to be assigned to cover the Boston Red Sox that season. Cam had known it—everybody in the sports room had known it—and any reason he might have given for denying her the assignment would have been feeble. She had done a series of feature articles on the Sox the previous year, articles that had appeared in the *Chronicle* well below the wire-service stories and the work of the senior reporters assigned to the baseball beat. But her work had been excellent, and she had been nominated for two prestigious awards on the basis of that series.

On top of that, Cam knew that the Red Sox were Diana's personal favorites. She could write well about any major league sport, but baseball was her first love, and her home-town Boston team held a special place in her heart. She had even been approached once to do a book about the team, but Diana had felt that her objectivity as a reporter would be compromised, and she had turned the offer down.

As a result of the previous year's feature series, Diana had been fairly certain of being assigned to Fenway Park that season. Then, just before spring training, Cam had casually announced, during a weekly story meeting, that of course Lou Columbo would be going down to Winter Haven that year, just as he had for the past twenty years.

Diana had been careful to hide her disappointment. Even when several other staff members approached her after the meeting and said they thought it was unfair, Diana refused to acknowledge their sympathy.

"Nobody ever said it was fair around here," she said in a level voice. She was a good writer, and she knew it, and she was not about to let her sex become an issue at this point in her career.

No wonder people at the *Chronicle* thought she had a great mind and not much heart.

So here she was in her hotel room getting ready to cover the Kentucky Derby, the first major horse-racing assignment of her career. What she didn't know about horses would fill a rather large book. Moreover, if she were any kind of reporter, Diana told herself sternly, she would pull herself out of this puddle of self-pity and get on the case. She would get her bearings quickly, review the background material on the Derby she had been reading ceaselessly for the past week and then get herself down to that Poolsider Bar and dive right in. Diana had been a sportswriter long enough to know that the best way to get information on a sporting event was to talk to the media. They often seemed to know more about what was happening than the people involved in the event themselves.

But if she were really honest with herself, Diana would have to admit that the real reason for her reluctance to go down to the bar was, quite simply, that she was shy. Not shy in the retiring, wallflower sense— no one would ever accuse Diana Jennings of that!—but shy about mixing socially with her peers. She never felt the difference between herself and a male sportswriter when she was in a professional situation; on the playing field, in a tour bus, even in the locker room, she felt she could hold her own with any man. But as soon as the

assignment was over and her fellow workers repaired to
the nearest pub to gossip about sports and other
sportswriters, Diana began to feel awkward and self-
conscious.

She had told herself many times that good stories
often emerged from those smoky encounters. Athletes,
coaches and other writers all spoke more freely with a
couple of beers under their belts, and Diana was as
eager as any man to get a scoop any way she could. But
she simply could not bring herself to relax completely
when she got out from behind the protective barrier of
her tape recorder and note pad.

Now, standing in front of her typewriter, still packed
in its steel-gray traveling case, Diana confronted her
image in the mirror above the bureau. Despite her
grave expression, a hint of amusement warmed the cool
green color of her wide-set eyes. Dark, rather unruly
brows drew straight across them on a slight incline,
feathering in at the top of her long, aquiline nose. Her
mouth was generous, although Diana thought her lips
were too thin and their line in repose too severe. Right
now they curved in a small, ironic smile, and she stuck
out the tip of her tongue, pink against her olive skin.

Diana turned away from the mirror with a sigh and
went to the closet, shrugging off her jacket as she
walked. She hung it on a hanger next to a blazer of
Alison's—a lavender and white seersucker affair with
lilac suede lapels and elbow patches. Alison, Diana
surmised, had surely read up on the appropriate appar-
el for Louisville in May. Without thinking, Diana
reached up and smoothed the pleats of her cream-
colored blouse and tan chinos. Alison's blazer looked
so tiny next to Diana's oversized, slouchy jacket! Diana
had a brief image of herself as equally oversized and
slouchy—a collection of big bones rather than a tall,
shapely woman.

"Yes, folks, watch Diana Jennings for a glimpse of
what the well-dressed, mature figure should *not* be

wearing in Louisville this spring," she intoned to her reflection on the back of the closet door. Then another of those ironic grins lit up her dark cheeks and pale jade eyes. Actually, it was a relief, at thirty-three, despite occasional twinges of insecurity, finally to feel at home in her five feet eight inches. The length of her legs and the width of her hips no longer occupied her embarrassed attention when she entered a locker room to do a story. She had learned to carry herself in such a way that while her female attributes were hardly invisible, they took second place to the determined intelligence in her eyes and the assured pride of her smile. Her manner communicated itself to her interviewees, so that by now only the greenest of rookies would venture to make her feel uncomfortable. Naturally, they never succeeded.

"Okay, Jennings. Enough with the self-pity. Either you go down there and join the city-room circus, or you get to work up here." Approaching the bureau once again, she put her hands on her hips and addressed this ultimatum to herself. But even as she spoke, her hands went to her typewriter, lifting the heavy case easily and transferring it to a small vanity desk in between the two beds. She brushed aside a collection of cosmetics and creams, presumably Alison's, and sat down resolutely. The best excuse of all for not going down to the Poolsider was this: Diana thought best with her typewriter in front of her, and she had to get a handle on the Derby before she went out to cover it.

All sports stories worked best when they had a specific angle going for them, and the Derby, Diana knew, would be no exception. In fact, one of Diana's strengths lay in her ability to provide that strong thread that held a series together, to provide the extra insight that made her work appealing to a wider range of readers. Despite her annoyance at Cam for denying her the Red Sox beat, Diana knew she had landed a coveted assignment in the Kentucky Derby, and she had no intention of giving it anything less than her best. It was only a matter of time and patience—and a little luck, perhaps—before she could hit on a perspective that would provide her with an angle to wedge behind the bare facts.

Slipping a piece of paper into the roller, she began to type. First, to get herself into the subject, she stated the obvious: the 107th Kentucky Derby, to be run at Churchill Downs, in Louisville, Kentucky, on the first Saturday in May. She listed the mechanics of the race—its length in furlongs, the number of entrants, the nature of the track. She listed the favored entrants in that year's race, smiling as she wrote about Diana's Folly, the long-shot filly that had attracted some attention by being the first female horse ever credited with a fighting chance at the title.

Then she went on to describe the human element— the jockeys, the trainers, the owners and the crowds that converged by the hundreds of thousands during Derby Week. She explained, largely for her own benefit, the intricacies of the pari-mutuel system of betting and named some astronomical figures in order to indicate exactly how much money would be changing hands during the course of the week and how much was at stake in the equally lucrative illegal pot.

All this material had been absorbed by reading everything she could get her hands on about the Derby and horse racing in general. Right now she was just typing it all out in the hopes that she would find some item to trigger her own interest and imagination. She had memorized the salient characteristics of each horse, from front runner Street Fare to a sure-bet loser named Our Colonel. The latter horse was old enough to have sired several other race entries and was entered every year as a nostalgic gesture by some well-heeled Kentucky gentleman who could afford to lose a bundle.

In addition to the information about the race itself, Diana had found out all about the other events traditionally scheduled as part of Derby Week. There would be a steamboat race, a balloon race and even a tricycle race for grownups, as well as a score of ballyhooed "grudge" matches scheduled for Kentucky's other favorite sport, basketball. All of these, Diana speculated, had been arranged to capitalize on the hordes of tourists that had descended on Louisville over the past day or so and who would continue to arrive until the population of the city had quadrupled on Derby morn.

The name of the game was money, of course. Money motivated everyone, from the owners of the great bluegrass breeding farms right down to that funny little bellhop she had frightened away. Why, the price of her hotel room had more than doubled from its usual rate for the week, and Diana knew that instant inflation had hit everything else as well. She had no objection to the practice; after all, the "season" was only a week long, and these people had to take advantage of it while they could. Besides, the name of the game was money for the *Chronicle,* too, which was the only reason they were footing the gigantic hotel bill and Diana's other expenses. She knew they expected her to make it worth their while.

But if money was the rule, then the rule had an unwritten corollary, and Diana was aware of that as well. Rumors of corruption were always rampant when a big sporting event took place, especially a one-shot deal like the Derby. Diana wondered what the particulars of those rumors would be around Louisville this week. Was someone fixing the odds? Were jockeys being bribed to throw the race? Horses drugged? Who was said to be incorrupt, and who, incorruptible?

As always, this train of thought led Diana back to her own role as a sportswriter and the role of her peers. Of course, every reporter, no matter what their beat, wanted to get a scoop and uncover a major scandal by their own investigative efforts, and Diana was no exception. If she could find an angle that led to a major revelation—what a trophy to bring back to Cam Davis! But Diana was sure that reporters far more knowledge-able than she were hoping for the same thing, and her chances were slim at best.

Not that there wouldn't be an opportunity. Major sporting events were conducted with all the confiden-tiality and secrecy of a three-ring circus. Everyone, from the Kentucky Horsebreeders' Association to the Louisville Chamber of Commerce, was looking for a little free publicity, and Diana's briefcase was filled with engraved invitations to dinners, luncheons and cocktail parties at which her presence as a member of the media was cordially requested. The request for a free plug in her paper was unwritten but just as clear. If she so desired, there would be ample opportunities to snoop behind the scenes.

"You made it at last!"

Diana's train of thought was suddenly interrupted by the sound of the door slamming shut behind her. Turning around, she saw Alison Chase framed in the doorway, her arms laden with parcels and plastic bags.

"What's this? Christmas?" Diana switched off her typewriter and rose to greet her roommate with a grin.

"Just about. These are welcome gifts—little tokens of appreciation, don't you know, from the sweet little ol' retailers of Louisville, Kentucky."

Alison's hazel eyes sparkled as she dumped her booty on Diana's bed. She was a short, well-rounded woman with a halo of soft blonde curls that belied her sharp mind and capacity for hard work. Diana knew her mostly by reputation, since their paths at the *Chronicle* rarely crossed. But she knew her well enough not to underestimate the woman simply because she wrote "soft" news like fashion and human-interest features.

"Let's see," Alison was saying, sitting on the edge of the bed to inspect her haul. "We have a complimentary copy of the history of the Kentucky Derby, four books of passes to local eating and drinking emporiums, two T-shirts that say "Meet Me at the Twin Spires"—hey, is this supposed to be suggestive or what?" She held up one of the T-shirts, which depicted the famous spires of Churchill Downs etched across the chest.

"Maybe that's what they meant," Diana said, grinning, "but on you the only thing it suggests is your knees."

It was true. The T-shirt stopped halfway down Alison's thighs, and the twin spires drooped comically around her waist.

"Ah, well," said Alison ruefully, "I guess this gift just wasn't meant for me."

"Neither was this." Diana leaned across the bed and picked up a shaving mug with the same picture of Churchill Downs. "Or this. Or this." In rapid succession, she held up a pair of jockey shorts, a huge white hat with "the Colonel" emblazoned across its brim and a garish pamphlet proclaiming to be a full-color guide to Louisville's adult-entertainment district. The two women exchanged bemused smiles.

"What? No complimentary lipstick or perfume flacon?" Alison gave an exasperated snort. "I guess I got off at the wrong airport or something. I didn't realize this was a men-only event."

Diana laughed and stared back down at her typewriter. "Welcome to the world of sports, honey," she drawled. "Where men are men, and women are girls, and the only real form of greeting is a hard slap on the back."

She was feeling a lot better than she had before sitting down to type. Diana had always thought that having a room to herself on the road was one of the nicest side benefits of being a female in a man's world. But Alison was nice, and her dry humor suited Diana's own. She suddenly relished the prospect of a little female companionship in the week ahead.

Alison now began to gather the things off Diana's bed and stuff them into a bureau drawer. "I'll tell you one thing, though. That real world down by the Poolsider is filled with some very fine looking specimens." She arched her thin brows expressively.

"Really? Do tell." Diana displayed polite interest but turned back to her typewriter as she spoke. She made it a hard and fast rule not to mix business with pleasure—ever. The closest thing to a newspaperman she had ever dated was a New York attorney who had defended a colleague of hers on a journalistic-immunity charge. The attorney had lost the case, accused Diana of refusing to use her influence to get her colleague to cooperate, and that had been the end of that.

Alison appeared to have no such compunctions. "Oh, my, yes," she murmured, throwing herself down on her own bed amid the confusion of clothes and bags. "I particularly like the ones with that delicious southern drawl—very backward of me, I know, but it sounds so seductive!" She wriggled her shoulders and rolled her eyes.

Diana folded her arms across the keyboard and shook her head. "Careful, Alison. I've heard that drawl can make an honest woman out of the most jaded New Yorker." She smiled and arched her brows. She might not agree with Alison on this topic, but she could certainly maintain her sense of humor about it.

"I don't believe anyone could make an honest woman out of me," Alison declared stoutly, softening the statement with a wink.

"Oh, but these southern men are in a league by themselves," Diana assured her. "Didn't you know that? Why, even that darling little bellhop nearly swept me off my feet—so charming and suave! And we all know what a hard nut *I* am to crack!" She raised and lowered her eyebrows dramatically, twirling an imaginary mustache.

But Alison's next comment took her by surprise.

"Are you?" she inquired. Her tone had grown quite serious.

"Am I what?"

"As hard a nut as that?"

To her credit, Alison now met Diana's long, cool stare without blinking or attempting to soften the frank question. Diana noticed that Alison did not attempt, as others often did, to *deny* that she was a hard nut. *My reputation,* Diana thought dryly, *has spread far and wide at the Chronicle.*

"Absolutely," she replied at last with deliberate emphasis. She had made peace with that image of herself long ago. Not only was it necessary to her career, both in the newsroom and in the sports arena, but, she had discovered, it held true in her personal life as well. Perhaps "hard" was not quite accurate. Diana had a gritty perseverance that was evident in everything she did. She even talked in the same style as she wrote—firm, somewhat clipped tones that allowed subtler shadings to shine through, like the slats in a Venetian blind. In her work, it was easy to read through those shadings. Face to face, it was not quite so simple.

So Diana was not so much surprised by Alison's query as she was by the directness with which it had been asked. And Alison, she was sure, was pretty good at reading between the lines. Right now, she seemed to be taking Diana's matter-of-fact affirmation in stride. "It shows in your work," she replied simply, and Diana took this as the compliment it was meant to be. "But I'm curious," Alison went on. "Whatever made you decide to become a sportswriter? I mean, you'd be good at anything." She wrinkled her nose and giggled. "Personally, I'd prefer doing the obituary column to doing the sports page!"

Diana laughed heartily at this honest admission. "That's the story of my life," she said, chuckling. "Girl friends who thought I was out of my head and boy friends who got miffed because I knew more about sports than they did."

"All your life?"

"Yup. All my life. And I can't even blame it on having four older brothers."

"Why on earth can't you?" Alison inquired, eyes wide.

"Because I don't have four older brothers. I have two sisters, neither of whom has ever displayed the tiniest interest in sports."

"You're kidding!" Alison threw herself back against the pillows. "Then it must have been something else. Wait, don't tell me! I've got it." She snapped her fingers. "Your father was a famous football coach."

Diana grinned. "He sells insurance."

"Your mother was a famous football coach?"

"She sells real estate. Although once she did take bids on a Little League field."

Alison rolled her eyes. "Well, then, your high school sweetheart was captain of the team."

"That's true," Diana admitted. "But he dropped me like a hot potato when I beat him in a football trivia contest in front of the whole school."

"I give up!" Alison raised her arms toward the ceiling. "You are a true freak of nature, turning a Columbia journalism degree to such dastardly use. But I'll forgive you—or I will if you promise to get up from that typewriter and come back down to the Poolsider with me."

Diana turned to her unfinished work. "I don't know," she said reluctantly. "I still haven't got what I want out of this material. And I have to do some clear thinking before the madness begins. Which, if I'm not mistaken"—she consulted her watch—"is due to happen in about two hours at the press conference down in the lobby."

"That's exactly my point," Alison exclaimed, jump-

ing off the bed to rummage through the pile of clothes
on which she had been lying. "All that dry stuff you've
got there isn't going to do you a bit of good until you
get down there and experience the madness. I truly
suspect that's the only angle to take on this Derby
nonsense."

Diana watched her forage. "Is that the angle you're
going to take?"

"I wish." Alison threw several lacy articles of clothing over her shoulder with sublime disregard. "My
features editor wants human-interest stories—stuff to
tug the heart, not boggle the mind." She held up a
black lace undergarment and considered. "However,
that's not to say I don't have a couple of angles I intend
to work on in my own time. I plan to profile the
quintessential bluegrass sportswriter. You know, an
in-depth type of thing. And boy, do I have my subject
lined up!" She giggled. "He's even got the quintessential name."

Diana was busy shutting her typewriter case, and she
spoke almost without thinking. "Beauregard Gatling . . ."

"How did you know?"

Diana looked up, surprised. "Beau Gatling? You
mean the ace word jockey? Star stud for the *Times
Union?* I was right?" She shook her head and snick-
ered. "Well, well, will wonders never cease."

Alison was on her way into the bathroom, but she
poked her head back into the room. "I didn't realize
you had already met him." Her smile was a mixture of
humor and regret. "My, that fellow does get around."

"I haven't actually had the pleasure yet," Diana
assured her. "At least, not in person. But I have been
treated to a brief sample of *Quotations from Chairman
Beau.*" Diana cocked her head and gazed thoughtfully
across the room. "Although I somehow doubt Mr.
Gatling would appreciate the comparison."

"Why not?"

Diana shrugged in the direction of the bathroom. "Maybe he hasn't even heard of the People's Republic of China," she offered.

Alison's face, covered with cold cream, appeared again. "Now, now. Let's not get chauvinistic. Louisville may not be the great Big Apple, Diana, but it's not exactly the city that time forgot, either." Alison wagged her finger and withdrew.

"Right. You're right." Diana walked briskly to her suitcases and began unzipping the larger of the two. "I'm being a perfect snob, and a bigot to boot." She spoke softly to herself as she rummaged through the neatly folded clothes for something to wear. "After all, I have to deal with discrimination all the time. Well, maybe not all the time, but I always know it's there. Take this assignment, for example," she addressed the ceiling imploringly. "Please, take it!" Then she clucked at herself in exasperation, shaking her head as if to rid it of such unworthy humor.

Diana lifted a dress of nubby blue Egyptian cotton out of the case. It had a blousy top, dolman sleeves and an elastic waist, and she usually wore it with amber beads and low sandals. It was one of her most comfortable dresses. She gazed at it for a moment and then looked vacantly in the direction of the bathroom where Alison's voice could be heard humming softly. Then, with an irritated little flounce, she shoved the dress back into the suitcase.

"You may fool the world, Jennings," she muttered to herself, "but your I-don't-care act doesn't fool me!" Rummaging through the contents again, she finally extricated a white linen shirtwaist with black piping around the exaggerated deep lapels and a wide, black patent-leather belt. It was a sophisticated dress, even a little outrageous for something as ordinary as a press conference. But Diana's day-long irritation had developed into a sort of devil-may-care impatience. She was impatient with herself, with her job—everything. The dress looked terrific on her, and with a pair of high black heels, made the most of her striking presence.

"What the hell?" she asked the dress. "It's a circus down there, isn't it?"

Chapter 2

DESPITE ITS GLEAMING, MODERN, CHROME AND GLASS exterior, the Galt House was a Louisville legacy. In an earlier incarnation, over a hundred years ago, it had been a roadhouse at the first Kentucky Derby. In 1875, dubious journalists had traveled down Fourth Street to the Louisville Jockey Club to watch a surprise victory by Aristedes on a track that was finished only moments before the race.

Today, journalists would be ferried to the track in scores of gypsy cabs rather than in mule-drawn carriages, and they would no longer be dubious about the fate of horse racing in Kentucky. Other than that, Diana reflected, one really could not say much had changed.

The Poolsider Bar was actually a misnomer. Situated on the mezzanine level of the hotel, the bar looked out across a spacious lobby, carefully dotted with topiary trees and tasteful conversation nooks. The only pool in sight lay behind the bar, not visible from the tall leather stools unless one was willing to vault the mahogany bar itself. Even then, it was not much to see, and Diana realized that nobody seemed disappointed or even the least bit interested in its whereabouts.

When Diana and Alison crossed the lobby toward the bar, all they could see was a crowd of men, their voices melted into a deep buzz of conversation punctuated by barks of laughter. At first, their presence did not make a dent in that wall of people, but soon Diana picked out a few familiar faces, and she was greeted by one of her colleagues from the *Boston Globe,* her old paper.

"Hey, Southie!"

As a lefty, Diana had earned herself that nickname the very first time she went out to cover a baseball story, and it had stuck as long as she was in Boston.

"What brings you out to the stables?" asked the man who had hailed her. "I thought you'd be spending the summer at Fenway Park?"

Diana grimaced good-naturedly. "So did Freddie Lynn, Chuck, and you know what happened to him!"

"Benched, huh?" Chuck clucked sympathetically.

"I wouldn't call this being benched," she replied, indicating the crowd. "After all, this is THE DERBY. The most exciting two and a half minutes in all of sports!"

"If you like your athletes on four legs, that is."

Diana looked around her. "By Saturday night," she commented dryly, "I'll bet the horses won't be the only beings on all fours around here."

Chuck looked at his empty shot glass and grinned. "Yup. Well, I guess whoever's left standing will get the scoop, huh? Hey, can I get you anything from the bar, Diana? Or how about your friend?" He looked over Diana's shoulder toward where Alison stood, looking over the crowd. Hearing Chuck's admiring voice, Alison directed her attention to him.

"Why, thanks!" she said, giving him the benefit of a grin. "I'd love a gin and tonic!"

"What? No mint juleps?" Diana asked. She didn't

want to drink before the press conference, especially since she hadn't eaten since early that morning. Already the conference was running twenty minutes late. At this rate, it would be midnight before she got to have dinner.

Chuck disappeared into the crowd to get Alison's drink, but before he returned, someone announced that they should move into the Bluegrass Room, where the press conference was being held. Allowing themselves to be jostled along in the flow of traffic, Diana and Alison were just about to squeeze through the double doors when a voice close behind them spoke.

"Hey, Miss Chase."

With some difficulty, Alison turned around. "Hey, Mr. Gatling." Her voice took on the same low, lingering inflection that his had. Because of the pressing crowd, Diana couldn't turn around to see the man who spoke, but he was so close behind her that she could feel his breath on the back of her neck.

"I was going to ask you what took you so long to get back down here," the voice continued, "but you look so pretty, I don't have to ask."

Diana rolled her eyes skyward. For heaven's sake! The guy was so close behind them, he probably couldn't even focus on the back of Alison's hair, let alone the silk print wraparound dress she was wearing. But Alison accepted the compliment with a delighted chuckle that only made Diana roll her eyes again. Oh, please!

By this time, they had entered the Bluegrass Room, where a long table had been set up on a raised dais. Behind the table sat a row of smiling men, partially obscured behind the cloud of cigar smoke that filled the room. Diana could barely make out the banners identifying the Churchill Downs Association, the Kentucky Horsebreeders' Association and the Louisville Chamber of Commerce. Sighing, for she knew already exactly what she was about to hear, she reached into her bag for her note pad.

"Courage, ma'am. This won't hurt too much."

The words were whispered softly into her ear so that even Alison didn't hear them. Diana smiled at Mr. Gatling's droll humor, but when she turned around, he moved back out of her line of vision. At that moment, one of the microphones was activated with a shrill whine, and the press conference was under way.

As she had expected, the first twenty minutes were filled with the usual pablum about what a great event was taking place and how glad the city fathers were to have the respected members of the press here to witness it. Diana dutifully took notes, still waiting for an idea to take root in her mind. Even while she thought and wrote, she was aware of Mr. Gatling's presence behind her. He made it very clear, humming to himself, muttering at the speakers up front and occasionally, it seemed, taking a deep swallow of some kind of drink. After each "sip," he sighed with exaggerated relief and then went back to his humming.

Next to her, Alison was having difficulty keeping a straight face at these shenanigans, although she did her best to keep her eyes focused on the dais. Diana, too, was having trouble concentrating. The man's presence was both amusing and irritating, and certainly more interesting than the smug drone coming through the microphone. If Mr. Gatling knew he was providing comic relief, he didn't acknowledge it. At the very least, Diana thought dryly, he could pass up his flask. She had changed her mind about wanting a drink.

Finally, the floor was opened up to questions. Diana recognized most of the people who raised their hands and spoke; UPI, AP, reporters from the *Times* and the *Post*. She made a mental note to go over and speak to Monty Parker, the syndicated sports columnist who was one of her few heroes. She had come to know him

casually through the years and knew he would have
some interesting things to say about the upcoming
baseball season, not that the subject would shed any
light on their present concern.

The questions were slightly more illuminating than
the speeches had been, and Diana jotted down several
points she thought worthy of following up. In particular, she noticed an uneasy and unusual silence from the
dais when one local reporter asked if the owner of the
odds-on favorite, Street Fare, a Mr. Derek Islington,
was going to break his traditional rule of silence to the
press. The answer, after a brief pause, was "no," and
something about the tone caught Diana's interest. She
had no idea what it meant yet, but she knew enough to
trust her instinct and jot it down. Then a voice called
out, "Yes, Mr. Gatling?"

All heads turned in her direction. Next to her, Alison
swiveled around, a broad smile on her face. Diana felt a
sudden and unaccustomed surge of discomfort. If she
turned around, she would be face to face with Mr.
Gatling, their bodies less than a foot apart. That would
be awkward. Yet it seemed just as awkward to be
standing with her back to the speaker, especially since
the eyes of everyone in the room were trained in her
direction. Irritated by her own indecision, Diana tried
to make it seem as if she were listening to him speak
over her shoulder. The position was strained and made
her feel even more foolish. She tried to keep from
biting her lower lip as he spoke.

"I have two questions, Mr. Daley." Beau Gatling
addressed the president of the Horsebreeders' Association, who seemed to know him well. "First of all, can
you tell us the latest odds on Diana's Folly, the first
female horse ever given odds to win? After all, she's
the only filly involved in this whole affair—aside from
these two lovely ladies, that is."

He was obviously indicating Diana and Alison, and a

wave of appreciative laughter swept the room. Diana
froze, her pen poised over her note pad. Out of the
corner of her eye, she could see that even Alison was
blushing uncomfortably. For the life of her, she could
not think of a single graceful way to handle the
situation.

Mr. Gatling was obviously enjoying the stir he had
created, and Diana did not doubt for a moment that it
had been a deliberate gesture. He did not join in the
general laughter, but Diana could feel him bustling
with satisfaction at his success. The ace word jockey
had done it again. Clamping her jaw, Diana decided
that serious action was called for and to hell with
graceful behavior. Abruptly, she spun around, making
sure to move slightly forward as she did so. Just as she
expected, this maneuver brought her face to face with
Beau Gatling—nose to nose would be more like it.

At first, he seemed delighted. She found herself
staring into crinkly brown eyes under surprisingly long
lashes and delicate eyebrows. His hair was very dark
and curly, not at all the short, manly cut she had
expected. The infectious grin he turned on her was
unexpected as well.

He was wearing the regulation alligator polo shirt in
a becoming shade of dark green that contrasted with
the pale skin and dark hair on his chest and arms. He
was well built but not large. In her heels, Diana was
exactly his height.

After a moment, during which Diana steeled herself
not to blink, Beau Gatling's smile lost some of its
powerful wattage. The laughter around them had died
down, but the man on the dais, obviously taken aback
by Diana's aggressive stance, had not yet replied to the
question. Diana forced herself to hold Beau's gaze,
which, despite his increasing discomfort, never wa-
vered from her face. The color of his eyes went from
dark brown to black, as if he were trying to obscure any

emotion. Diana could see her own face reflected in the opaque irises, her forehead and eyes distorted oddly on the concave surface of his vision.

They remained in that exact position for what seemed like hours, neither one batting an eyelash. Then a strange smile flickered across Beau's features, lighting up his eyes to their original warm brown.

"I can see," he said without a trace of repentance in his voice, "that you are hardly a filly, ma'am."

"Mr. Gatling." Diana's voice was low and ominous. "Do you usually make it a habit to ridicule your colleagues in public?"

The flicker of a challenge deepened his eyes again. Beau Gatling obviously did not expect to make any more of an apology than that.

"Most of my colleagues have a rather well-developed sense of humor," he replied, as if that were excuse enough.

Diana could tell that the people who stood closest to them were straining to catch their words—Alison among them. She was glad Beau had enough sense to keep his voice down. "Well developed in adolescence, no doubt," she said. "But I doubt they've matured since then, if your remark is any indication."

The tension between them fairly crackled through the air. Diana refused to let the matter drop. She had every intention of staring the man down even if it took all evening. And, somewhat to her surprise, she found she was enjoying the exchange much more than she should have.

Beau seemed to be enjoying it as well, if the deepening crinkles around his eyes were any indication. Suddenly, Diana felt as if they were alone in the room, the only two people who understood the humor in the situation as well as the tension. Despite her annoyance, she felt a certain kinship with the ace word jockey. He might have the manner of a twelve-year-old, but he had a sharp enough mind.

"That's us." Beau chuckled softly under his breath. "Just a bunch of good ol' boys at heart." Diana couldn't tell if he was poking fun at himself or at her image of him. "Anyway, ma'am," he went on with a tiny inclination of his head, "I'm mighty pleased to welcome you to the club."

Diana arched her brows. "Don't hold your breath."

After another pause, during which they still held one another's gaze, Beau winked, nodded and lifted his eyes over her head toward the dais. This series of small gestures broke the spell. Clearing his throat rather loudly, Mr. Daley, who had been waiting uneasily for a chance to answer Beau's original question, spoke with some relief. "I'll be glad to talk about Diana's Folly," he said heartily. "We're mighty proud to have her with us. Of course, her odds really aren't that great—even if she were a he, it would still be a long shot. But she's performed well and consistently in the three-year-old qualifiers, and her lineage is undoubtedly impressive. Her recent Derby track times have been promising, too—for a filly, of course. We're all rootin' for the little lady, I can tell you that!" He paused and mopped his brow. "Part of the magic of the Derby lies in the long shot coming up from behind," he began to drone. "It's tradition here in our great bluegrass state to set much store by the underdog. That's Derby for you!"

It was clear that Mr. Daley, once he got started, was prepared to continue his speech all night long, but a whispered message from another man on the platform cut him short. After a moment's confusion, Mr. Daley got back to the business at hand. "You have another question, Beau?"

By this time, Diana had turned back to face the front of the room. She was no longer paying much attention to what went on around her. Instead, she was going over in her mind the confrontation she had just had with Beau Gatling. Why on earth hadn't she been stronger in condemning his sexist jibe? Why hadn't she simply ignored it, risen above it as she had learned to do from years of experience? Why on earth had she enjoyed it all so much?

Now she listened with only half an ear to Beau's next question, something about qualifying rules for the horses, and listened not at all to Mr. Daley's long-winded reply. By the time she got caught up with what was going on, the conference was over, and everyone was drifting toward the door for dinner.

She turned around to see if Beau was behind her. He was there, but his back was toward her as he greeted some friends. A stolid-looking man with a National Turf Writers' badge pinned to his rather shabby jacket came up and pounded Beau heavily on the back.

"Beau, you ugly coon!" he rasped jovially. "You sure do have a knack for asking the wrong questions, don't you?"

"Amen to that," muttered Diana under her breath.

When Beau did not reply, the man went on. "Now, you can make people itchy here, but I expect you to behave yourself when you speak at our dinner tomorrow night, you hear?"

Diana had already begun to move away, but she heard Beau's reply quite clearly. "That's not what you really want me to do, though, is it, Ed?" There was something harsh, almost mocking, in his voice.

Ed, however, appeared not to notice and guffawed loudly. "You're right about that, I guess, Beau." Diana could hear the thud as Ed pounded on Beau's back again. "Well, you can make all the filly jokes you want, I suppose. Just you keep away from that other stuff. You know what I mean? Don't go gettin' all hot under the collar about you-know-who again."

Diana pursed her lips. Apparently, she had missed something in Beau's second question, something that had touched more than one nerve in the roomful of reporters and officials. It was quite clear that this Ed fellow did not regard tasteless filly jokes as being in poor taste.

When Beau spoke again, the bitterness that had been simmering in his voice surfaced with a vengeance. "Of course, Ed. I wouldn't dream of upsetting anyone for Derby Week. I've learned my lesson.

The sarcasm fairly dripped from his voice, but Diana was at a loss to understand why his mood had changed so fast. He had gone from being a southern gentleman with Alison to being a rather rude, if interesting, adversary with her, and now this fierce bitterness . . . *Ah, well,* Diana thought with a small shrug, *what should it matter to me, anyway?* She began to move out of hearing range, but the last thing she heard was Beau saying shortly. "I said I'd behave, didn't I?"

"Amen to that, too," said Diana, and with a ferocious toss of her head, she went off in search of that drink.

Diana would have liked to forget about the entire incident. As soon as she was out of range of Beau's face and voice, she was able to re-establish her professional detachment. He was rude; that was all—just rude. If it took different forms with different people, well, then, he was just *creatively* rude. But whatever his game was, it had nothing to do with her. And she intended to see that it stayed that way.

But Beau Gatling was not so easily shaken off either in her mind or in the flesh. Just when Diana, vodka and tonic in hand, had gotten settled in to a good discussion about baseball with Monty Parker, there he was. Diana saw him approaching and concentrated hard on what Monty was saying, hoping that Beau's southern up-bringing had taught him not to interrupt other peoples' conversations. But apparently southern chivalry did not extend to discussions about sports. He sailed right

up to them and began pumping Monty's hand even
before Monty finished his sentence. One look at
Monty's face, which lit up at the sight of Beau's, and
Diana knew she was outnumbered.

"Monty, my man! What a delight to see you down in
my neck of the woods. What brings you off the baseball
beat?"

Beau's style had changed again. Now he was playing
the worldly sophisticate, with just a touch of down-
home humor to make it interesting. His broad smile,
revealing impossibly white teeth, included Diana without singling her out. Diana found herself feeling curiously irritated at being left out.

They were talking about baseball. Hadn't *she* just
been talking about baseball with Monty? What gave
this guy the right to just butt in and assume all of
Monty's attention? She knew just as much about the
sport as *he* did, didn't she? And Monty had been plenty
interested in what *she* had to say before Beau's interruption.

"Don't be silly, Mont," Beau was saying, that hon-
eyed drawl making it sound more like a compliment
than an argument. "There's no way Jim Palmer could
match pitches with Catfish Hunter. Without a good
rotation system, his arm just wouldn't hold up."

"Excuse me." Diana's well-modulated voice cut
through the tight net of their conversation. "But you
happen to be wrong, Mr. Gatling. Last year, Palmer's
stats beat out Hunter's even before they were adjusted
to account for all discrepancies." She paused for dra-
matic effect. "In games where he pitched against the
same lineup as Hunter, he consistently outpitched the
man, shot for shot."

Beau's head swiveled around on his neck during this
recitation, his eyes growing wider with every word.
Diana might have thought he was getting angry except
that a huge grin was eating its way across his entire
face. As soon as she saw it, her carefully restored

professional composure was shot all to bits. Once again, she had the sensation of sallying forth into battle with him. Once again, she had the feeling that they were both enjoying it very much.

By the time she finished speaking, he was positively beaming at her. Although his eyes never left her face, he spoke to Monty. "Who *is* this fascinatin' lady, Monty?"

"You mean you two don't already know each other? From the way you two faced off in the press room, I would have thought you were old enemies."

"I must confess she's a perfectly new enemy," murmured Beau, "although the oversight is surely mine."

"Beau," said Monty, "allow me to introduce you to Ms. Diana Jennings of the New York *Chronicle*— talented sportswriter, fascinating woman and the smartest baseball freak I know, aside from me. She's right about Catfish, by the way."

Beau's eyebrows arched wickedly. "Then I guess this is not Diana's folly, but Beau's. Right ma'am?"

"Quite right," Diana murmured demurely, her eyes sparkling at him through slightly lowered lashes.

Monty must have realized that something out of the ordinary was going on because he interrupted with a touch of impatience. "Of course, Diana, you have already heard from and about Beauregard Gatling of the *Louisville Times-Union*. After all, he is one of the best turf men in the business."

Beau raised his hand to offer a handshake. "It's an honor to meet you, ma'am. And Monty is being generous, I assure you."

The hell he is, Diana thought. *He's miffed because I'm not acting like a properly impressed little lady in front of his friend. Well, I'll give them both something to think about!*

Beau's hand remained outstretched, but Diana didn't offer hers in return. She thought she could see his hand trembling slightly, and she allowed the pause to stretch into an awkward moment before she began to raise her own arm, ever so slowly, to meet his.

"You are *the* Beau Gatling?"

"Yes, ma'am." Although both Beau and Monty were staring at the extended hand in helpless fascination, she could hear the pride creep into Beau's voice at the thought that his reputation had preceded him. Diana made her fingers inch even more slowly upward.

"The famous Ace Word Jockey of the Bluegrass State?" She made the capital letters apparent in her voice.

"The very same." Diana did not take her own eyes off Beau's twitching hand, but she could tell he was preening at the praise.

Their fingertips finally met, and she could feel him gathering her fingers into his palm. Pleasure vibrated right through his fingertips into hers—whether because of Diana's compliments or Diana herself, she couldn't tell. She let the grip last a while.

Then, raising her eyes in measured cadences to his, she smiled sweetly as she delivered her punch line.

"Never heard of you before in my life," she said clearly. Then she dropped his hand, turned around and walked away to find Alison.

Chapter 3

"I SWEAR," ALISON GRUMBLED, STARING OUT THE WIN-
dow of their taxi the next morning.

"So do I, on occasion," replied Diana. "But what are
you swearing about in particular this bright, sunny
morning?"

It was bright and sunny, a crayon-blue sky reflecting
light and heat down on the long line of cars that was
snaking slowly toward Churchill Downs. Diana and
Alison were both looking for their first glimpse of the
famous twin spires, but at the rate their cab was
moving, it might be well after noon before they got to
the Downs.

Not that they would miss much. The scheduled event
for the day was a balloon race, and although every
journalist in Louisville was dutifully on the way to
cover it, neither Alison nor Diana could work up much
enthusiasm for the prospect of spending the day craning
their necks and squinting their eyes for a contrived
publicity stunt like that.

But they knew their respective editors were expecting copy, and so they waited in the endless line of taxis with the other members of the press, hoping to find some angle that would make even a balloon race seem worthwhile.

"What do you swear, Alison?" Diana repeated.

"I swear I don't know why some of these guys even bother to go out there and watch the race; that's what I swear."

Diana laughed. "They go to see who wins, of course."

Alison gave an exasperated sigh. "It doesn't seem to matter much, though, does it? I mean, all this talk about race fixing, drugged horses and officials with their hands in the till. I ask you, what kind of a race is that?"

Diana shrugged. "That's horse racing," she said.

"Diana! How can you be so cool? You know damn well it makes you mad, too. Why, last night, who was it raving about the tight old-boy network and how unfair it was?"

"Me."

"And who complained that anybody who's not male and southern doesn't have a chance to get an inside break on a story here?"

"That was me."

"And who said it was disgusting the way those guys sat there all night drinking and telling jokes and trading stories across the bar so that they wouldn't have to go to the trouble of writing their own?"

"That was you, I believe."

Alison scowled. "All right, so that was me. But I actually saw it, Diana! I saw two guys trading typed copy so that they could phone in two stories for the price of one! Doesn't that make you mad?"

"It'll make their editors even madder, I'm sure."

"How will their editors know?"

"Believe me, Alison, sports editors are not as dull-

witted as that." She leaned forward conspiratorially.
"Why, I've even heard that there are some sports*writers* who have integrity! They actually go out and cover a
story and do a damn good job of it! Do you believe it?"

Alison grinned sheepishly. "All right, all right. I
guess I deserved that. Sorry to poke fun at your
hallowed profession, Diana." She sighed. "I guess I'm
just miffed because there's no one in sight whom *I* can
trade stories with. Could you imagine the look on one
of those guy's faces if I went up and asked if he had
anything hot on what the well-dressed jockey is wearing
this year?" She giggled, her good humor restored.
"Oh, look, there they are! The twin spires!"

Diana craned her head out the window on her side of
the cab. At first, all she saw were the domed tops of
several brightly colored hot-air balloons clustered in
the distance. Then she saw the white-painted spires
with their slatted towers, and she felt a tug of excitement in spite of herself. Balloon races might not be her
cup of tea, but Churchill Downs was a major landmark
in the world of sports, and Diana was enough of a
sports enthusiast to appreciate her first glimpse of the
rambling buildings and perfectly coiffed inner track.

Actually, there was very little that could dampen her
good spirits this bright morning. She told herself that
she always felt this way once she really got into an
assignment, that she was beginning to get a feel for the
magic of the Derby, and although she couldn't put her
finger on it yet, a feel for the angle her story might take.

In fact, there was something else that buoyed her
spirits, and although she would never have admitted it
to Alison, it did have something to do with that old-boy
network they had seen in operation at the press conference the night before.

Yes, it had been disappointing and frustrating to
watch all those men trading little tidbits of information
and clamming up so obviously whenever Diana approached. True, she was tired of having to fend off the

not-so-subtle innuendoes that a woman could never cover sports the way a man could and that her colleagues would rather be trading something a bit more titillating than press gossip with so well endowed a writer as Diana.

But the entire evening, and that morning as well, had been colored with a sense of expectancy that Diana had not experienced in years. She ought to be more put out, she knew. She ought to be more annoyed that things were the way they were. She ought to be more determined to get the best story possible out of the Derby, with or without the aid of her peers.

Instead, she just felt excited, like a kid getting ready for a school vacation. In spite of what long, hard experience had taught her, she saw only good things in the days ahead.

And it wasn't until they got out of the cab and filed into the lush green inner field of Churchill Downs that Diana finally admitted to herself the reason for her exuberant anticipation.

She was going to see Beauregard Gatling again.

The crowd swirling around them seemed to be in an exuberant mood to match Diana's. Alison, who had stopped grumbling as soon as they reached their destination, quickly attached herself to a family of eight, all of whom wore T-shirts proclaiming, "Oregon loves the Kentucky Derby!"

"I may not have good friends in the right places," whispered Alison to Diana, "but I sure do know a good human-interest story when I see one!"

Winking, she made off with her new friends, and Diana could hear her asking the mother of the brood, "What makes you come all this way just to see a horse race?"

Diana chuckled. The old-boy network could use a few more like her, she thought. Sure, it might just be a feature angle, but Diana had no doubt that Alison would use the same bold approach even if she were talking to, say, the reclusive Mr. Islington, owner of Street Fare. Even Diana herself seldom resorted to such head-on tactics. She watched Alison disappear with her family into the crowd, chattering away as if she had known them all her life.

"A beautiful day for a balloon race, don't you think?"

She already recognized the voice, and the mirrored sunglasses that greeted her when she turned around did not really come as much of a surprise.

"It's a beautiful day for anything," she replied with a wide smile.

"Not a bad outfit you're wearing, either," Beau added. Although she couldn't see his eyes, she could feel their close appraisal of her legs and hips in the corduroy culottes she wore with an open-weave cotton sweater and low heels.

Diana raised one brow. "You southern gents sure do know how to hand out a compliment," she said dryly.

"If last night was any indication, you northern girls are no slouches at it, either," he retorted promptly. "And you seem to have a knack for leaving the scene of the crime, too."

"My mother always taught me to walk away from a fight," Diana told him.

"Not until you've taken one last swing, though, right?"

This conversation was conducted in complete good humor. Instead of the excitement she had felt with Beau the previous night, Diana now felt a complete sense of ease in his presence. He had accepted the rebuke she had handed him in front of Monty with no rancor, and it made her realize that he had not intended to rankle her, either. They spoke the same language, that was all, and if it seemed rather sharp and elliptical to other people, she was quite sure that they understood each other.

"Of course," said Beau, tucking her arm under his as

if it were the most natural thing in the world to do, "it doesn't matter that neither of us knew each other from a hole in the wall. Someday we'll both be household words."

"Of course," Diana agreed confidently. "Woodward and Bernstein have nothing on us." They were strolling slowly toward the press grandstand on the far end of the field. On all sides of them, people paraded past in high spirits, and Diana was reminded of a medieval country fair she had once attended in upstate New York. That was a good image, and she made a mental note to use it in her copy. After all, she was here to work, wasn't she?

"Just think of this as absorbing the local color," Beau commented, and Diana realized with a start that he was still on the same wavelength as she. It was one thing to trade wits with the man, but sharing thoughts was a little out of her league.

"Yes," she said, making an effort to sound calm and professional. "I do need to beef up my copy. Can't let it get too serious, now, can I?"

"Good God, no! At Derby, that's practically illegal!"

Diana turned and tried to read the expression in his eyes, but all she saw was a reflection of her own face. She had heard that same edge of bitterness in his voice that had sounded so odd the previous night after the press conference. It occurred to her that Beauregard Gatling, while one of the boys in every sense of the word, might not subscribe to the complete network party line. Diana had the notion that his perceptions were considerably more astute than those of his local colleagues. She suddenly remembered Beau's discussion with the man from the Turf Writers' Association.

"Who's you-know-who?" she asked suddenly.

There was a minute pause before he replied. "Beats me," he said smoothly. "How many guesses do I get?"

"Only one," Diana retorted. "And it had better be

right. What was that boor talking about last night when he told you to watch your step at the dinner tonight?"

"Boor . . . yes, Ed Toller is certainly a boor." Beau was stalling. "I'll have to remember to call him that the next time I see him. He's sure not to have the slightest idea what I mean." He chuckled, but there was no humor in his voice.

"Who's you-know-who?" Diana repeated, "and why doesn't Ed Toller want you to bring the name up?" Beau stopped walking and turned to look at her. "And take off those silly glasses," Diana added impatiently. "I want to look at you, not at myself." Normally, Diana would never have allowed her impatience to surface with someone she had only just met. But Beau was different. She felt as if she knew him well. The only uneasy sensation was the feeling that he knew her as well as she knew him.

"Your loss." Beau shrugged and took off the glasses. Their eyes met for a moment in a brief challenge. Diana knew he was silently debating whether or not to tell her any more. She felt that much hung in the balance of this small confidence. If he refused to tell her, it would confirm what she and Alison had been talking about. If Beau would not speak, then surely no one else would, at least not among the members of the press. And Diana doubted that the male-dominated world of jockeys and trainers would be much more help. If Beau refused to tell her what every other journalist who covered horse racing already knew, then Diana knew she would be left with little more than local color for her stories.

It would also mean she had been wrong about Beau.

The pause stretched into minutes. Then, without speaking, Beau took her arm and began walking again, leading her through the tunnel that led under the track and out beyond the grandstands to the broad rows of neat stables behind the Downs.

The stables were divided up by breeders, and each farm had placed a silk banner above the row of stalls proclaiming its name. At the farthest end of the block was a gray and pink stretch of silk that covered a half-dozen stalls.

"Fleur D'Isle," read Diana. "That's Street Fare's farm, right?"

"Right."

"So? Where is he?" The double doors of the stalls were all shut, and there seemed to be no sign of recent activity.

"Good question." Beau smiled humorlessly. "Nobody knows. And I doubt anyone will get to see him until the day of the race, if I know Derek Islington."

"Derek Islington," Diana repeated slowly. As she said it, two dim memories coincided in her brain. She looked sharply at Beau. "You know something about Derek Islington, don't you? He's you-know-who."

Beau shrugged guardedly. "Everybody knows something about Derek Islington," he said off handedly. "It's just that nobody knows much."

"But you've got your ideas, haven't you," Diana went on, her voice gaining conviction. "You know more than the other guys around here, but either you're not telling, or nobody around here is willing to listen."

"I would say," Beau said slowly, "that it's a little bit of both." He seemed to have a grudging admiration for the accuracy of Diana's reportorial instinct.

"So, what is it? Why all the secrecy about Islington and Street Fare? Isn't it against pari-mutuel rules for a racehorse to be off limits before a major cup race?"

"Depends on whose rules you play by," Beau clarified. He didn't seem interested in giving out any more information, and Diana was annoyed. He hadn't told her anything, really, that she didn't already know. Now he turned to walk back in the direction of the Downs. Diana started to follow him, ready to press for more.

But he had only taken a few steps before he stopped short, putting out his hand for Diana to do the same.

"See that guy over there?" Beau spoke in a whisper, directing Diana's attention to a narrow alley between two sets of stalls. Craning her neck and squinting to see down the shady path, she noticed a striking-looking man in a cream-colored suit. He stood among a knot of people in a little cul-de-sac at the end of the alley. She couldn't hear what was being said, but it was clear that the well-dressed man was doing the talking and that the others were listening closely to every word.

"Who is he?" she asked.

Beau cast her a swift look of impatience. "For a smart lady," he hissed, "you don't catch on to everything so quickly, do you? That's Islington. Derek Islington."

"That's him, huh?" She looked more closely, letting her reporter's eye memorize all the details. Then she turned back to Beau. "So? What's the big secret? Isn't he supposed to be here? After all, he's got a fortune invested in that horse."

Beau was shaking his head. "That's the point. I didn't even expect him to be in Louisville at all. He usually makes it a point to stay far away when his horses are racing."

Diana liked the way Beau said the name of his city—*Louvul.* It sort of rolled off his tongue and made it sound like a small town.

"But why should he? Street Fare's favored two to one, isn't he? Why shouldn't he want to stick around and watch the money roll in? He sure doesn't look like the hermit type to me."

Beau shook his head. "He has his reasons, believe me."

"I'm sure he does," Diana retorted. "I just want to know what they are." She glanced back at the silent stables, so different from the bustle of activity that was going on in front of all the other stalls. "And why is it

such a morgue back there? You would think the
atmosphere would be positively festive."

"Islington doesn't give a damn about this Derby or
who wins it. Now come on. I'm sure he doesn't expect
to be gawked at, especially not by a couple of press
hounds like us." He pulled her away, but Diana held
her ground.

"How would he know we were press hounds?" she
asked. "And why doesn't Derek Islington care who
wins?"

Beau looked exasperated. "Maybe it's because he's
had so many winners that it's lost its thrill."

She would not let herself be budged. "That may be,"
she conceded, forcing herself to think clearly despite
Beau's urgency. "But if he's not in it for the glory, then
surely he's in it for the money. And winning makes a
big difference in stud prices, doesn't it?"

"Don't ask questions if you already know the answer," Beau snapped.

Diana was watching the group in the alley. Islington
was talking now to only one of the men in the group,
although they all stood perfectly still. Then the man to
whom he was speaking shook his head, and Diana
could clearly see the whole group stiffen, as if preparing
for a blow. Islington clamped his mouth shut and
shoved his way through the group, stalking off out of
Diana's range of vision.

"Seen enough?" Beau inquired.

"I wonder." At last, Diana allowed herself to be
moved forward. She looked at Beau, who had replaced
his mirrored glasses and was again expressionless.
"What do you know about Derek Islington, Beau? Is it
an exclusive?"

"It would be if I had anything real," Beau replied.
"But I don't."

"Then why can't you share your theories with me?
Why doesn't anyone want you to talk about it, even
other press people?"

Beau sighed heavily. "Look, Diana, it's nothing worth bothering with. It doesn't really have anything at all to do with this Derby, I swear. The Derby purse is small potatoes to someone like Islington. He doesn't really give a hoot about racing at all."

"What does he give a hoot about?"

This time, Beau's lips clamped shut with obvious finality.

"What's the matter, Beau?" Diana was irritated by her inability to make sense of the whole situation. "Can't talk to me because I'm not one of the boys? Is that it?"

He stopped short and considered the tense figure before him. "Well, Miz Jennings," he said in an exaggerated drawl that dripped sarcasm, "I guess you can take the boy out of the country, but . . ." he snorted derisively. "You know the rest, I'm sure."

"You bet I do." They had reached the inner field again. Diana stood fuming under the bright sun. Suddenly, all the festivities seemed ridiculous. She was annoyed at Beau's obstinate refusal to explain what was going on, but she was even more annoyed with herself for having been sucked into feeling good about him in the first place. Obviously, her initial impression of him had been right; he was party line all the way.

"Look," he said now, facing her without removing the offensive sunglasses. "I've got to talk to some of the boys." He seemed impatient to be going. "I'll probably see you later. All right?"

Diana glanced at him coldly and then looked away. "I doubt it," she retorted. "I have quite a bit of research to do." She was sure he would understand what she meant. "After all, some of us plan to get some serious writing done down here," she added deliberately. "And that means a lot of work."

"Work?" Beau grinned his biggest, most winning grin. "That's a dangerous word during Derby. It's against my religion!"

She opened her mouth to tell him exactly what she thought of him, but he had already turned to greet one of the good ol' boys.

The balloon race had been filler material, Diana decided. It was just one of the activities that had been planned to keep the crowds busy and the money flowing until Derby Day. Diana found herself more and more grateful that Alison had been sent down to cover the human-interest angle. It meant that she herself would not have to bother wringing copy out of essentially frivolous events.

It was not that Diana thought such work was beneath her. On her way up to her present position on the *Chronicle*, she had spent enough time doing exactly that, and she knew full well that it was sometimes harder to write "soft" copy than it was to cover "hard" news.

But Diana had something else on her mind as the brilliant blue afternoon drifted lazily by, and she didn't want anything else to be distracting her. Her confrontation with Beau and the strange little scene she had witnessed between Derek Islington and his men had fueled all those vague half thoughts that had been swirling around in her mind since the press conference the day before. And now, even while she tried to control her irritation with Beau's transparent techniques, she knew that his attitude had only focused her determination. There was a story to be written, and it had to do with Derek Islington, and nobody around there seemed to have the nerve, or the desire, to follow it through. Well, that left the field open for Diana, and she had every intention of getting to the bottom of the whole situation. It might prove to be nothing more than the idiosyncrasy of a rich and powerful Kentucky horse breeder who enjoyed building up a mystique. That in itself would make a good angle—to compare Islington's jaded lack of enthusiasm with the wild crowds that had come to see his horse win or lose.

But Diana's nose for news told her it was not that simple. There was something going on beneath the surface here, something that Beau Gatling was either unwilling or unable to share with her. And that, somehow, made it even more important for her to know what it was.

The only trouble was that Diana didn't like the feeling that Beau had made it even more important. She wasn't used to having her professional decisions affected by personal considerations. It had occurred to her, as she wandered around the Downs that afternoon picking up tidbits of conversations from trainers, owners and jockeys, that perhaps Beau wasn't acting purely out of chauvinism when he refused her information. Perhaps he had something he honestly had to conceal. But if it was facts he was hiding, Diana fully intended to be ruthless until she uncovered them, either with his help or alone.

At the moment, she hoped it would be alone. She could think of no greater satisfaction than coming up with a story on her own. She was better off working solo, anyway, especially if the alternative was working with someone who had a habit of calling her "ma'am." Still, Diana dressed for the Turf Writers' dinner that night with the uncomfortable sensation that she was taking more care with her appearance than she would under normal circumstances. Somehow, her dark-blue Egyptian cotton wouldn't hang right over her hips, and she kept tugging at it irritably while she made up her face.

"Jennings," she warned herself, "if you take off that dress and put on something flashy, I will simply refuse to accompany you to that dinner!"

As usual, the self-confrontation restored Diana's perspective. Alison was not attending the dinner. She had hooked up with a fourteen-year-old girl who exercised horses and who planned to be the first woman jockey to win racing's Triple Crown. In her excitement at finding a "ready-made story," Alison didn't even notice that her roommate was talking to herself. She left in a flurry of perfume and mohair, and Diana went down to the lobby alone.

The Turf Writers' Association was holding its dinner in another hotel several blocks away from the Galt House, but Diana was pleased at the chance to take a stroll in the pleasantly cool evening. Alison had been right; Louisville was hardly the Big Apple, but it did have a charming atmosphere, a suave serenity that was an excellent replacement for big-city sophistication. By the time she reached the hotel, she was both relaxed and hungry, and the prospect of spending an evening wasted in media hype didn't bother her as much as it usually did.

But there wasn't any hype. Rather, there was, but something else captured Diana's attention and held it for over an hour.

After the compulsory fruit cup and chicken dinner, washed down with an overly sweet dessert and equally saccharine opening remarks, the master of ceremonies prepared to introduce the next speaker of the evening. Recognizing the MC as Ed Toller, who looked as shabby in a dinner jacket as he had in a sportcoat, Diana got ready to tune out the rest of the evening by doodling on her ever-present note pad. Her short-lived patience with media hype was at an end already.

But then Ed Toller began to read from a magazine article he was holding, and despite his dismal reading skills, Diana quickly realized that what he was reading was terrific.

It was an account of a young jockey named Elmo Stewart who had come East from Missouri as a stableboy for a large breeding farm. Elmo wasn't terribly bright, but he knew horses, and he knew when they were "on." His reputation for calling winners spread quickly along the Triple Crown circuit, but the owners of the breeding farm where he worked kept him under close wraps, fearing that his premonitions would lower the odds on their own racers.

In a simple, straightforward manner, the reporter recounted Elmo's crusade to get a heavily favored two-year-old out of the lineup. He felt that the horse was "ill fated" and warned that he would never get around the track. In fact, Elmo himself was the only one who could get the animal to cooperate at all, and some stable hands who were interviewed were sure that the horse had "been spooked."

The owners insisted that there was no such thing as being spooked. Elmo would not say what he thought was wrong with the horse, and every vet who was sent in to check him gave him a clean bill of health. So the owners, instead of pulling their costly colt out of the race, decided that they would run him in the Belmont Sweepstakes as planned—except that Elmo Stewart would be on his back instead of the regular rider.

By the time Ed Toller got to the last paragraph, not a sound could be heard in the roomful of sportswriters. Two hundred people sat perfectly still, waiting for the end of the tale, although most of them probably knew what was coming. Diana had tied her linen napkin into knots in her lap, and her eyes never left the podium. She had an uneasy feeling in the pit of her stomach that was not, she knew, only due to the gripping tale.

Dark Star, the two-year-old, suffered a massive cardiac arrest during the Belmont Stakes. He fell heavily, pitching forward over the inside railing of the course. Elmo Stewart was thrown thirty feet and died instantly when his head struck a stone. Dark Star was shot that night.

"Gentlemen," said Ed Toller, pausing dramatically

when he put the paper down, "I give you the winner of
the 1982 Turf Writers' Award, our own Mr. Beauregard Gatling!"

Diana applauded as loud as any of the men at her
table. She had, of course, known that Beau was going
to speak at the dinner. It was only during the course of
Ed's reading, however, that it dawned on her that the
story was Beau's. She couldn't remember when anything had affected her so deeply. Not only had the
subject been riveting, but the style was perfectly suited
to the content. She found herself going back over what
she had heard, mentally checking to see if all the points
in a good story had been properly covered. Yes, the
facts had been stated early in the piece, the characters
described without editorializing, the race itself brought
into sharp, succinct focus, and all the quotes had been
carefully credited.

Even more, the piece represented something that
Diana hoped to do in her own work. It reported on the
event itself—the Belmont Stakes—but it also told a
parallel story that gave the readers a deeper insight into
the nature of the event. If she got anything out of the
story she was planning to write on the Derby, she
hoped it would be like that.

And Diana realized that she had once again been
wrong about Beau. He had taken pains to make it seem
as if working hard was a worthless effort in his business.
He had made it seem as if his opinions were not worth
repeating, or if they were, they were not his own. He
had gone to a great deal of trouble to present himself to
Diana as the archetypcal southern boy—charming and
suave and shallow as a lily pond.

But the story of Elmo Stewart had not been written
in a smoky bar over a couple of drinks with the boys.
Now she watched Beau thread his way among the
tables, pausing every few steps to shake someone's
hand. He was wearing a tan suit, well made but

obviously not his accustomed attire. A dark blue shirt and paler blue tie made a striking contrast between his suit and pale skin. From where Diana sat, his eyes were shadowed beneath his brows, but she could tell that they were beaming with pleasure, and every once in a while he threw his head back to laugh at someone's humorous compliment, revealing the sudden flash of white teeth and the ripple of curly dark hair.

Diana toyed absently with her amber necklace, her green eyes picking up faint hints of the amber as they followed Beau's progress up to the microphone. There, he shook Ed's hand, using his free hand to accept the small gold trophy, a miniature of the huge Derby Cup. He stepped up to the microphone and waited for the applause to die down.

"Thanks." He spoke easily to the crowd, with the same intimate drawl Diana remembered against her ear earlier that day. She felt a chill running along her arm and brushed it impatiently away. "I accept your applause, your honor and your esteem. The trophy"—he held it briefly aloft—"I accept as well, although by rights it should go to the man who earned it." He bowed his head for an instant, but when he looked up, his voice was strong. "For Elmo Stewart," he said, and stepped firmly away from the podium.

The M.C. tried in vain to get Beau to come back and elaborate on his gratitude to his peers for honoring him so well, but Beau only shook his head and laughed. Whatever emotion he had been feeling on Elmo Stewart's behalf appeared to have passed, and there was no trace of sadness on his fine features. "I *told* you I wouldn't behave, Ed!" he called back gaily over his shoulder.

"But you're the honored guest!" Ed spluttered.

"That doesn't mean I have to sing for my supper!"

"But . . . what will I do up here?"

By this time, Beau had reached the back of the room.

"Do what I do when I can't think!" he hollered. "Buy these dumb hacks a round of drinks and let *them* do all the talking!"

He departed amid a huge roar of laughter and a rising chant from the tables demanding liquor. Poor Ed was left alone at the microphone, vainly trying to explain that he had not planned on an open bar. From the mad scramble to the service bars that ensued, it was clear that Beau had had the last word of the evening.

Diana was still chuckling and shaking her head as she got up and left the room. She had no desire to fight her way to the bar, and the evening was still early enough so that she could walk back to the Galt House. The Turf Writers' dinner had delivered a far more enlightening evening than she had expected, thanks to Beauregard Gatling.

What a name! Everytime she said it to herself, it made her smile. That name made Rhett Butler sound like a Yankee! But Diana could not deny that Beau had risen considerably in her estimation—for the second time in twenty-four hours. Only this time it was not his personal magnetism that had changed her mind. It was the very real talent that she had recognized in his work. As she had once said to a feminist friend who couldn't understand how she put up with her more unliberated colleagues, "I don't care how long their arms swing as long as they can write a good story."

Despite her leisurely musing, Diana walked with her usual long, determined strides, and she was back at the Galt House in less than twenty minutes. Since most of the hotel's population was still at the Turf Writers' dinner, the lobby was virtually empty. Diana made her way over to the elevator, then paused, changed her mind and retraced her steps back to the Poolsider Bar for a nightcap.

"I thought you'd never get here."

Beau spoke over his shoulder to her the moment she entered the alcove. He must have seen her coming in the mirrored glass behind the bar. Surprised, Diana stopped for a moment and then came up beside him, hooking one low heel over the brass footrail and leaning both elbows on the counter just as he did.

"I don't believe you," she retorted promptly. "How could you possibly have known I would be here? Surely you expected me to take advantage of your generosity over at the dinner? Everybody else is."

Beau snorted and picked up the trophy that stood in front of him. "I'm quite sure of that. Ol' Ed will probably make me turn in my trophy to pay for the bar bill over there."

"I doubt the Derby Cup itself would foot that bill," Diana remarked blandly.

Beau arched one brow and chuckled. "Darlin', I doubt the whole of Fort Knox would cover it."

Diana laughed. "Still, I'm surprised you're not over there yourself," she said carefully. "After all, you do have quite a number of people waiting back there to shake your hand and slap your back."

Beau looked at her carefully. "Backslapping and handshaking are practically a national occupation in this neck of the woods," he said quietly. "And besides, I told you I was waiting for you."

She met his gaze levelly, waiting for him to continue.

"I wanted to apologize for this afternoon. I acted like a jerk."

A small smile played around Diana's lips, but she didn't dispute him. "I owe you one, too," she said. "I should know better than to try and horn in on someone else's story."

Beau, in turn, made no attempt to dispute her. For a moment, they smiled at each other in silence, their eyes sending little sparks of humor and warmth across the small gap between them.

"Anyway," said Beau, his eyes never leaving her face, "I wanted to know what you thought of my story."

Diana was surprised at the simple honesty of this request. And she could tell that he was slightly nervous —his lips were dry, and his fingertips drummed incessantly on the bar.

"You really want to know?"

"Of course I do." He licked his lips swiftly.

Diana gave him a wide, happy grin. She was inordinately glad that her opinion mattered so much to him. "I thought it was terrific," she said emphatically. "Really top-notch." Then, as an afterthought, she reached out and slapped him on the back.

The pressure, although hardly great, took him by surprise. He pitched forward with an exaggerated "Oof!" and lay supine across the bar. "Jeez," he muttered, his head cradled on his arm, "and I thought you were different from all the other guys!"

Suddenly everything seemed so right again. Diana and Beau were laughing heartily together, as much from relief as from the humor of the situation. The bartender approached and placed two wineglasses in front of them, smiling at their merriment. Without asking or even looking, Beau reached over the side of the bar and produced a dark green bottle, the label of which looked impressively aged.

"My, my, what have we here?" Diana murmured. She prided herself on her knowledge of good wines and even admitted to being a bit of a snob about it. The bottle didn't look like anything she had expected to find in a bar in Louisville, where the only thing available in some places was bourbon, bourbon, or bourbon.

Beau's brows lifted with a flourish, and he turned to the bartender. "See, George? I told you she was a lady of taste." A slow grin spread across his face as he accepted the corkscrew George proferred and inserted it into the cork. "Or at least," he added, "a lady who's impressed by a fancy label."

"Hmmph!" Diana pretended to be offended as she

watched him pour the dark red liquid into his glass, lift it and swirl it around before taking a sip. "You're the type who would put a classic label on a bottle of Thunderbird just to catch a faker, aren't you?" she demanded.

Beau stared at her over the glass, his eyes wide. "What a marvelous idea!" I'm sure I would have thought of it myself, but I doubt I could have found anybody up to the test in these parts." He poured some wine into her glass and held it out. "Why don't you try it and tell me what you think?" he offered. His smile was positively wicked.

Diana accepted the glass, watching him watch her drink. The wine was dark and full flavored, with a woody hint and a burnished touch of gold beneath the fruitiness. Diana was quite sure it was an excellent vintage—French, for certain—but the glint in Beau's eye made her hesitate. Was he trying to fool her or not?

"Mmmmm." She wouldn't deny that it was good. Then she added, more hesitantly, "It's French, isn't it? Chateau Lafite, perhaps?" She took another sip, a longer one this time, to hide her embarrassment. Whether Beau intended it or not, she certainly felt like a phony right now!

A curious smile flickered across Beau's lips, replacing the grin with something a little less readable. "'Fraid not, ma'am," he replied with his most courteous drawl. "As a matter of fact, it's just a little ol' thing my mammy brewed up right in our back yard. Not up to your highfalutin' city standards, no doubt, but it does just fine for us country folk."

During this ridiculous speech, Beau's hand crept forward stealthily and turned the bottle around so that the label was out of Diana's sight. But Diana saw the motion and reached out quickly, grasping the bottle by the neck.

"Chateau Lafite '68," she read, clicking her teeth

against her tongue in exasperation. "Now what on
earth was that little performance about?" she demanded.

Beau shrugged. He didn't seem in the least cha-
grined. "Not much," he replied, refilling their glasses.
"Just trying to establish some perspective."

Diana started to reply, but something in his face
made her stop. Beau seemed to be looking at her as if
seeing her for the first time. His flickering dark eyes
broke the lighthearted mood into something that made
her slightly uneasy because it had come about with so
little warning. He seemed to have a habit of doing that,
of switching moods without giving any prior indication.
Diana, who was used to picking up subtleties as fast as
they were issued, found herself at somewhat of a loss.
But she was fascinated by the way his pupils changed,
even in the dim light of the bar, from brown to almost
black and back to brown again. She was also aware of
his body, so still and strong as it leaned against the bar,
and of her own fingers, twirling the stem of her
wineglass nervously around and around.

Beau must have noticed that, too; the color of his
eyes changed again, and the corners of his eyes lifted
into a smile. "Let's drink up, shall we?"

Diana was only too glad to comply. She drained her
glass. But Beau put his hand over it before she could
refill it. "Not here, though." He glanced over his
shoulder. "I'm afraid the thundering hordes will be
returning soon. And we don't want this Chateau Lafite
'68 to get caught in the crush of bourbon and branch,
do we?"

Diana smiled. "Most certainly not." She was glad the
mood had broken.

"Then may I suggest," he said, stepping away from
the bar with a flourish, "that we repair to a quiet corner
so that we may share our wine and our life stories
without fear of any boorish interruptions?"

"Mr. Gatling," Diana said graciously, "it would be a pleasure."

"Please, Miz Jennings," he murmured as they walked over to a small alcove hidden behind a drooping Ficus tree in a terra-cotta pot, "won't you call me Beauregard?"

"Beauregard." She tried to say it the way he had, letting the vowels spill like bubbles out of her mouth. But she giggled as she spoke, and it ruined the effect.

"I'll try," she promised, "but you must call me Diana."

"Da-ana." He pretended to be testing the word on his tongue. "Dah-anna. The goddess of the hunt, right?"

Diana nodded inanely. She hoped he would say her name again and again. As a matter of fact, she hoped she could listen to his honey-and-gravel voice all night long.

Three hours later, Beau and Diana were still sitting in their hidden alcove between the bar and the lobby, leaning back against the cushions of the high-backed banquette and talking in low, urgent tones. The lobby had long ago filled up with returning journalists, but their boisterous high spirits barely filtered into their hideaway, so engrossed were they in sharing their life stories and the excellent wine.

Diana had forgotten all about the things that separated her from Beauregard Gatling. Their upbringings, the cities in which they lived, their professional attitudes. Even his steadfast southern chivalry was unimportant in the steady flow of words that rushed between them. She felt as if she were talking to somebody she had known forever, and there was never a moment when she judged what Beau said against her own world. Only the positive things stood out, the things they shared. He loved to write and had always had a passion for sports. He loved reading British detective fiction for relaxation and had never in his life had the patience to complete an entire crossword puzzle. He loved good wine but didn't know a thing about gourmet food. And he had always, always, known what he wanted to be when he grew up.

It was only when the lobby finally began to empty out again and the quiet intruded on them more clearly than the noise had that Diana looked at her watch.

"I don't believe it! It's two-fifteen!"

Beau's eyes reflected her own droll expression of amazement. "I believe it," he said, and indicated the small coffee table in front of them. Three bottles were neatly lined up on it, and only one of them held any wine. "It's early yet," he went on. "We still have half a bottle to go, and I'm only up to my junior year in college!"

"No. No, absolutely not." Diana realized she was grinning in spite of her firm statement, and the idea made her grin even more broadly. "I make it an ironclad rule to be in bed by midnight when I'm on the road. I already owe myself two hours."

"What happens at midnight?" Beau inquired. "Do you northern girls turn into pumpkins or something?" Although he was smiling, too, his manner had suddenly changed. In spite of all the wine, Diana could sense the difference. They weren't just two friends talking anymore. They were man and woman.

"Do southern women? Turn into pumpkins, I mean." She wanted to keep it light.

"Nope. They turn into peaches. Ripe, juicy, southern peaches, just as sweet as they can be." He moved slightly forward as he spoke, his eyes smoky under half-closed lids. Diana had to hold herself in check to keep from swaying toward him as he brushed two fingers lightly down her cheek.

"Oh."

She considered her alternatives for a moment and

decided to behave rationally despite all inclinations to the contrary. "Well, I'm afraid we northerners are a bit more prickly than that," she said in a tight voice. "Especially when we have a full day's work ahead of us."

"Yeah. Those tricycle races are going to be pretty heavy going for a pro like you." Beau seemed to acquiesce easily, but she could feel his fingers dropping reluctantly from her face.

Diana sighed. "I had a nice time talking to you," she said forlornly. "Really I did."

She tried to hold his gaze steadily, but she knew he was aware of her struggle, just as she had been aware of his unspoken intentions. His eyes left hers and traveled up and down her body as if calculating the odds for one last attempt. Then he nodded.

"Tell me something, Dah-anna." His voice was husky. "Do they make 'em all like you back up there in New York?"

There was something prickly about this statement, but Diana chose to ignore it. "No sirree." She grinned, standing up quickly. She seemed to wobble slightly as she stood. "They broke the mold when they made me."

Beau chuckled deep in his throat and stood up slowly in front of her, stretching each limb so that Diana had to look away to avoid gaping. In her lower heels, she was an inch or so shorter than Beau, and from the way he flexed his shoulders when he stretched, she suddenly got an impression of strength. She shook her head once to clear it of the woozy image. When she looked back at Beau, he was smiling down into her eyes.

"I'll bet," he whispered. "I'll just bet they did."

Then, since Diana could not seem to think of a single thing to say in reply to that, Beau bent forward and kissed her on the mouth.

It was a brief kiss, and anybody who might have seen it would not have thought it any more romantic than a parting gesture among old friends. But anyone watch-

ing would not have felt the sudden, hot imprint of his
lips against hers or the sharp flash of his tongue
between her teeth, quick as metal. And unless they
were very close, they would not have seen Diana flush
and sigh and grip the amber beads around her throat as
if clinging for support.

It was all over before anyone could have seen. Beau
waited until Diana had opened her eyes once again, the
pupils inky black against pale mint green. She saw his
Adam's apple twitch as he swallowed heavily, and she
realized she was doing the same thing. For a moment,
she couldn't think of what to do next.

Then she realized it was out of her hands. The wine,
the conversation and the growing awareness of a physical desire acted like a drug on her brain, making it
impossible for her to make any rational decision. Her
brief effort at sanity had been useless, and any attempt
to restrain herself would be useless as well. Even if she
had been capable of logic, Diana could not have come
up with a single reason not to go to bed with Beauregard Gatling just then.

Quite clearly, Beau had reached the same decision—
or nondecision. Without saying another word, they
moved through the deserted lobby to the elevators.
Beau pressed the "up" button silently, and they stood
waiting, their eyes glued on one another so intently that
neither of them noticed when the elevator doors slid
open invitingly. Neither of them moved. It was only
when the doors began to shut again that Beau made a
sudden lunge to hold them, and the gesture made
Diana jump.

Beau grinned crookedly at that, and it seemed to
break the tension somewhat. He stepped into the
elevator and gestured broadly to usher her in. "Why
don't you just come on up and I'll show you my
etchings?" he urged huskily.

Diana giggled. "Etchings—hmmph!" She still felt
giddy and totally without conscience, but at least the

facility for speech had returned. "What are they? Great horses you have known?"

Beau leaned across her shoulder to press the button for his floor, and the nearness of his body made her feel all watery around the kneecaps. "You might say that," he whispered against her ear, letting his breath lift the stray hairs along her neck. "Of course, I prefer to concentrate on the fillies."

Diana blinked and pulled back to stare at him. But his affected leer was so expressive that she burst into laughter instead of berating him for the sexist comment.

They were still laughing when they entered his room. It was the same size as Diana's and Alison's, but instead of the second double bed, there was a pair of chairs and a small settee up against the window. His room was on the opposite side of the building from Diana's, and the view of the Ohio River, just a few blocks away from the Galt House, was magnificent.

"Beautiful, really lovely," she murmured, staring out into the still blue light.

"Yes, indeed," Beau added, and when he came up behind her, she fell into his arms.

It was so swift and so artless that they didn't even have time to reach the double bed. Instead, they slipped down to the thick carpet in one motion, melting together so heatedly that Diana was unaware of the encumbrance of clothing that separated her bare skin from his. It was as if she could feel, through two layers of clothing, the warm, satiny friction of his chest against her nipples, and they hardened so abruptly that it felt as if an electric current had turned her on.

Then she became aware of a low, moaning sound and realized slowly that it was the sound of her own sighs, magnified against Beau's mouth. He, too, was sighing, but it was a deeper sound, more like a growl in the pit of his sternum, and it rumbled against her chest like the excitement of an approaching train.

Suddenly, the clothes were a tremendous obstacle; they bound and manacled their bodies and kept them cruelly apart. Cursing under his breath, Beau literally ripped his from his body, and his fevered fingers leaped to help Diana's, made numb and clumsy by desire.

Then they paused, on their knees and face to face, holding each other at arm's length to marvel at how right their combined intuition had been. Diana was unable to pick out details; her vision seemed as swollen and blurry as her lips felt. But she knew that he was delightful. She had a sense of smooth planes and beveled edges, of the pulsing of muscle and the coursing of blood through taut veins. Beau's face seemed to glow with the reflection from an unseen light, which Diana thought might be coming from her own glittering eyes. As her eyes traveled down lower, she saw his groin arching up and out with trenchant desire, and her body responded of its own accord, her spine bending inward as if drawn by a magnetic force.

The carpet was thick and rough beneath her as they rolled down to it, and she relished the grainy pattern against her buttocks. Then he entered her, his arms gripped tightly around her back so that his hands reached clear around to the tender source of her breasts beneath her armpits. And it seemed to Diana that the carpet fell away beneath her as they rocked skyward at a precipitous rate. Her head fell back on her shoulders, and she could feel the springy coils of Beau's hair as he bent his head against her neck.

It took them a long time to climax. Each time one of them felt the ultimate shudder approaching, they held back, concentrating instead on giving pleasure and maintaining the rich rhythms they had established together. Although the ability to reason was long since lost in the need to experience union, they both realized intuitively that to waste this moment would be a cruel trick. Fate had brought them there, and fate would hold them together until the last possible moment, when both bodies communicated that the moment was at hand and that the time was now.

Diana was fairly experienced in the nature of sexual satisfaction. But never before had she reached a climax with such a complete lack of forethought and control. It was a purely instinctive response, as free from guile and manipulation as the act of breathing. Diana felt the angle of their ascent tip steeply forward; then she felt the usual twinge that reminded her that her contraceptive device was in place, and suddenly, all hell broke loose.

Considering the enormity of her response, it was all over very quickly. They lay meshed together in total abandon on the carpet, their limbs thrown wildly outward from the force of their combined climax. But she found herself recovering her normal rate of breath all too quickly, and the room became quite still.

She could not see his face and did not know whether she cared to. As sanity regained a foothold in her body, Diana began to realize the extent to which she had compromised herself. Certainly she had never intended for this to happen with any man, much less this one. Oh, he was pleasant enough, and a good deal smarter than she had given him credit for at first, but this—! This was unacceptable!

She struggled upright. "Beau," she began.

"Hmmm?" His voice was calm and reassuring and gave her the courage to turn to face him.

"I . . ." She smiled lamely. "I just wanted you to understand . . ."

"Please." He reached up one languid arm and placed a finger across her mouth. "Please, don't go into it now, all right?" His smile was genuine, not patronizing but patient. "I just feel too good right now. And so do you." He gave a shrug that was endearingly awkward. "Let's not bother, okay?"

This was fine with Diana. Now that the deed had been done—and she could not persuade herself that it had been altogether a mistake—she only wanted to escape its consequences. If they could manage to savor the experience without attaching any importance to it whatsoever, then Diana would consider herself lucky.

And it appeared Beau was willing to do just that. They lay idly together for a few moments more, just long enough to avoid seeming rude. Then Diana washed and dressed, with Beau's solicitous but not overbearing help. When his hand brushed against her body, it was a tender but not possessive gesture—just what Diana wanted. He saw her to the door of his room, traded a last pliant and knowledgeable kiss and then closed the door with just the right touch of regret—not too little but not too much.

It was only when she fell into bed that she realized she was still a bit tipsy. The thought gave her some comfort, and she fell asleep immediately with a smile on her face.

Chapter 4

DIANA GOT UP VERY CAREFULLY THE NEXT MORNING. Between the wine she had consumed, her experience with Beau and the fact that Alison had risen loudly at four A.M. to join her girl jockey at the track, she had not slept well at all. Experience had taught her that such mornings needed to be handled gingerly in order to minimize the risk of ruining the entire day.

That day, in particular, Diana took pains to probe gently at her mood, like a child examining a new tooth. It was not like her to go to bed giggling and even less like her to wake up with a smile still on her lips, especially after what should have been a major disaster in her life. She knew that while the wine might have been responsible for her lack of discretion the previous night, it was more likely to leave her scowling the morning after being consumed so liberally. But the face that greeted her in the mirror looked astonishingly peaceful and rested, and the glint of laughter in her clear green eyes was unmistakable.

"You sure can hold your liquor, girl," she announced

to her reflection with a swagger. But the laughing eyes mocked her, and she knew that Beau Gatling was responsible for her mood. Not only because he had let her ease out of what might have been an embarrassing situation with all the grace she could muster, but also because that embarrassing situation had been so damned much fun. Now, if only the gentleman would oblige her by continuing to act as if nothing at all had happened between them, Diana would be content to savor her physical memories and get on with her life.

She switched on the local radio station. A man's voice entreated her to come on down and make herself at home at the Derby Bar and Grill. Idly, she wondered if Louisville was any less emphatically southern during the fifty-one weeks of the year that were not Derby. She suspected that the entire city went out of its way to charm visitors.

Diana gathered her hair into a loose knot at the back of her head, turning critically from side to side to examine the effect. Was Beau Gatling doing the same thing as that radio announcer, she found herself thinking? Going out of his way to charm visitors? Had their lovemaking merely been his contribution to the Chamber of Commerce? Diana hoped so. But she also hoped not, and as soon as she recognized that forbidden impulse, she dropped her hands and let her hair fall heavily across her bare shoulders.

"Come on, now," she reminded herself sternly. "Rules are rules. You broke them this time, but let's just make damned sure it doesn't happen again. No mixing business with pleasure. You've got work to do today!"

The announcer was now urging her to attend the great bicycle race being held that afternoon at the fairgrounds. "Great bicycle race, great balloon race . . . doesn't anybody care about the great horse race?" she asked the radio. The announcer apparently didn't, so Diana tied up her hair, pulled on her favorite sweatsuit for heavy writing and sat down at her typewriter to type out her notes.

So far, she really did not have much to go on. She managed seventy-five lines of copy on the atmosphere in Louisville and the kinds of events that set the stage for the Derby, and she prepared that for submission via teletype to Cam Davis back in New York. Then she got down to the business of sorting out her thoughts on the subject that really interested her—the mysterious Derek Islington and his odds-on favorite Street Fare.

There were even fewer facts to go on there. Everyone she had spoken to the day before had only confirmed what Beau had told her—that Islington was notoriously reclusive, that he never spoke to the press and that his appearance, even behind the scenes at the Derby, was something of a surprise. She also learned that he had a reputation for wheeling and dealing and that he had some very powerful connections in the state legislature. But no one was willing to admit that they even suspected the man of wielding influence for personal gain. Just like Beau, everyone she spoke to seemed to lower their eyes or look the other way.

Of course, this only made Diana more determined that there was something going on behind his cloak of secrecy, and that if everybody else in Louisville ignored it, it didn't mean she had to do the same. She decided to start by focusing on the curious lack of activity at the Fleur D'Isle stables at Churchill Downs. Looking back over her notes and recalling the frantic pace she had witnessed while wandering around the other stables, she decided there was definitely something odd about Street Fare's absence. A call to the racing board produced no clear answer as to whether this was common practice, and several phone calls to other authorities produced a similar lack of result. Diana began to think that the conspiracy of silence went beyond Beau's unwillingness to share his "scoop" with her.

By the time she got up from her typewriter four hours later, she had finished a pot of room-service coffee and eight pages of speculation.

"Not much to go on," she muttered, making a face as she pored over what she had written. The only thing worthwhile as far as she was concerned was a series of questions she had prepared to ask Derek Islington. And Diana realized that one clear thing had come out of her morning's work, after all: she was bound and determined to meet this reclusive gentleman and ask him those questions face to face.

Then she went to her closet to get dressed. "What on earth do you wear to a bicycle race?" she asked herself. "Alison, where are you when I need you most?" Finally, deciding that bicycle races and balloon races required much the same dress codes, she pulled out a flowered challis skirt and a pale cotton blouse with a notched stand-up collar and cuffed sleeves. Then, after stopping at the Galt House coffee shop long enough to consume a turkey club sandwich and two newspapers, she set off by cab for the fairgrounds.

During the ride, Diana had congratulated herself several times on having gotten through the morning without once daydreaming about the time she had spent with Beau the previous night. It was a sign to her that she had managed to keep the occasion in its proper perspective and her own emotions well under control. It had been a pleasant way to while away the evening; there was no doubt about that. But life—meaning work—went on.

In that frame of mind, it was something of a shock when, having arrived at the fairgrounds, she spotted Beau almost at once, waving broadly to her from among a circle of men just beyond the press stands. It was even more of a shock to feel the giddy lurch of her heart at the sight of him and to understand that she had been hoping to see him all along. Diana took the time to marshal her common sense before she returned the wave and made her way toward him through the crowded stands. Beau was watching her all the while, and she noticed that his cronies were trying hard not to do the same. Despite her fluttering heart, a little voice inside her head kept chanting, "Be on guard, Diana. Be on guard."

When she got to the cluster of folding chairs where they sat, Beau rose, and the other men shifted uneasily in their seats to greet her. Most of them were quite a bit older than she was, and Beau was easily the youngest man present.

Diana knew this sort of crowd well. It was clear they both appreciated and resented her presence among them, and she could almost hear them all thinking to themselves that it was all well and good to be a pretty woman writing sports columns, but a lady had to do a lot of proving before they, for one, were gonna believe it!

The situation was a common one to Diana. What was not common was Beau's steadfast chivalry in the face of his peers' unspoken resentment. He made a great show of holding out a chair for her, brushing it off quickly and then making sure it was positioned out of the direct glare of the sun. Normally, Diana would not have allowed such elaborate courtliness on her behalf. But she knew that Beau was deliberately setting her up to make the men most at their ease. And that was exactly what she wanted—at first.

"Miss Diana Jennings of the New York *Chronicle,* I'd like you to meet . . ." Beau went around the circle naming his friends, all of whom wrote for various southern newspapers. Diana recognized a few of the names, but not many, and from the cagey nods she got in return, it was clear that nobody recognized hers. Only her gender, it seemed, was an established fact. After Beau's introductions, there was an awkward silence. Diana, having decided that she was going to milk this situation for any information she could get, readied herself to handle it.

"We were just discussing the pari-mutuel odds, Miss Jennings," Beau explained. He spoke slowly and solicitously, and Diana wondered if he wasn't carrying the gentleman bit too far. It was clear from the formal way in which he addressed her that he had no intention of letting these men know what friendly terms they had been on the night before. She looked over at him sharply, but he ignored the challenge in her eyes.

"You know," Beau went on, "that the odds change every day. Every time a horse works out, every little bit of information that leaks up from the training circle to the betting window has an effect. The closer it gets to Derby Day, the crazier it gets."

Diana allowed her gaze to linger a bit longer on Beau's smiling face. What did he think she was, a moron? It was one thing to make a show of courtesy, but he had no right to talk down to her in that manner just to make his friends feel more at ease.

"I was aware of that," she murmured quietly. Then, looking from one face to another, she continued blandly, "But it does seem strange to me that some horses never get out there where people can see them. I suppose that means the odds on those horses don't change, doesn't it?" She paused, but not long enough to let anybody break in. "Take Street Fare, for instance." She could feel the circle tense up. "Why, I just realized this morning that his odds haven't changed in four days!"

She looked around her innocently, aware of the shock waves she had generated. Beau was carefully avoiding her eyes.

"Where'd you hear that bit of information?" one man asked her tersely.

"Hear it?" Diana allowed herself a small smile. "Why, sir, it's right there for the world to see. As a matter of fact, I was able to compare his prerace

standings in all major races for the past year by looking
at the pari-mutuel figures for the week preceding each
race Street Fare ran." She leaned forward in her chair.
"Why, do you realize that his odds remain constant
right up until the evening before the race, in every
single case?"

She thought she heard Beau groan, but otherwise
there was complete silence around her. Finally, another
man spoke up after exchanging several glances with his
colleagues. "I'm sure you've done your homework, Miz
Jennings," he said, "but if I were you, I sure wouldn't
put much store by what you read." He gave a short,
humorless laugh. "Figures do lie, you know."

"That's funny," murmured Diana. "I thought it was
people who lied."

The man who had spoken first cleared his throat. "As
a matter of fact, ma'am," he said, emphasizing the title
heavily, "you happen to be wrong. Street Fare's odds
are changing this afternoon. And it's still four days to
go before the race."

This was news to everyone. "Where'd you hear that,
Jack?" Beau asked instantly. He had leaned back in his
chair, and since Diana was sitting next to him, she
could no longer see his face.

"I got it straight from the horse's mouth," Jack
replied. "Lou Belvedere himself." He watched Diana
for her reaction to this earthshaking bit of news, and
when none seemed forthcoming, he elaborated. "Lou
Belvedere's Street Fare's trainer, you see, ma'am."

"His trainer?" In spite of her efforts to remain calm,
Diana's eyes widened. "His trainer told you that the
odds were going to change later today? And he's still
being kept off the track?" She spread her palms upward. "How could his trainer possibly know what the
odds were going to be?"

Jack realized he had made a mistake. "Belvedere
knows what he's talking about," he muttered.

Diana shook her outstretched palms impatiently. She

didn't remember ever feeling so completely outnumbered, so hopelessly defenseless. "He's hardly an objective source," she said tightly. "Wouldn't you agree?"

Beside her, she could hear the legs of Beau's chair slamming down. "Look," he said, sounding as impatient as Diana felt. "There's a lot you can learn by listening to an insider like Belvedere. He must know that Street Fare has something going on, even if no one else knows about it yet. He was probably just offering a good guess, not a hard fact. Am I right, Jack?"

Jack nodded miserably.

"Anyway, there happens to be a perfectly legitimate explanation for Street Fare's absence from the public eye. And there has been for every race he's ever run."

Diana turned on him furiously. "Oh, really?" she snapped. "Like what? It's supposed to be illegal for a horse to remain in seclusion after the betting's opened. And if he is under wraps for some reason, then the odds aren't allowed to change. So what's the story with Street Fare? From an objective source like yourself, of course."

She heard, very clearly, the sound of Beau's jaws clamping shut in anger. For a moment, they sat there, their eyes blazing dark against light, their anger all out of proportion to the situation. The curls quivered on Beau's head, although he sat very still. "You want to know the reason?" he hissed. "Go find out for yourself. You're the hot-shot lady reporter from New York. We're just a bunch of lazy hicks."

Diana heard a chuckle of relief from somewhere else along the circle, but neither she nor Beau reacted. It was quite clear that they were conducting business on two different levels. Diana was more convinced than ever that there was something happening with Derek Islington, and she was sure Beau and the boys knew more about it than they were letting on. But the conflict between them now was about something altogether

different. It was about Diana's insistence on being
treated as a complete equal and about Beau's contempt
for the image he knew she had of him at heart. It was
about acknowledging that the previous night meant
more than they cared to admit.

They might have remained in that angry face-off for
hours if Jack hadn't gotten up the courage to interrupt.
"That's just horse racing, lady," he said smugly. "Nobody ever said it was objective. It's all a matter of
instinct. And you gotta trust the instincts of a guy like
Lou Belvedere. He knows the score."

Diana responded without taking her eyes off Beau,
but the icy precision in her voice could not have failed
to effect Jack as well. "I'm quite sure that Lou Belvedere knows the score," she said slowly. "As a matter of
fact, it's beginning to sound as if he sets the score, too."

Beau's eyes narrowed. "Watch yourself, Diana."

"Watch yourself, Diana," she mimicked. For a moment, she was too angry to think of what to say and
incapable of regaining composure despite the shocked
silence of the men around her. "Why should I watch
myself, Beau? What's the big secret that all you reporters are trying to hide?"

She knew this wounded him by the way his jaw
twitched before he spoke. But his voice was steady and
quiet. "I wouldn't make unsupported statements about
someone like Lou Belvedere if I were you, that's all."

"I'm sure you wouldn't," she retorted. "But tell me,
Mr. Gatling. Did you write Elmo Stewart's story by
listening to people like Lou Belvedere? Is that your
idea of getting at the truth?"

"Lou helped." Beau's voice was dangerously calm.

"He didn't help Elmo," she snapped.

There was a scraping of wood as one of the men
moved to leave the area. But Beau waved an impatient
arm out, and the sound stopped abruptly.

"You don't know a thing about the Elmo Stewart
story, lady, and if you did, you wouldn't have the guts

to do a damn thing about it. So I'd just cut the New York superior act and start paying attention to what's going on down here in the real world."

The angry embers in Beau's eyes had died down, and now they were a curiously flat brown color. She could feel how far away from her he was slipping, and this only increased her anger until, even to herself her voice sounded tight and out of control.

"I have been paying close attention," she hissed, "and I've decided that it's time someone around here got off their ass and began asking some real questions." Although Diana had very little control over what she was saying, an idea had begun to form in her mind even as she spoke. "And I'm beginning to see just where I should begin, too."

The light changed again in Beau's eyes. Now they watched her expectantly, as if he already knew what she was going to say.

"Lou Belvedere was Dark Star's trainer, too, wan't he, Beau? And that means that Derek Islington was the owner of that horse. *He* was the one who let Elmo ride to his death two years ago." Beau's silence and the complete stillness of the men in the circle were all the answer she needed to hear.

"And you've never forgiven yourself because you couldn't touch Derek Islington, have you? A man rode to his death, and Derek Islington walked away without a crease in his fancy suit." She looked around at the shocked, slack-mouthed expressions of the other men. Jack was sweating profusely. "None of you," she went on bitterly, "can touch him. And it hurts, but you don't do a thing about it. You don't talk about it, you don't write about it—you just sit around in your cozy little circles patting each other on the back."

Her wooden folding chair scraped backward with a harsh shriek, and Beau winced. Standing above them all, Diana had a sudden image of herself as seen from the outside: a tall, imperious woman, her green eyes dilated with pain and anger, her wide lips trembling to contain irrational tears. The perfect picture, she thought bitterly, to confirm their image of women as creatures of instinct and unpredictable passions.

But she was past caring. And she didn't trust herself to cast a last look back at Beau. Despite her frightening loss of control over her emotions, she was suddenly thinking with perfect clarity. She knew what it was she had to do, for a number of reasons, and she couldn't wait a minute longer to do it. She spun sharply around and began to walk away.

"Where are you going?" It was Beau's voice, imperious and betraying, for the first time, the extent of his anger. *Of course,* she told herself. *I've embarrassed him in front of his buddies, and he has to try to save face.* She kept on walking as she tossed the answer over her shoulder with venomous satisfaction. "I'm going to talk to Derek Islington."

Diana had to force herself not to run. Her body was trembling, and she was breathing in short, angry puffs. Her mind was moving way ahead of her body, recalling the bits of memory that had led her to piece together the truth about Derek Islington and Elmo Stewart. But while occupied with that, she had no idea where she was walking and had to change directions suddenly several times to avoid running into people or objects. She finally came up short in front of the grandstand itself, and finding people blocking her path in both directions as well as in the way she had come, she simply stopped short. She stood there, forcing herself to take deep, steadying breaths, while clenching and unclenching her hands on the splintery banister.

You should have known, she told herself. *You should have known better than to walk into the middle of that circle of old . . . old hacks and expect to come out unscathed. You should have known which side Beau would take. You should have figured out that Beau knew something about Islington, something that he wouldn't tell because he didn't have the guts to use it himself. But you were careless and cocky, and you lost control of the situation. You're paying for last night today, girl. Did you imagine you would get away unscathed?*

"Never again," she muttered under her breath. "That won't happen again." She stared sightlessly across the grandstand to where the great annual bicycle race was going on amid great hilarity. Grown men pedaled furiously around the course on small tricycles, their faces red with embarrassment and exertion. Diana put her hand to her own cheek and felt the heat there. She rubbed hard, trying to erase the telltale sign, then passed her fingers wearily across her brow. The hoots and hollers of the crowd made a gray wave of noise, and the antics of the contestants blurred her vision. But Diana ignored all that. Instead, she heard her own futile arguments with herself and saw, over and over, the bitter look on Beau's face as she got up to leave.

Whatever had possessed her to think of him as an ally? He had seemed so familiar the night before, so willing to play the game her way. How could she have failed to recognize the familiar syndrome, she who had taken such pains to explain to Alison that she never got involved with journalists and that southern men held no appeal?

Diana felt unfamiliar tears of frustration stinging her eyes. She had nobody to blame but herself, she thought, blinking them back and forcing herself to focus on the gyrations of a man on a tricycle in front of her on the field. And, of course, there was nothing to do about it but to go on, once again, to prove that she could do as good a job as they could—better, because none of them were willing to bother. She would have to be better, and it wasn't fair.

Catching her lower lip between her teeth to steady it, Diana began to sort out her options. She had every intention of going for that interview with Derek Islington. But *how* she was going to get it was another issue.

Usually, a letter of introduction, or its verbal equivalent, was necessary to get in to see someone like Derek Islington. Since he made it a rule not to give out interviews, a letter from her editor would hardly open the door in this case. The only other alternative was a good word from a mutual friend, but there was no one whose acquaintance they had in common—no one except Beau Gatling, that is, and Diana was bleakly aware that there was no way she could expect help from him. On further reflection, it occurred to her that after the story Beau had written about Elmo Stewart, there was probably no love lost between him and Islington. That would explain Beau's reluctance to confront the man the day before at the stables.

All in all, it looked pretty hopeless. As a matter of fact, in her current state of mind, it looked completely hopeless. But Diana had every intention of willing herself out of her mood of despair and of working up a nice healthy steam of anger. There was nothing like a tantrum to set things in motion, no matter how helpless they might seem. . . .

"Diana."

When she spun her head around, Diana realized that she was already angry. So angry that Beau flinched at the sight of her taut, pinched face. But he spoke before she did.

"God," he said wearily, "I'm so sorry."

The simple, heavy cadence to his words and the bewildered furrow to his brow took some of the bitter wind right out of her sails. He shook his head slowly from side to side. "I'm so sorry," he repeated, as if he could think of no more eloquent way of expressing himself.

Diana considered him for a moment, her face framed against the afternoon sun. Angry comments and accusations flicked through her mind like projections on a screen. Although she didn't speak out loud, it seemed to her that Beau could read each thought as it passed by and that he sadly acknowledged every one.

Finally, she understood that there was no reason to say it out loud. "So am I." She sighed and turned back toward the field. The winners of the tricycle race were frolicking forward to get their awards, and someone was booming their names through the loudspeaker. As Diana watched, all her anger evaporated into weariness.

Beau moved up beside her, also looking out on the scene. "That doesn't happen to you much anymore, does it?"

She cast a swift, oblique glance at his profile, not sure if she understood what he meant.

"Getting pushed up against a wall because you're a woman, I mean." His expression didn't change as he spoke, but his brows drew closer together over his straight nose. Diana found herself watching his mouth, entranced by the slight fullness in his lower lip.

"It doesn't happen so much anymore," she replied carefully, unwilling to let her surprise show. "But it still happens. And I never have learned how to control myself in that situation."

"I don't know what could have come over me," Beau muttered, half to himself. "To have invited you over and then behaved so rudely." He seemed to be truly amazed.

Diana allowed herself a small, dry smile. "You weren't exactly the model of a southern gentleman."

He caught her softened expression but did not smile back. "I wasn't exactly the model of a mature person, either." He shook his head again. "I sacrificed you back there for a bunch of old coots who call themselves my friends."

"You didn't want to make them look foolish."

"That's right. I didn't. Because I knew it would make me look foolish right along with them." He thought it over, pursing that lower lip. "So I tried to make a fool out of you instead."

"And I rose right to the occasion," she added. "I didn't exactly handle myself well, either."

They both turned to look out at the field. Diana felt a soothing breeze lifting the hair off the back of her neck. For a moment, neither of them spoke. There was some comfort, she reflected, in realizing that, by mutual consent, the previous night would not be discussed.

"Trouble is," Beau continued, "it's hard to make a fool out of you, Diana Jennings." He had turned to face her, and although she still faced out to the field, she could feel his dark eyes traveling over the angle of her olive cheek and jaw. "You've got more brains in your little finger than all those guys put together, Diana."

There was something so insistently warm in the way he repeated her name that Diana turned back to him in spite of herself. He was smiling now, and his eyes were a clear velvet brown.

"And I'm glad," he finished in a whisper, leaning slightly forward so that the hubbub around them was momentarily blanked out by his voice. "Because you're worth more as a friend than they are."

Diana felt herself slipping into the inviting pool of his smile, and she drew back with a visible effort. "That's kind of you, Beau," she said stiffly. And then, thinking better of it, she faced him again. "I mean, it's really nice. Thank you," she corrected herself with a shy smile.

Beau seemed to understand the effort it took for her not to pull away, and he nodded, smiling back. They stood there, smiling and nodding until they both realized simultaneously what a silly picture they were making.

"Well!" Beau broke the mood by rubbing his hands together briskly. "I guess the excitement is over for another day."

Diana glanced back at the emptying grandstand and

chuckled. "If you can call it excitement," she commented.

"Listen, don't knock tricycles," Beau advised her, his good spirits returning rapidly. "Have you ever tried to steer one of them babies around a dirt course?"

Diana was feeling better fast, too. "Not in the past thirty years," she told him, "but you know what they say: Once you learn . . ."

". . . You can never forget!" he finished with her, and they both laughed. Together they fell in with the crowd headed for the exit.

"Were you serious back there?" Beau had a habit of changing subjects quickly and without apparent reason. But, curiously enough, Diana had no trouble picking up on his train of thought.

"About getting an interview with Derek Islington?"

"Um-hm."

Diana looked at him, shading her eyes against the slant of the sun. "Why?"

He caught the meaning of her look and shook his head. "No, no. I'm not gonna start that line again. I was just curious to see if you meant it, that's all." His voice was casual, but Diana knew better.

"I meant it, all right. I had planned on doing it even before I saw you today." She made a face. "That little encounter only made me more determined."

Beau grinned. "I figured as much. Well, look, I just might be able to help you, that's all."

"But I thought you said Islington doesn't give interviews."

"He doesn't."

"And I gathered there was no love lost between you two."

Beau grimaced. "That," he said, "is an understatement."

He gripped her arm and steered her away from the crowd toward another gate farther from the main exit. "But I do have a pretty good relationship with Lou

Belvedere. It survived Elmo Stewart, and . . . several other rather tense occasions. He might be able to give you a leg up, so to speak."

"Why?"

"Why what?"

"Why are you trying to help me get an interview with Islington? He may have a personal reason not to see you, but he doesn't see anybody. What good would it do?"

Beau pursed his lips and shrugged. "There's no reason why you shouldn't give it a try, is there?"

She watched him cautiously. "Because of last night?"

He allowed himself the smallest smile. "That's the obvious reason, of course. But actually it's because you're good. And because you're determined. And"—he shaded his eyes and squinted before continuing—"because you haven't had a chance to get scared and lazy like the rest of us have around here."

"Why should you be scared?"

"That's an excellent question. Why should we be scared?" Beau laughed bitterly. "Just think of it as a Louisville tradition, right? And you are a tradition buster if ever I saw one."

Diana was not sure she wanted to be flattered in this manner. Something about his tone of voice made her nervous.

"You know," she said warily, "somehow you just don't strike me as the type to give away secrets to the competition. And the *Chronicle* is the competition. Why, Beau?"

He shook his head. "Because I don't know myself, that's why. But if you're game, if you think you've got an angle that will work on this guy, then I'll give you a hand."

A warning bell sounded in Diana's mind. "I don't want any favors I can't return, Beau," she told him. "No *bedroom* tradeoffs for me, you understand?"

His brows shot up. "You've made yourself quite clear

on that issue," he said dryly. "But I assume your great
code of the north doesn't include a simple letter of
introduction to Lou? You could talk to him first, see if
you even want to bother."

"Oh, I want to bother," she put in quickly.

He ignored her interruption. "Then, if you can
interest Lou in helping you finagle an appointment with
His Honor, that's totally up to you."

"Sounds fair to me," Diana said. She stopped and
put her hand on his shoulder. "But that's as far as it
goes, friend or no friend. I'll take it from there on my
own."

Beau grinned. "Lady, I had no intention of lifting
another finger where Mr. Islington is concerned."

She grinned back. "Then I accept." she extended her
hand.

He took it, reached out and picked up her other hand
and imprisoned them both between his own.

"So do I," he said emphatically. "So do I."

Beau told her he would arrange things with Lou
Belvedere right away. He and Diana planned to meet
later that night, back at the Galt House, after attending
a dinner and press party being held at Churchill Downs
by the Kentucky Horsebreeders' Association. They
considered going to the dinner together, but Beau said
he had already made plans to sit with the rest of the
staff from the *Times-Union,* and Diana, after the events
of the afternoon, politely declined to join him there.
Smiling, Beau told her he understood.

By the time she went to meet Beau after the dinner,
however, things had changed considerably. Diana had
already had her first interview with Derek Islington.
What's more, she had arranged with him for an even
lengthier discussion to take place the following day.

Diana would have found it hard to resist being just
the tiniest bit smug about the whole thing in the face of
this unexpected coup, but the truth of the matter was

she had practically fallen into the situation and was as surprised as anyone that it worked out so well.

She had arrived at the clubhouse of the Downs along with Alison, who had been deeply engrossed in relating the story of her girl jockey all the way from the hotel. Diana was wearing a simple black sheath of lightweight wool with a strand of Lucite beads glistening against her exposed collarbone and another on her lanky, tanned wrist. Except for the scooped back, the dress was subdued and chic. Alison, on the other hand, was wearing a short beaded bolero jacket in pale peach over a soft gray circle skirt. With her bubbly pouf of blonde curls and her animated face, Diana had remarked that she looked good enough to eat. To which Alison had replied, quite calmly, "Yes, I know."

Given the contrasts in their outfits, Diana just assumed that the stir caused by their entrance was on Alison's behalf. But a short while later, while standing alone at the huge glass windows that overlooked the racecourse, a slim stranger approached her with a diffident smile.

"Are you aware of having caused a mild sensation?" he inquired, lounging gracefully against the glass.

Diana recognized Derek Islington at once from the glimpse she had gotten down by the stables the day before. That spare figure, oozing monied elegance, was impossible to mistake for any other. But she made an effort to mask her reaction and to control her surprise at seeing him there tonight.

"When you walk into a room with a woman in pink sequins," she remarked coolly, "it's something you learn to expect." She smiled obliquely and bent her head to sip her wine. What on earth brought the hermit to a press party, she wondered furiously? They were fairly well concealed from the rest of the crowd, and there was no way Diana could unobtrusively scan the crowd for Beau. Instead, she concentrated hard on the man in front of her.

"On the contrary," he replied with a suave smile. "Women in pink sequins should learn to expect it when they make an entrance with brunettes in classic black." His eyes, a subtle mixture of blue and gray, traveled appreciatively over her figure.

"To each his—or her—own," Diana replied, and paused briefly before finishing. "Mr. Islington."

The eyes narrowed, and the body inside the impeccable European suit stiffened perceptibly. He seemed genuinely taken aback by the fact that his identity was known, and Diana took pains to keep her smile light and unrevealing. Then he nodded, as if to acknowledge her advantage.

"I'm afraid I can't return the compliment, Ms. . . ."

Diana couldn't fail to notice the emphasis he put on the title or to be impressed by his courtly manner of speech. She noticed that his accent was much less obvious than Beau's and wondered if he was a Kentucky native. But Beau, she remembered, was able to control the amount of honey in his voice at will. There was no reason why Mr. Islington could not do the same.

"I'm Diana Jennings," she said warmly, extending her hand. "From the New York *Chronicle*."

The hand that grasped hers was cool but firm, and the pressure of the handshake was prolonged for just a moment. "I should have known," he murmured, turning her wrist slightly to examine the lucite bracelet.

"That I was a reporter?"

"No, that you were from Manhattan. They don't sell Elsa Peretti jewelry in Louisville, as far as I know."

He looked up, eyes glittering, and Diana blushed. He had uncovered her weakness for expensive costume jewelry—a very perceptive man.

"Is that fact or just ugly rumor?" She allowed him to hold her wrist briefly before pulling it gently back.

Again, there was a quick narrowing of the eyes before he replied. "I don't deal in rumors, Ms. Jennings," he said evenly. "Only facts."

"I couldn't agree with you more, Mr. Islington," she responded promptly.

Now his eyebrows arched, and he looked at her more closely. Both of them were aware of what was being communicated between the lines, and Diana knew this was a critical moment. Mentally, she went over the questions she had been preparing earlier in the day. Control, she reminded herself. Keep your cool and don't blow this opportunity. But her heart was beating rapidly against her ribs, and she knew her eyes were glittering with excitement.

A small smile had begun to appear on Derek's face, and Diana let her breath out slowly through her teeth. She wasn't going to have to ask out loud the question that hung in the air between them. Islington was going to agree to give her an interview; she could feel it in her reporter's bones. She had no idea why, but she knew he would say yes.

"You want to do a story on Street Fare, don't you, Ms. Jennings."

"No. I want to do a story on you." Now was the moment, she told herself. Lay it out for him before he gets nervous and backs off. Show him what you can do. "Not the rumors but the facts. Why you're in this business and why you think of it as a business and not a sacred ritual like some of the others do." She saw him flash a smile and knew she was on the right track. "What the Derby means exactly, whether you love it . . . or whether you don't give a damn. Why you make it a rule not to come to the races and why you're here at this one."

He looked up sharply. "Who told you I never come to races?"

She chose to ignore the question. "But I want the real story, in your own words. From the horse's mouth, so to speak."

She ended on a smile, and he smiled back. "So to speak." He looked down at the darkened track, tapping slender fingers idly against the glass. "So to speak," he repeated under his breath. Diana, watching his profile, thought she saw a hint of cruelty in the angle of his jaw. She thought briefly of Elmo Stewart but decided Islington's role in that story was not her business. Diana was very good at reading people's expressions, but she had always tried not to let her reading color her judgment of an interview subject early on. One needed an open mind to be able to listen carefully for the truth.

"All right, Ms. Jennings. . . . Diana, is it?" He turned back to her as he asked the question, and Diana nodded. "Let's give it a try, shall we?"

"Whenever it's convenient for you, Mr. Islington." She made a point of not returning the familiar form of address, and Islington's wry smile showed he knew it. He made no attempt to correct her.

"Then you'll be my guest for lunch tomorrow?"

"I'd love to." There was no need to manufacture the enthusiasm in her voice.

"Fine. My car will pick you up at one. The Galt House, right?"

It was a statement, not a question, and Diana's nod was taken as a farewell more than assent. With one last, gracious inclination of his smooth head, Derek Islington turned and walked away. Diana was careful to wait for a few moments before returning to the crowded clubhouse tables. She wanted to avoid an awkward second meeting, and she also needed time to compose herself.

Still, she could not avoid one quick crow to her reflection in the window before turning away.

"Ooooh, boy!" she whispered exultantly. "Wait'll Beau finds out about this!"

Chapter 5

SHE NEED NOT HAVE WORRIED ABOUT RUNNING INTO Derek again. He had apparently left Churchill Downs before the festivities got under way; Diana did not run into him again that evening. Several times during the course of the dinner, she tried to figure out what had brought him there in the first place. Surely he had not intended to mingle with the press—the man who had sworn never to give an interview. But then again, he *had* agreed to be interviewed by Diana, hadn't he? Either Beau and his colleagues had overstated Mr. Islington's aversion to journalists, or Mr. Islington had his own reasons for breaking his silence at last. Diana realized it would put her at an advantage to know *why* he was planning to talk and why he had decided to talk to her.

But for the moment, speculation was useless. Diana reconciled herself to an evening of light laughter and entertainment with Alison and several of their New

York acquaintances. She did catch sight of Beau once
or twice during the meal and the inevitable speeches.
He was sitting at the opposite end of the room, at a
table that was surely the loudest and most boisterous
among a roomful of loud and boisterous people. Diana
knew better than to try and venture near, but she
couldn't help smiling secretly once or twice at the
thought of the bomb she would be able to drop into his
lap later on.

When she arrived back at the Galt House lobby with
Alison and the others from her table, she saw that he
was already waiting in their old alcove beside the bar.
Alison went immediately upstairs to bed, pleading
another early morning ahead of her. Soon after, Diana
also excused herself and went to join Beau. She was
surprised at the shiver of pleasure she experienced as
he watched her approach.

"There's nothing like a black dress to make a woman
look like a woman," he said as she sat down next to
him. Diana chuckled. The compliment was not quite as
gracefully stated as Derek Islington's had been, but it
was nice all the same.

"There's nothing like another endless evening of
self-serving speeches to make a woman feel like her
skull is vibrating," she countered. The noise level at the
Poolsider was not much better than it had been at the
Churchill Downs clubhouse, and Beau winced sympathetically.

"An affliction not restricted to the fair sex alone, my
dear," he told her. "Shall we go somewhere a little less
thunderous to confer?"

"A.S.A.P.," Diana replied, using the familiar short-
hand lingo for "now." "Is there a quieter room we
could sit in on the mezzanine?"

Beau shook his head. "How about going up to your
room?" he inquired casually.

"Sorry, won't do. Alison has another four A.M.

reveille tomorrow morning, and I'm sure she wouldn't appreciate our presence." It was only as she spoke that Diana realized the importance of their conversation. She had been so absorbed by the coup she was about to reveal that she had forgotten to be on guard. Now she had to force herself not to react and to keep her voice as light as Beau's had been. "My room's out," she added unnecessarily.

"Well, then, I guess it'll have to be my place." Beau got up and extended his hand to help her rise. He did not bother to add the word they both heard on the end of that sentence—"my place . . . again."

Diana stood without using his outstretched hand, but she fell companionably into step beside him, trying to smile as if it were the most natural thing in the world to be accompanying him to his room—again. "By the way, why do you have a room here? You live in Louisville, don't you?"

"Actually, I don't live in town. I have a little place about twenty miles out. Fine for your everyday work schedule, but during Derby Week I do need to be here all the time." He pressed the button between the two elevators and watched Diana blandly, as if challenging her to change her mind.

That, of course, she refused to do. They rode up in the elevator, which was mercifully empty, and she waited beside Beau in the hall while he hunted through his pockets for his key, pretending that she was not sneaking nervous glances up and down the hall.

Once inside the room, she marched purposefully to the windows and fixed her gaze on the river. Behind her, she could hear Beau fumbling through the towering piles of papers on his cluttered desk, muttering to himself about having to clean up his act. Diana wondered when she should break the news about not needing Beau's help to get her interview. She wondered if anybody noticed them coming upstairs together. She wondered if she was crazy for being there and if Beau was as nervous as she.

"I talked to Lou this afternoon," he said, sounding perfectly normal. "He seemed to think you had a chance. He even gave me a little note for you saying he knows you—you can bring it straight to Islington, if you get that far. Ah, here it is." He waved a slightly rumpled envelope and sat down on the settee, motioning Diana to sit down also. "But I think you should know that I have some serious reservations."

She had some serious reservations about sitting beside him, but she could not refuse. "You sounded pretty confident this afternoon," she said.

"That was this afternoon. I talked to Lou, and well, let's just say I'm having second thoughts." He caught Diana's warning look and amended his words hastily. "I know, I know. I promised I wouldn't interfere beyond this. But can I just give a word of advice?"

Diana smiled. "Can I say no?"

"No, you cannot say no." He looked at her severely. "A word of warning does not constitute a favor, even in your great code of the north." He had made no move to get closer to her on the couch.

"Warn on, MacDuff." Diana made an effort to control the sparkle in her eyes. She felt a lot more comfortable and couldn't wait to see the look on his face when she told him her news.

Beau glared but went on. "Derek Islington's a very smooth operator, Diana," he said seriously. "Some people even call him dangerous."

"A tough cookie, huh?" *Diana,* she scolded herself, *you have no right to be enjoying this so much.*

"Why do I get the feeling you're making fun of me?" Beau demanded. "I'm not casting aspersions on your skill as a reporter, believe me. But I have had some experience with the man, and it hasn't been nice." Diana opened her mouth to say something, but Beau held up his hand in protest. "Now listen to me, Diana. I'm sure you'll get in to see him, with this letter or without it. And I'm sure you'll do just fine. Just be on your guard, and don't take anything at face value, that's all. Don't expect to outmaneuver the man."

He sat back against the upholstered arm of the couch and lay the envelope on the cushion between them.

"Why are you telling me this? What's behind it all?" In spite of her smugness, Diana was intrigued. Every time she talked to someone about Derek Islington, she got the same sense of avoidance, as if people were holding back more than they gave out. At this point, Diana was eager even for the innuendo—anything that might provide grist for her story mill.

Beau sighed and leaned forward. "What you said about Street Fare and the odds being set this afternoon hit a nerve, Diana. Those guys—myself included—were uptight because it's something we all sense but can't prove. Most of us avoid it by unspoken consent. Those of us who try to dig deeper meet up with closed doors and brick walls. Derek Islington is a powerful man, and his influence reaches far and wide."

"Hasn't anybody ever pinned anything on him, or is it all just theory?"

He shook his head. "Islington was indicted for race fixing in 1974. That was the last time anybody was able to prove it."

"But you think he's done it since."

"If he hasn't, he's made it pretty hard to prove his innocence. He's got a security net so tight no one can even look at it without trespassing. Keeping his prime racer off the track does more than just stabilize the odds. It keeps old Derek clean."

"How does he get away with it? Isn't it illegal?"

He flashed her a look that said, *See how little you know?* "It isn't if you help make the laws. Or change them when they don't suit your purposes."

"But don't all the horses get checked over before the race? I mean, even if he was hiding something, it would show up in a prerace exam, wouldn't it?"

"It's not just the possibility of tampering with the horse. It's speculation—setting odds—that makes this Derby worth a fortune. And Islington can control that simply by keeping Street Fare out of sight and only letting the pari-mutuel people know what he wants them to know. Besides," he added grimly, "I'm not so sure anything would show up in a prerace exam even if he had doped his horse."

"Why not?"

"Because the rules on prerace exams were relaxed the year before last. Thanks to Mr. Islington's influence. Now an owner has the right to choose the so-called independent examiner from among a group of certified veterinarians. And you can bet there are a whole bunch of those boys in his pocket."

"Can you prove that?"

"Damn it, Diana! Don't you think I would if I could?" Beau's voice exploded with all the pent-up frustration she knew he must be feeling. To be so certain, and yet have no way to prove it! It was a journalist's nightmare.

She took a deep breath. "Well, maybe I can."

He looked at her for a long moment and then shook his head. "Haven't you listened to a word I've said?"

"I've listened very closely." She refused to back down, and she knew her determination was reflected in her eyes.

"Diana." Beau leaned forward and placed both hands carefully together in his lap. "I know what you're thinking," he said.

Diana looked at his hands. *I'm thinking how strong and slender his fingers are,* she thought irrelevantly, and looked up with a funny smile on her face. "Do you?"

But Beau would not be distracted. "You're thinking

you might have a fresh angle to go on. You're thinking you could go in there with a clean slate and maybe get closer to the truth than the rest of us. But believe me, Diana, stronger men than you have . . ." he broke off with a short laugh. "Excuse me. For a moment I forgot myself." His eyes lingered on her bare collarbone. "I don't see how I could have made such a mistake," he added softly.

Diana grinned. "You're excused." Apparently, she was not the only one whose mind was wandering from business to pleasure. She felt a strange inclination to giggle all of a sudden, an urge to do something outrageous. Part of it was in anticipation of the shock she was about to administer when she told Beau about her meeting with Derek Islington. Part of it was an urge to show him that while she was definitely more of a prickly pear than a juicy southern peach, she did not enjoy being taken for one of the boys—especially after last night's experience.

And then there was that part of her that could not stop thinking about what it would feel like if those strong, slender fingers were to reach up and caress her bare collarbone. . . .

"I've already met him."

"What?" She had spoken so abruptly that Beau was taken aback.

Diana swallowed. "I said, I've already met Derek Islington."

"You *what?*"

Diana nodded. Beau looked so stricken that some of the fun had already gone out of the telling. "Tonight. At the Downs. He was there, and I just met him. By accident."

"By what?"

"Beau, do you think you could stop squawking like that? I'm telling you, I met Derek Islington tonight at the clubhouse. I was standing at the window looking out over the track, and he came over to me. We got to talking and . . . and I asked him if I could interview him." She took a deep breath. "And he said . . . yes."

Beau looked quite ill. All the color had gone out of his face, and he sat there, slowly shaking his head. "I don't believe it," he muttered over and over again. "I don't believe it."

"Well, it's true!" Boy, he really wasn't making this easy, was he? "We spoke for a while and made plans to have lunch together tomorrow."

Beau's eyes seemed to focus for the first time. "He just walked up to you?"

"Yes."

"And started a conversation?"

"Yes!"

"And let you introduce yourself, right?"

"Beau! Stop that!" She made her voice loud enough so that he had to listen. "You're making me nervous," she added in a softer voice.

"Because I'm right, right?"

She glared at him. "So what? So I introduced myself. What is it, a crime in Kentucky for a woman?"

But Beau didn't catch her sarcasm. "And then you set up a meeting, and then he left," he was saying, mostly to himself. "Right?"

"What are you trying to get at?" she demanded.

He looked up and blinked. "Nothing. Nothing."

She put her hands on her hips. "I don't believe it. You're thinking about something. You've got some kind of theory simmering in your little brain. And I want to know what it is."

"I know you do." He considered her for a moment, his expression more gentle than it had been since hearing the news. "But if I tell you now, you won't believe me, and anyway, it wouldn't help you get your story, would it?"

"Ohhh! So now it's okay for me to get the story again. I have your permission?" She was getting annoyed with Beau's highhanded refusal to include her in his theories. After all, she was the one going out there to do the dirty work, if there was dirty work to be done.

He caught her grimace and returned it playfully. Then his voice changed again. "Of course you can go get the story," he said placatingly, placing both hands on her shoulders and smiling easily into her eyes. "I never would have dreamed of stopping you!"

"Hmmph!" she snorted. "As if you could have."

"Exactly." His drawl was amplified, soothing as syrup. "All I want to do is keep an eye on you. Sort of like . . ."

"Like a paternalistic wise guy."

He chuckled. "Nooo. I was thinking like a respected colleague and equal."

She lifted her chin slightly. "I'd rather do it myself," she said stiffly. Even to her wounded pride, that sounded silly.

Beau laughed out loud. "I'm sure you would! And I have no intention of helping you." Diana had to work to maintain her stern visage in the face of Beau's good humor. Also, there was the small matter of his hands, which had not left her shoulders and were becoming increasingly hard to ignore.

"But I just want to make sure you understand what you're getting involved with here," Beau was saying. "This whole thing could blow up in your face. It could be . . ."

"Diana's folly?" Now she did smile. "Why not? After all, I'm just a long-shot filly, just like that horse. We really have a lot in common, that old mare and I—just a couple of fillies in a colt's race!"

It was Beau's turn to be serious. His fingers tightened on her shoulders, and she could feel the warmth through the thin material of the dress. It was particularly intense where his finger tips touched her bare skin. Her smile broadened.

"For God's sake, Diana, this is not a joke!"

"You're right about that, Beau. This is not a joke."

Then, suddenly, neither of them was smiling anymore. They both stared at one another, perfectly
serious, eyes wide and unblinking. What is happening
here, Diana asked herself? What is going on?

She had no idea when it had started, but Beau's
thumb had begun to rub gently against the bare skin of
her collarbone. The small circles he was absently
etching left bright eddies of flame in a concentrated
area of her flesh, and the sensation was slowly radiating
outward in waves of heat, staining her arm and chest
and neck with warmth. Whatever it was they had been
talking about had been erased from Diana's consciousness like a distant memory. In its place was a single
emotion—pure desire.

Her expression must have registered on Beau, or else
he was experiencing much the same thing at the same
time. As if on cue, their eyes moved together to watch
the hypnotic rhythm of his thumb as it moved in those
tiny circles to the base of her throat. They both stared,
transfixed, as if the motion of flesh on flesh had nothing
to do with either of them. Then, with a more deliberate
gesture, Beau moved his palm an inch to the side so
that it was resting just above Diana's breast. The
motion of his fingers didn't change, but the meaning
behind it had altered dramatically.

As his fingers traced a widening arc across her neck
and throat, Diana felt herself slipping into the numb-
ing, erotic rhythm they created, as if her whole being
moved to that silent, circular dance. Slowly, as if drawn
by an invisible ribbon, she felt her face moving closer to
his. The distance between them, hardly more than
inches, seemed an endless pool of passion that could
only be bridged with excruciatingly deliberate care.

Then their lips finally met, and at once the waters of
desire closed over them, engulfing them in a silent
world of sensation. Their arms lifted, tangled and

enveloped one another as if they were creatures of the sea and not the land. Diana felt her body floating up against the length of his. When she opened her eyes, she was not surprised to find herself stretched out beneath him on the tiny couch, although she had no recollection of moving on her own.

"Diana." His whisper against her mouth sounded miles away, muted by the sea of kisses he was raining across her face. "I didn't mean for it to be like this," he finished thickly, and she knew that Beau meant he had lost the struggle for reason and rational behavior just as she had—*again*.

"I know, I know." Her fingers were helplessly entwined in the springy expanse of his black hair. "I know . . ." And she added, almost to herself, "We agreed not to let it happen again. . . . It's just one of those things . . ."

He pulled up on his elbows, cradling her face in his palms so that his fingers framed her face with little tendrils of desire. "It is not one of those things. That's precisely it. It's different. For me, it's different. And if I made any deals to ignore it, it was only because you—"

She put two fingers across his lips to silence them. Then, when she was sure he wouldn't speak again, she removed her fingers and hooked both elbows tightly around his shoulders. For a long moment, they remained imprisoned in one another's grasp. Diana's green gaze, smoky with passion, searched every corner of Beau's still face until she was absolutely sure she had seen what she wanted to see.

Then, without a moment's hesitation, she knew what she was going to do. "I want to make love to you again," she murmured.

Beau grinned, but she saw his jaw tense. "What about your principles?"

"I'm making an exception in this case," she whispered. *What principles?* she asked herself. *All I want is this man—now*. His reply was half a chuckle, half a groan. "Isn't it supposed to be my job to do the asking?"

"Not where I come from," she replied, nipping hungrily at his cheek. Oddly enough, she felt no desire to explain to Beau that this sort of thing didn't happen to her often, either. She felt elated, outside of herself, and she couldn't think of a single reason why she should not stay feeling that way for a good, long while.

Beau's dark eyes narrowed as he marveled at her beauty. "Where *do* you come from . . . into my life like this?" he whispered. Then he shook his head quickly. "Don't answer that. Please. Just . . . stay."

The lights from the river far below twinkled over his body as he stood up in the quiet, dimly lit room. He gazed down at her for a moment and then began to unbutton his shirt. Diana lifted her arms above her head to release the clasp on her dress, but Beau stopped her.

"No. Wait." He moved her hands gently away and helped her up so that she stood facing him. Then, moving with tender grace, he reached back, unclasping the lucite beads and then the dress hook with one deft gesture. Letting the beads slide heavily through his fingers, he slipped the dress over Diana's shoulders and slithered it down her arms. "Slowly this time."

Diana stood motionless before him, her eyes closed against the rush of sensations—wool against silk, silk against skin, and finally, skin against bare skin. When she finally reopened them, they were both standing silhouetted against the navy sky, and Beau was letting her slip fall to the floor in slow motion. Diana knew that it was her cue. Taking a small step forward, she reached up and began undoing the buttons of his shirt, one by one, taking deliberate pleasure in studying Beau's features as she worked.

When she had finished, they stood naked in the soft half light. This time her vision was clear, her senses sharp. Beau's body became a series of planes and angles, separated into light and shadow like a chiseled sculpture of blue marble. She had never seen skin so pale or perfect. His eyes traveled along her flanks and breasts, and she could see him catalogue, memorize, worship, every curve and swell. The tension between them palpitated with barely controlled desire.

Having come this far, Diana suddenly felt a delicious lassitude envelop her. Except for the aching need to press herself against the length of Beau's torso, she was perfectly content to stand there, trembling slightly in expectation, allowing the potent tension of their bodies to mount to its natural conclusion. All her life, she had been a woman who relished determining her own fate. Right now, with no warning at all, she had relinquished the moment to a charming man with a drawl. It struck her as delightfully absurd to be feeling this good with this man, and she found herself smiling dreamily with half-closed eyes as she whispered his name.

"Beauregard Gatling." The words were a caress.

But Beau's voice, when he answered her, was anything but gentle. "Diana." he called out harshly, and Diana knew, from the urgency of his tone, that the moment could be suspended no longer.

He covered the space between them in one swift motion, and the impact of their bodies connecting for the first time left Diana literally gasping for breath.

There was no more sleepy bemusement on her face as he carried her over to the bed. Instead, her eyes were opened wide, and her mouth made a small oval of astonishment. *This is not like last night,* she remembered thinking as Beau knelt to cover her breasts with kisses. *This is serious.* She could see only the top of his curly head and the muscled arch of his back as he bent to her nipples, one after the other. She saw her own hands, stroking upward on either side of his broad ribs, her fingers trailing lightly under his arms and up across the taut sinews of his neck. She had a brief moment of utter detachment, as if she didn't recognize her own lean, dark body curved up against the harder pale one. *This is me!* she flashed—*me!*

Then Beau's hands slipped across the angular expanse of her hips and down along her thighs—a swift, sure dance of arousal across her heated loins. And then Diana was nowhere but in her body, reveling in the sight of Beau's face rising above her, the sound of his grated breath against her neck and, above all, in the sensation of his body entering hers.

At first, their hips and groins moved together in slow, measured cadences, drawing out every rush of feeling, every twinge of delight. Just as it had been when Beau's fingertip first began to navigate the skin on her shoulder, now they waited together, looking inside themselves and each other for signs that the experience was being shared in full.

But soon it became clear that careful pleasures would have to be abandoned. Time, which had been so exquisitely drawn out, suddenly contracted and intensified, and their world became a compact mine field of sensation, exploding without control as they spiraled upward together toward a mountainous release.

Afterward, they lay wrapped together in a cocoon of pleasure, the climax they had shared settling down around them like motes of gold in a glass paperweight. This time there was no need to escape. Diana was nestled into the cozy crook of Beau's shoulder, her ear pressed against the slowly diminishing thunder of his heartbeat. She could feel the warmth of his breath on her hair as his breathing became steadier, and the rhythmic sound helped to calm her own racing pulse. Diana felt as if she had all the time in the world.

Absently, her fingers traced sweeping arabesques onto the curve of his back, mirroring the arches he was etching on her shoulder blades. Gradually, she stirred herself out of her sated half slumber and pulled her head back to look up at Beau's face.

"That was awfully nice," she murmured sleepily at him.

"Awfully nice. Mmmm." His fingers slid around the slope of her neck and over her chin to weave delicate patterns across her lips. "Is that all you can say about it? That it was awfully nice?" He stroked up to the prominent arc of her cheekbone, sweeping away a minuscule eyelash with proprietary care. "Or maybe," he continued lazily, "they call that a high compliment where you come from."

"Where I come from?" Diana laughed deep in her chest, very much aware of the pressure of her breasts against Beau's rib cage. "You make it sound like I come from another planet!"

"Well, you do, sort of."

"Come off it. Do you mean to tell me you've never . . . you've never been with a woman from north of the Mason-Dixon Line?"

He smiled, still studying her finely chiseled features with tender fingertips. "I don't kiss and tell," he intoned solemnly. "Anyway, that's not the point."

"What's the point?" She caught his fingers and guided his hand across her face and neck, letting it trail like a feather over her skin.

"I just meant that . . . around here . . . well, a woman, I mean—" He broke off and stilled his traveling hand. "It's just that 'awfully nice' doesn't really cover it in my book."

"Well, it was just a figure of speech. After all, I'm not the ace word jockey." She laughed. "Word jockey. If only they knew of your real talents. You don't need to say a word ever again as far as I'm concerned."

He pulled his hand away. "And that's another thing. Where I come from, women aren't quite so bold with their talk. I mean, you come in here, make yourself right at home . . . not that I have any complaints, mind you, but . . ."

Diana swiveled around so that she could prop herself up on both elbows and still maintain that delicious contact of flesh on flesh. "Why, Beau! I do believe I've shocked you with my wanton ways."

He laughed. "Your wanton ways are fine," he assured her. "It's just that I'm usually the one who does the wantin'—and the askin'."

A deep laugh, full of mischief and delight, bubbled up in Diana's voice. "I *have* shocked you! I think you're accusing me of seducing you!"

"I am not!" He sat up so fast that Diana was tumbled to one side, and his sinuous smile was replaced by a look of true alarm. "I would never accuse a woman of that!"

"Course you wouldn't! You're too much of a gentleman to accuse a lady." Diana reached over and fiddled with a thatch of curly hair just above Beau's ear, keeping her eyes demurely downcast. "On the other hand, there's no denying it. I was the one who asked if we could make love again, wasn't I?"

Beau started to object, then caught the fun in Diana's voice and grinned. "You were, weren't you?" He hooked his thumb through imaginary suspenders and crowed. "I just can't keep 'em away, can I? They're poundin' on my door right and left."

Diana cocked an ear toward the door. "Sounds suspiciously quiet to me out there," she offered helpfully. "Anyway, you said it yourself—those southern peaches, juicy though they may be, don't do much of the askin'. Come on, 'fess up."

He reached out and pulled her back against his chest. "They don't, and that's the honest truth. And what's more, I'll pick a prickly pear over a ripe peach any old day—as of right now."

"That's funny," Diana murmured, settling happily

against him. "I could have sworn the prickly pear picked you."

"Boy, you don't let up for a minute on that, do you? You're pretty proud of being in control, aren't you? Won't give ol' Beau one ounce of the credit, huh? Huh?" His jaw thrust out aggressively, he pinned one of Diana's elbows behind her back and began to tickle her under the armpit. They tussled amiably for a moment until Diana came up for air.

"That's right," she gasped. "I believe in giving credit where credit is due." Somehow, despite the good humor of the moment, Diana realized that she was not entirely jesting. What had just happened between her and Beau had been an unusual experience, unusual because of the intensity of feeling that had accompanied the impulsive act. She wasn't used to feeling impulsive or intense, and somewhere in her mind was that familiar warning voice, reminding her to hang on to that important sense of control.

Beau was watching her face and stroking her warm, thick hair away from her face. "That's all right, Miz Dah-anna," he murmured with surprising gentleness. "I don't mind, really." He smiled softly. "As long as you don't forget what it means."

"What does it means?" She smiled back, but her voice was a little strained.

"I hope that it means our lovemaking *this time* was more than just *a fluke,*" he whispered, his brow creased into a straight line. "And I hope it was more than just a way of showing me that you're in charge of your life."

It wasn't true, of course, but it was close enough so that Diana actually winced. "I don't make a habit of this, you know. Despite the fact that I live in the big, sinful city, this is not a common occurrence." It was suddenly very important to Diana that Beau understood how special it had been for her. She held her gaze steady, inches from his, but she slipped out of the hand

that lay over her head, twisting her head over on the
pillow on top of her streaming hair. "I did it because I
wanted to," she added quietly. "And because a woman
has a right to do what she wants."

"I'll drink to that," said Beau, and he bent down to
take a long draft from her lips. Diana's defensive
posture slid away, and she settled back against the
pillows with a little sigh of pleasure. She had made her
point, satisfied that little voice inside her head. Now it
was time to satisfy the rest of her.

The first time they had come together, it had been a
stunned, and stunning, meeting of bodies and minds.
This time, as if in response to the conversation they had
just had, it seemed that Beau was bent on maintaining
control every step of the way. It was all right that Diana
had taken the initiative the first time around, he
seemed to be saying. But equality meant just that, and
now Beau was determined to take his turn.

Diana was amazed that he had learned the language
of her body in such a short time. He seemed to know
every secret spot, as if he had been giving her pleasure
for years and years. Every time Diana moved to
explore the terrain of his body, the firm, glazed con-
tours of his back or the spiny ripples of his thighs, he
would gently persuade her to concentrate on the sensations he was arousing in her, alternately making her
gasp and sigh with desire and relief. In the tiny recess
where reason still functioned, Diana understood that
this was *Beau's* power play, his way of handling the
prickly pear. But, at the moment, she was not in a
position to protest.

At the last moment, just as Beau was poised above
her, he slipped his lips against her ear. "A man has
certain rights and responsibilities, too," he whispered,
the effort at control making his voice ragged.

"I don't think it's the time to be talking about
rights," Diana muttered breathlessly. Her body was

aching with expectation, and her mind dimmed with desire. Any conversation seemed pointless under the circumstances, but she, for one, was not about to admit it. "And besides," she added with some difficulty, for Beau was manuevering deliciously, "men's rights and women's rights aren't mutually exclusive propositions."

"I guess it's sort of like being a woman sportswriter, huh?" Beau said, his voice muffled against her neck.

"What?" Diana's eyes flew open.

He pulled his face away and looked into her eyes. "You know," he said innocently. "Not necessarily a contradiction in terms."

She was about to explode in laughter, but Beau, with expert grace and timing, moved inside her at that moment, and the explosion was of a different sort altogether.

"Beau? Beau!"

Diana opened her eyes with a start. A minute before, it seemed, she had been drifting easily on a sea of satiation—long, comfortable silences punctuated by short, equally comfortable bursts of talking. She had been lying nestled against his chest once again, staring out at the blue-black Kentucky night.

Now, lying in exactly the same position, she saw that the sky had changed to a pearly gray and was tinged with the blush of certain dawn.

"Diana, Diana," he responded from somewhere up above her head, his voice tangled in her thick hair.

"Beau, it's nearly dawn already."

"Why, so it is." She felt him shift lazily to look out the window. "And it's going to be a beauty, too."

"Be serious, Beau." Diana struggled to sit up.

"I am being serious. Never more." He ran his fingers down her bare back as she sat up, and she looked back at him reproachfully.

"No, really. I've got to go. I really have to go."

"You have to . . ." He leaned forward, the pale yellow bed sheets pleating around his muscled groin like a Grecian robe. "For God's sake, Diana, why?"

Diana looked at him longingly for a moment before pulling herself away. "Because I fully intend to be back in my own little bed when morning comes."

"I repeat. For God's sake, why?" He drew both knees up under the sheets and draped his elbows over them, surveying Diana's burnished back and thighs with unabashed longing. "I want you to stay."

Diana closed her eyes and sighed. "I'd like to, but I can't. It just wouldn't be . . . professional."

"Oh, right. Of course. How provincial of me." He turned toward the window and narrowed his eyes against the growing light. "I forget. It's just not done that way in the big city, is it?"

"Don't be smart," Diana snapped, and then, in a softer voice, she added, "Don't ruin it, all right?"

He took a moment to turn back to her, but when he did, he was smiling. "You're right," he agreed ruefully. "Shouldn't ruin it." He laughed quietly and surveyed her as she stood before him at the side of the bed. "As if I could."

There was an awkward silence. Beau's frank stare, more than any words of entreaty, made it hard for Diana to turn away and get dressed. But with the coming dawn came a growing sense of reality. She did not want Alison to wake up and find her gone. It would mean too many explanations. And besides, one had to maintain *some* rules somewhere along the line.

"No," she decided firmly, "I really do have to leave." She turned and picked up her dress from the back of the couch where it had been discarded.

As if he had been waiting for her final decision, Beau fell back against the pillows and closed his eyes. "All right." He sighed. "You win. Give me a minute and I'll walk you down."

Diana stopped with her dress halfway up. "Beau," she said incredulously, "I'm only going three floors down and across the hall!"

Beau had already swung his legs over the side of the bed. "I don't care if you're going to the loo," he said. "I escorted you up here, and I'll escort you home."

"You didn't seem to want to bother last night."

"Last night was different, and you know it."

Diana huffed in exasperation. "For God's sake, Beau, this is not prom night in old Atlanta!"

He rattled his thick brows. "I wish prom night had been this good."

She stared at him, hands on hips. "Is this what they mean by southern chivalry? Useless gestures that serve no purpose?"

"This is what I mean by rights and responsibilities," he retorted promptly. "Making a commitment and recognizing that it has repercussions."

She made a face. "You make it sound like a visit to the dentist," she grumbled.

"I never said falling in love with me would be easy."

She stared at him, speechless. "For God's sake," she began, but he cut her off by putting his finger to his lips.

"Uh-uh," he warned, reaching for his slacks with his free hand. "That's my line. Besides, you don't have a choice on this one. I'm taking you home." He buttoned his slacks and reached for his shirt.

Diana was annoyed. The idea was to slip quietly into her room, not to parade through the Galt House like a high school couple. There probably wasn't a soul awake, but then, one could never tell with newspaper folks. And who, she wondered, had brought up falling in love? Certainly not her.

"I really wish you wouldn't," she began tightly.

"And I really wish *you* wouldn't." Fully dressed, he stood in front of her, his arms crossed over his chest and a determinedly bland smile on his face. Diana started to speak, thought better of it and with a deep sigh, turned her back to him. "Do up my button, then, will you?"

"Why, surely, ma'am," he drawled, and Diana realized that she had hardly been aware of his southern accent all night. *It just goes to show,* she thought grumpily. *Some things run deep.*

The walk back to her room was as uncomfortable as she had expected it to be. Beau insisted on holding Diana's elbow every step of the way, except when he stepped in and out of the elevator to hold the doors open with a flourish. It was clear that he was putting on the Rhett Butler act to needle her, because he was annoyed at her decision to leave. But, she reflected, he didn't *have* to get out of bed with her. What she did was her own business, after all, wasn't it? Diana began to feel the strain of exhaustion creeping up on her with each step, and with it, the hard reality of what she had done grew more perplexing.

"Here we are, ma'am. Door to door." He bowed but had the good sense to keep his voice low.

"Cut it out. Alison's due to get up any minute. She's got a date with a girl jockey." Diana smiled halfheartedly. She wished she didn't feel so annoyed. It would have been nice to end the encounter on a light, positive note. After all, these things did happen, and as long as one kept them in perspective, there was no sense in her getting all upset about it, was there?

Beau's persistent chivalry, however, was rubbing her the wrong way. What's more, he seemed to know it.

"So," he said, leaning amiably against the doorjamb while Diana fumbled with her key. "What's on your agenda for today? Can I see you again?"

Beneath the careful mannerisms, Diana could see that he meant it. Then she recalled what *was* on the agenda for the day and slapped her forehead in despair.

"Oh, no! I completely forgot. I'm having lunch with

Islington in just . . . eight hours!" She consulted her watch and looked up in alarm.

Beau stiffened slightly, but his expression didn't change except for a slight elevation of the brows. "Mercy me," he murmured. "Don't we have the full social schedule!"

Diana's eyes narrowed. "Good night, Beau." Suddenly, she wanted him to leave, wanted to be alone in her own bed to think—and to sleep. "And thanks."

She meant thanks for his help in talking to Lou Belvedere. But even as she said it, it sounded terribly lame. She bit her lip at the look of sorrow that crossed his face like a shadow. It hadn't come out the way she wanted it to, and it surely didn't reflect what she felt about their night together. But she couldn't retract it now.

"Don't mention it," he said sardonically. "The pleasure was all mine."

"No, it wasn't." Impulsively, she grabbed his hand and pulled him closer. "It was mine, too, believe me."

He looked straight into her eyes, his jaw working slightly. For a moment, she thought he might pull her against him, and for a moment, she wanted him to do just that. But instead, he considered her face, inch by inch, as if memorizing it. Diana recalled his fingers doing what his eyes were doing now, only over her entire body, and she felt a rush of heat from the pit of her stomach.

Just as she was beginning to sway toward him, Beau broke eye contact and took a deliberate step backward.

"I believe you," he said with only a trace of reproach in his voice. He leaned forward and placed a chaste kiss on her forehead. "Get some rest," he advised her. "And have a good day. Good luck with Islington."

He turned and walked a few paces away. Diana stood with her hand on the doorknob, unable to turn away.

"And Diana?"

"Beau?" She could not hide the expectant gleam in her eyes.

He smiled that skewed half smile and raised an admonitory finger. "You be careful around him now, you heah? I don't want to have to come rescuin' you now, do I?" He laughed silently as she started to retort, then turned away. "Good night, prickly pear."

Chapter 6

"IMPOSSIBLE!"

Diana lay on her side, her back to Alison's still-sleeping form. For almost an hour now, she had been making a determined effort to fall asleep. But however tightly she screwed her eyes shut, they insisted on popping open, like trick candles bursting into flame on a birthday cake. And the more she tried, the more tense she got, until she found herself screwed up in a tangle of bedclothes and nerves.

It was impossible to sleep, impossible to think clearly about the upcoming interview and impossible to clear her mind of Beau Gatling. He, of course, was the most impossible of all. Where did he come off with that knight-in-shining-armor act? The chivalrous Lancelot escorting his Guinevere back to her castle. What a lot of jive! And that southern accent was probably jive, too, she thought treacherously, since it seemed to ooze out of the man whenever he wanted it to.

What on earth had made her do it? Diana hitched the

covers up with a resentful tug, cursing quietly when that left her toes exposed. *Okay,* she cautioned herself, *let's be reasonable. Let's approach this from a logical angle. He's smart; I'll grant him that. And he's a damn good newspaperman, although that's supposed to be beside the point in cases like this. And he's kind of cute, in a rough-and-ready sort of way, which is definitely not beside the point!* A tiny laugh bubbled up in her chest without warning, and Diana did her best to suppress it.

"He's also full of surprises, which is actually in his favor, seeing as how so many men are too predictable for words these days . . ." Diana's stern inner monologue broke off at this point, and she found herself smiling vaguely at the linen drapes. Yes, that man was full of surprises . . .

With another muffled oath—this time her personal favorite, reserved for only the most extreme circumstances—Diana flung herself over onto her other side and found herself staring directly into Alison's big tan eyes.

"Good morning," Alison chirped. "Have a good night?"

Diana moaned and yanked her pillow over her head.

"Well, I did." Alison continued, sitting up in bed and stretching prettily. "I must admit, I was truly beat when I came up here last night. I didn't even hear you come in." She swung her legs over the side of the bed and fluffed up her curls with both hands. "What time did you come in?"

Diana could just see a wedge of lavender nightie from her position under the pillow. But she watched it closely as she replied. "Late."

The wedge of nightie turned into a wedge of leg as Alison got up. "Well, I can *see* that. *That* much is certainly evident." The legs came up to Diana's bed, obviously so that their owner could survey the limp form in striped flannel pajamas. "Tsk, tsk," said Alison cheerfully. "But your pajamas are cute."

She pranced away into the bathroom, and Diana could hear her humming. "Even on a good day I don't look that good when I wake up," she grumbled into the pillow. Then she readjusted it to drown out the happy sounds.

Of course, there was no use holding it against Alison. Diana felt badly, and there was no one to blame but herself. It wasn't so much that she regretted what had happened between Beau and herself the previous night; she was far too urbane and in control to tear her hair out over that sort of thing, she thought. But how had she allowed it to happen so quickly. And with another reporter? Where were her rules, her professional ethics?

And why on earth had it been so special?

It wasn't the kind of thing she wanted happening to her, not at this point in her life, and certainly not while she was on assignment. Relationships were fine; she had had several wonderful ones, and one that came close to being THE one. But Diana had never had any trouble keeping things in their proper time and place. And this was neither the time nor the place to . . . well, to fall in love.

"Bite your tongue, girl!"

"Did you say something?" Alison appeared from the bathroom, looking even better than she had when she went into it.

Diana hadn't realized she had spoken out loud. "Nothing important." She sighed, extracting her head from the pillow and sitting up on her storm-tossed bed.

"Must have been quite a night at the Poolsider," Alison observed, pursing her lips at both the bed and its occupant. "I thought you didn't go in for drinking with the boys and all that cronyism."

Diana let out a snort of humorless laughter before climbing out of bed. "Believe me, neither did I."

"Hmmmm." Alison tapped one manicured finger against her cheek. "Anyone I know?"

Diana threw her a cool, warning look. "Are you done with the bathroom?" she inquired.

"Okay, okay," Alison replied quickly, holding her hands up in an attitude of surrender. "It's all yours."

"Thanks." Diana stopped at the bathroom door and turned around, flashing a rueful grin. "Don't they teach you the cardinal rule over there in the feature department?" she asked, shaking her head.

Alison planted her fists on her hips. "Which cardinal rule are you referring to?"

"Never ask a reporter a leading question," Diana said with a wink, and shut the door.

"Oh, *that* cardinal rule!" Alison hollered through the sound of the shower. "I thought you were going to tell me the one about not getting involved with other reporters. You know, the one you were so adamant about?"

"Knock it off, Chase!" was the reply from within, and Alison giggled.

"Yes, ma'am!" She saluted the door smartly. "And just to show you there are no hard feelings, I'll order up some breakfast before I leave."

"Chase, you're a peach!" was the response to this, but Alison couldn't figure out why it was followed by a sudden oath.

Ten minutes later, just as Alison was tipping the room-service waiter, Diana emerged from the bathroom. She was wearing a thick white terry-cloth robe and a pale green hotel towel turbaned around her wet hair. Alison, carefully turned out in a white corduroy pantsuit, whistled.

"I can see you're one of those disgusting people for whom less is definitely more," she observed, narrowing her well-made-up eyes. "Must be all those extra inches you carry around." Diana made a face, half sarcastic, half appreciative, and moved toward the desk, where her breakfast lay under silver domes. "Or maybe," Alison added, "it's just the glow of new love."

Diana swung around and walked back to Alison, moving in very close so that Alison had to crane her neck to look her in the eye. "Don't you have someplace you're supposed to be?" she demanded in her most threatening voice, although her green eyes twinkled.

Alison took a step back before replying, with mock belligerence, "You may scare those Confederate scandalmongers down at the Poolsider, honey, but you don't scare me!"

Diana broke into a wide grin. "I'll bet I don't," she retorted with a laugh. "Come on. Aren't you going to eat with me?"

"Nope. I really do have someplace I'm supposed to be. But why don't we try to meet for a drink later on? I don't know what's on the agenda for tonight, but I'm sure we'll be needing some fortification, whatever the Derby organizers have got up their sleeves."

"I think tonight's our one free night," said Diana, sitting down and lifting the nearest silver cover to peek underneath. "Of course, that doesn't mean we won't be needing fortification." She took a slice of toast and shook it in Alison's direction. "As a matter of fact, I have a feeling I'll be needing a transfusion by the end of this afternoon." She saw Alison's delicately questioning eyebrow and decided not to leave her completely in the dark. "I've scooped an interview with Derek Islington," she confided. "You know, Street Fare?"

Alison's eyes widened. "Are you kidding? Hey, he's quite the catch, isn't he? Listen, you may not need a transfusion; you may need a replacement." She pressed three fingers to her heart. "And, Diana, dear, I do hope you'll think of me for the job."

"I wouldn't think of turning him loose on anyone else," Diana vowed. "Or vice versa, for that matter."

Alison grinned at the compliment. "Thanks. I needed that." She grabbed her bag and reached for the door. "So we'll meet back here to reconnoiter around six, all right?"

"See you!"

After she had gone, Diana attacked the large breakfast with gusto. She was feeling surprisingly good, considering her sleepless night. The meal finished, she put the tray aside, refilled her coffee cup and got out her notes on Derek Islington. She was determined to cope with only one predicament at a time, and the upcoming interview clearly took precedence over any personal confusion she might be feeling.

Armed with good, strong coffee, an intriguing subject and a firm refusal to let her mind wander, Diana passed several hours in fruitful preparation. She meticulously studied her growing file on Islington's background and called Cam in New York to ask for more information. His assistant read off the facts, and Diana nursed them into some kind of overall picture.

Derek Islington had been born in Kentucky but had spent much of his youth back East, in expensive preparatory schools. He had inherited a modest breeding farm and had turned it into a major source of Triple Crown contenders through hard work and shrewd dealing. His influence was apparently felt in many circles, both locally and statewide, and was not limited to horse racing. Another call to Cam revealed that Islington's contributions to political campaigns were frequent and well chosen to protect his interests.

The race-fixing conviction, she found, had been overturned in a superior court. Diana wondered if there was any connection between that reversal and the appointment of two new judges a few months before Islington's case came up for review. That was the sort of thing a good reporter would look for, and it crossed Diana's mind that Beau would have been looking for the same connection.

But she could find no way to tie the judges to Islington and no way to connect any of them to the subsequent change in the racing rules that relaxed the prerace medical exam for the horses. Despite Beau's hint that Islington was involved in that decision as well, there seemed to be no evidence in the available records.

Diana only got up once, when room service insisted that they had to have her tray. Then she realized that she had only a half hour to get dressed before her luncheon date. This time, there was no hesitation about what she should wear. With a silent prayer of thanks directed out the window toward the cool gray skies, she put on a raw silk long-sleeved shirtwaist in a minty green that matched her eyes perfectly. The delicate fabric was woven with occasional threads of cloudy blue and mauve, and the overall effect was, Diana knew, smashing.

She brushed her hair back carefully from her face but left it loose, in thick, chestnut waves to her shoulders. After applying touches of dusky pink to her cheeks to warm up her olive skin and highlighting her eyes with blue-black kohl, Diana slid into silky neutral pantyhose and bone-colored pumps with two-inch heels. That brought her to about five feet ten, but Diana knew she would need every imposing inch if she wanted to make a favorable impression on Mr. Islington.

It was hardly the kind of outfit she would have worn to interview the owner of the Red Sox, she reflected ruefully, pausing to apply orchid-colored lipstick before leaving the room. But then, part of her professionalism lay in her ability to adapt to different situations. Moreover, in this situation, a certain amount of grandeur was absolutely essential, she was sure, both to put her elegant subject at home and as a protective coloration. Grandeur was probably not what Islington got from the local press, Beauregard Gatling included.

She waited for the elevator, taking quarter turns in the hall mirror to examine the overall effect. Nervously, she checked her tiny tape recorder, although she had checked it carefully already. Somehow, although she couldn't admit it to herself, her success at this

interview was tied up with the confusing night she had
spent in Beau's bed. There had been a definite and total
loss of control in that situation, and Diana had no
intention of letting it happen again. Perhaps, by doing
well with Derek Islington, Diana would prove to
herself that she could regain that control, that she was
all the things she wanted Beau to believe she was—a
damned good reporter as well as a woman. She needed
to recover her own perspective on that, since, as of last
night, the woman in her was doing a good job of
eclipsing the reporter altogether.

Somehow, Diana focused on Beau's last-minute
warning. That said it all; the new lover immediately
assuming control over her life where the professional
colleague would never have dared to presume. By
advising her to be careful, Beau was putting her in
exactly the position she wanted to avoid—the weak
woman who needs a man to help her along. Hadn't her
behavior the night before proved that that was hardly
the case? Hadn't he realized that she was not a peach
but a prickly pear? What happened to the cool-headed,
sophisticated newswoman she knew herself to be?

"Damn! Where is that elevator?" Diana pressed the
button impatiently, tapping the toe of her shoe on the
tiled floor. She would simply have to make a success of
this interview. A whole lot was riding on it—more than
she cared to admit.

When she finally stepped out into the lobby, Derek
Islington's chauffeur was waiting for her. She recognized him by the pale gray uniform he wore, accented
with an ascot in the Islington racing colors of hot pink
and cream. He stood easily by a pillar near the door,
carefully ignoring the curious stares of the press
hounds, who knew his colors. He must have been
briefed on what to expect, for his eyes registered only
the mildest surprise when Diana strode across the lobby
toward him. The press hounds were noticing her, too,
she was sure.

"Good afternoon, Miss Jennings," he purred in a quiet drawl. "This way, please." He swung the bag containing Diana's tape recorder and notebooks into his own hand before she could protest and guided her discreetly toward the revolving doors with practiced ease.

A Galt House doorman held open the door of the dove-gray Mercedes sedan, and Diana slid into the rear seat. Almost immediately, the car pulled away, making the same purring sound as the chauffeur's throaty drawl.

As the Louisville business district slipped by, Diana surveyed her luxurious surroundings. From the outside, it had looked like just another Mercedes. Inside, it was clear that a more lavish hand had taken over. The seats were upholstered in cream-colored saddle leather with chevron stripes of pink running across the thin piping. The door handles had been replaced by brass stirrup fittings, and the crystal bud vases by the opera windows contained deep pink miniature orchids rather than the more pedestrian rosebuds.

Diana settled back among the loose pillows with a smile. Whatever else one might say about Derek Islington, she thought, one had to admit he had style. Rather than being oppressive and showy, she found it all rather witty and carefully noted her first impressions in her ever-present notebook as the car swept out of the city.

Twenty minutes later, her impression was not only confirmed but elevated to a new respect as Diana was ushered through the foyer of the main house at Fleur D'Isle Farms. The hallway was formed by an atrium that rose two stories above the marble floor, and a circular skylight at its apex let in a wash of light despite the gray skies. Fresh flowers—more orchids—filled several oriental vases on side tables, and from somewhere out of sight, she could hear soft chamber music.

A tall butler in the same gray and pink uniform led her through the room toward the sound, and Diana set her jaw against a sudden, fluttering sensation in her chest. If Derek Islington had carefully chosen his home environment to appeal to all of Diana's weaknesses, he could not have scored more perfectly. She thought of Beau's warning. Distance, she reminded herself, running her eyes across the Monet haystack study that graced the hallway—distance and objectivity made a good story—and a good reporter.

The butler showed her into a long, narrow room with French windows running its entire length. They looked out onto a lush expanse of pasture that suddenly made Diana clear as to the origin of the term "bluegrass." Everything seemed to be in the same subdued tones; the deep blue of the walls, the dark paneled wainscotting, the steely sky—even the horses, looking like miniatures in the distance, were in sober shades of roan and dappled gray. Diana was more glad than ever that she had chosen her raw silk dress. She fit in so well.

The view was so arresting that it took Diana a moment to notice Derek Islington, standing in half shadow beside an elegant mahogany highboy in a corner of the room. He was watching her watch the view, and Diana had to compose her features into an expression of cool approval to avoid looking startled.

He stepped forward, a narrow smile on his face. "Miss Jennings. Diana. Welcome to the farm."

The farm. Nothing pretentious about that. Or it might be a sort of reverse snobbism, as if every other farm in Kentucky needed to be identified by name, but this was just *the farm*.

Diana smiled and held out her hand to accept his. "The Monet is superb," she murmured gracefully, "but your view rivals it."

"Now it does," he replied, his eyes taking in her outfit with approval. "Come, shall we sit here for an aperitif? Lunch will be ready in a few minutes."

"Thank you, but I try not to drink while I'm working."

"Really?" His brows rose eloquently. "Then you are an anomaly in your profession, Diana."

Diana smiled. "In more ways than one." Islington chuckled, and she used the moment to press her advantage. "I was hoping I could ask you a few questions before lunch," she went on. "That way we wouldn't have to be interrupted."

"Ah, but I'm afraid that's impossible," Derek replied, still smiling. "My cook is an absolute martinet about punctuality, and I've already ordered the meal for one-thirty." Without pausing to see if this met with Diana's approval, he led the way to an oval Chippendale table facing the center window. Her tape recorder lay ready in front of one chair, and a lacquered tray bearing two crystal glasses and a decanter of wine stood in front of the other.

Diana raised her eyebrows in mild surprise. "If your horses run as smoothly as your staff does, Mr. Islington, I can see why Street Fare is a shoo-in."

"I work very hard to achieve that effortless effect both with my staff and with my horses," he replied, pouring two glasses of wine and handing one to Diana despite her earlier protest. Diana accepted it, because not drinking, she understood, would be more of an issue than drinking. "But Street Fare is hardly a shoo-in, as I'm sure you're aware." His eyes glittered over the crystal. "And I wish you'd call me Derek."

He really had lovely eyes, Diana thought, sipping the exquisite Beaujolais in silence. Sort of smoky blue gray, just like the room. Derek wore a sleek Italian suit in neat dark blue. His chiseled, smooth-shaven features and the angular lines of his body reminded Diana of the male models in European fashion magazines. Rather, the way a European fashion magazine might depict a southern gentleman. Certainly the sight of Derek leaning over the polished Chippendale table, silhouetted against the muted bluegrass in the distance, called to her mind a carefully arranged photograph. But a nice photo, Diana decided, and she allowed her smile to warm up considerably as she nodded her consent.

"All right, Derek. And thank you for helping me break my rule with such a delicious wine." They both drank, their eyes meeting in silent acknowledgment of affinity. Relaxed and pleased, Diana decided that there would be plenty of time to conduct business—on her own terms, not his.

Lunch was impressive. The butler lit a fire in the fireplace in front of their low table, and they sat before it eating delicately grilled fish and crisp vegetables that appeared and disappeared without any apparent human assistance. Over the meal, Derek talked delightfully, telling Diana more about his childhood in a small town outside of Lexington, the state capital, and his clumsy indoctrination into the intricacies of a northeastern boarding school at twelve. (Diana could not imagine Derek Islington ever being clumsy, not even at twelve, when she herself had been a brittle collection of teeth and limbs.) They talked about New York, where Derek still maintained an apartment for frequent business trips and "my seasonal fix of culture."

"I can't believe there isn't enough to keep you happy and busy right here on this farm," Diana said, refusing a second helping of raspberries and clotted cream. "This place seems like the essence of civilization."

Derek smiled sardonically. "Compared to Broadway and Fifth Avenue," he confided, "this is strictly the Dark Ages as far as I'm concerned. After all, a man can only take so many shades of blue green. After a while, one longs for a hint of dirty gray pavement, a patch of neon to relieve the beauty of it all."

Diana laughed. "I suppose that's one reason you aren't considered one of the local squires, isn't it?" The question was casual, but Derek must have been aware of the careful calculation behind it.

"Who said I wasn't?" he countered, settling back in his chair.

"It's not what they say," Diana replied. "It's what they don't say. And your reputation is, shall we say, conspicuous in its absence?"

He paused to light a narrow cigar. "I prefer to think of it as people respecting my right of privacy," he said, and she could hear the care behind his seemingly casual tone.

"There's no such thing as privacy on Derby Week," Diana said. "It's written in the rules."

She was still smiling—they both were—but Derek threw her a sharp look that spoke volumes. He knew she was getting at something, and Diana was sure he knew what it was. But he would not let on.

"Oh, those rules," he scoffed lightly. "That's like saying there's no such thing as life after Derby Week."

"But there is, isn't there? For you especially. What else is there besides Derby, Derek?"

"There's fine wine, good cigars . . . beautiful women . . ." He nodded suavely in her direction. "There's life."

"And business." When he didn't reply, she pressed on. "You have other interests besides horse breeding and racing, don't you? Professional, business interests, I mean."

"Horse breeding and racing is a business, Diana, and don't let those sentimental hacks out there tell you any differently." For the first time, she heard a hint of anger in his voice. But he collected himself admirably before going on. "The Derby used to be a true test of skill and a celebration of the great art of horse breeding, but no longer." He shrugged eloquently. "Everybody knows it, of course. I'm just one of the few people who is willing to admit it."

"And to do something about it?"

This time, Derek made no attempt to hide his uneasiness. "Diana, I don't know who has told you what, but you seem to be laboring under the impression that I have some unsavory dealings in my involvement with the Derby."

Diana saw it was time to back off. "Nobody has told me anything," she said quickly. "At least, not that I would believe. But the facts are there."

"What facts?"

She took a deep breath. "Race-fixing conviction in 1974."

"Overturned."

"New prerace medical examination rules legislated in 1977—with your help."

"And the help of every other stable owner in Kentucky. I just happened to be more . . . articulate in my support, shall we say?"

"The death of Dark Star . . . and Elmo Stewart."

Derek's chair slid back heavily from the table. He was smiling, but without humor, and Diana remembered the flash of cruelty she had seen in the angle of his jaw the night before. "Miss Jennings," he said in a low, tight voice, "I offered you the opportunity to interview me because you seemed to be a cut above the usual grimy hack they send out to cover this event. I had made the decision to talk to the press for reasons entirely of my own, and you happened to be the first likely suspect to catch my eye. But I must make it quite clear to you that you are not going to learn anything more about my allegedly seedy past than your weak-minded predecessors. Not because they were not up to the task of finding the truth—which they were not—but because I didn't choose for them to know it." He smiled then, and the cruelty she had suspected was written as clear as day on his face. "Besides," he added, "there is nothing at all to find out, and the records, I am sure, bear me out."

Diana considered her options. She could give up and leave right away and agree with Beau Gatling that the man was playing a game with them all. She could try and ferret out the truth that lay so tauntingly beneath the surface despite Derek's obvious assurance that she would not succeed. Or she could continue with the interview, on his terms, and see what developed. And really, given this intriguing situation and the intriguing man who sat smiling before her, she had no choice.

"You're quite right, Derek," she said, rising to stand as he did. "I was merely testing the waters." She reached out and hooked her arm in his proffered elbow. "Any good reporter would do the same thing, you know."

"And any good horse breeder would make sure she didn't." Derek smiled, his good humor restored. "Now, shall we take a stroll through my stables?"

The whole incident was chillingly civilized. But Diana was up to the challenge, and her only regret was that she had not thought to put the tape recorder on "record" before beginning to talk to him. Not that he said anything revealing, but as Cam always told her, it was what they didn't say that mattered.

They moved through the long drawing room and out the double French doors into the misty afternoon. Except for the expansiveness of the rolling hills in the distance and the occasional droop of a weeping willow tree behind the red brick buildings, she might have been in rural England on a foggy fall afternoon. Derek had donned polished black English riding boots that completed the illusion, and as they strolled down the clean, broad center hallway of the main stable, he rapped a leather riding crop against his side.

They walked down what seemed like miles of hallway, bordered on each side by wide stalls with heavy double doors. Sweet-smelling hay mingled with the unmistakable pungency of the animals. Diana was disappointed that so few of the stalls were occupied.

"No, Street Fare isn't here," Derek said, in answer to her unspoken question. "And it is not because I'm hiding him from the public eye, as is so often rumored. He's simply out on the far course with Lou, getting a little action."

Diana would have loved to press him to reveal why Street Fare was keeping such a low profile, but the failure of her efforts to be direct at lunch warned her off. Instead, she smiled sweetly at this bit of information and moved on.

"I didn't come here to interview Street Fare," she told him. "I came to find out about you."

"His loss, my gain. Ask on." He was apparently confident that no more leading questions would be asked and that, in any case, the tape recorder had been left indoors.

"You mentioned that the Derby is just business to you. Why?" Diana got out her small note pad. There would be time, she told herself. Time to ask those leading questions or, if not, to make sense out of what Derek did not say and use that to get at the truth.

"The Derby is big business," Derek replied. "One plays to win, and one uses all the tools at one's disposal. Computers, advertising, shareholding, anything that works. It all enters the race now, along with the horse."

"Even politics?" She could not resist.

But he didn't seem to mind that question. "Even politics. Especially politics, in this day and age. Why, practically every big owner today is involved in politics in one way or another."

"How are you involved, Derek?"

They emerged into the daylight at the far end of the stable. Derek looked at her swiftly, arched his brows and then actually laughed aloud. "I should have known better than to think I was going to get off easily with you, Diana Jennings," he said, chuckling. "You are as clever as you are beautiful—a combination that's as rare these days as . . . as an honest race."

"Can I quote you on that?" she inquired promptly.

"No, you may not. But you may keep on trying, my

dear. Because I am having a delightful afternoon in your company."

"So am I." To her surprise, Diana found that she wasn't merely being polite. Despite their constant game of cat and mouse, she felt an affinity with Derek, a level of understanding that went deeper than their professional standoff. He was bright, witty, well read and well traveled, and she loved listening to him talk about his horses as they toured the outdoor paddocks behind the stables. As he spoke, Diana tried to filter his words through her own intuition. She wasn't sure, but she doubted that a man who had as little love for his animals as Derek claimed he did would constantly refer to them as if they were people. They were more than a business proposition to him, those two-year-olds and yearlings who came when he called. Underneath that steely, opaque exterior beat the heart of a horseman, she was sure.

Diana was also sure that Derek would not reveal anything else that afternoon—and she was right. The rest of her tour was carefully orchestrated, as was Derek's conversation. He let her ask questions, then easily guided his responses so that they revealed only what he wanted them to reveal. Beau had been right— he was a smooth operator. Diana knew she was being fed processed fare—it had happened too many times to her before. She would need patience to get beneath that calm, contrived exterior, but she was more curious and more determined than ever to find out what it was all about. And Beau had nothing to do with it, or hardly anything.

They finally stopped back at the paved courtyard to the side of the main house, and Diana saw the gray Mercedes swinging up the long drive. Diana knew it meant the visit was over, and she tried to think of a way to extend it or secure an invitation to return.

"It's all been very interesting, Derek, and quite lovely. What's that building over there?" She pointed

to a small white building slightly behind the stables to
the side of the compound.

"That's my trophy room," Derek told her, taking her
tape recorder from the butler and handing it to her.

"I'd adore seeing them," she gushed hopefully.

"I'm sure you would." He turned to open the car
door for her. "Perhaps another time."

"I'd love it," Diana said. "When?" She knew she
was pushing, but she had no choice. And she had
noticed something shutting off in Derek's eyes when
she mentioned the trophy room. It had been a perfectly
innocent question, but Derek hadn't even looked to see
where she was pointing when he told her what it was.
Probably nothing, Diana knew, but she had been
reduced to grasping at straws.

"I'm afraid my schedule is rather tight for the next
few days out here," he said, standing beside the open
door. "But perhaps we can get together in town." He
was still evasive.

"I'd like that."

Derek smiled, realizing that she was not going to
leave without a more specific plan. "I have to come into
town this evening to do some business," he told her.
"Perhaps we could meet for dinner late? I know a
wonderful little place downtown—as close as you can
get to New York without crossing the Mason-Dixon
Line."

Diana made a pretense of considering the invitation.
It wasn't an invitation to the farm, but . . . She
thought only fleetingly of Beau before replying, "I'd
love to. What time?"

"Nine. And I'll have Geoff pick you up again, if you
don't mind." He gave a little smile. "Your colleagues
must be green with envy as it is."

"I'm sure I can protect my interests as well as your
privacy. But I'll be waiting for Geoff. Good-by,
Derek."

She reached her hand out the window of the car to

grasp his. He held it for a moment, looking at it before turning her wrist around and placing a swift, light kiss on the inside of her palm.

"I hope," he said deliberately, "that you intend to mix pleasure with our business, Diana. Because I certainly do."

Diana let her hand linger in his for a moment without replying. Then she withdrew it inside the car, and Geoff pulled smoothly away.

She got back to the Galt House a little after four and spent the next few hours prowling around the press room that had been set up in one of the conference rooms off the lobby. She told herself she was looking for Alison to save herself a trip up to the room at six. But the truth was that every time a curly head popped into view or a rich, ticklish laugh filled the room, her head whipped up like a filly that's been given her lead.

None of them was Beau.

The press room had the stale, pregnant air of all waiting rooms, which was exactly what it was. This was the one day of Derby Week that did not seem to have been scheduled up with all the rigidity of a summer camp. There had been steamboat races on the Ohio River that afternoon, but due to the threatening weather, only the hardiest of feature writers had bothered to attend. The sportswriters, dryly declaring that steamboat races were not covered in their contracts as bicycles and balloons had been, had elected to remain behind, vaguely hoping for some spectacular scoop to materialize out of the dim corners of the Poolsider Bar. By now, the press room was almost empty, and many of the reporters had long since forgotten about the first order of business as they traded stories across the mahogany bar.

Diana read through the latest UPI and AP releases on the teletype and called Cam in New York to see that her copy to date had been well received.

"Well, Jennings," came his gruff voice over the wire. "Find anything on this Islington kid yet?"

Diana smiled into the phone. "Not yet, Cam. I'm not even sure there's something to find."

"Diana. There had better be. This is Derby Week. And I want a good Derby story from you. If he's a dead fish, go fishing somewhere else. I've got . . ."

". . . A paper to sell. I know, I know. Listen, Cam. Can you plug into the Louisville microfilm computer from up there?"

"Are you kidding? They don't even know what a computer is down there, do they?"

"Of course they do, Cam. And I want you to get Freddie, or one of the other interns, to see if he can get a list of the names of all the judges who have been appointed to the Kentucky Racing Authority."

"Yeah."

"In the past eight years."

"Sure."

"And a short bio on all of them, too."

"Anything else?" he inquired sourly.

Diana laughed. "Yeah. You can let me know how spring training is going. Bye, Cam."

After hanging up, Diana picked up the Louisville papers and sat down to read. She doubted if Cam could get his hands on that kind of information from New York. But she was hoping he could, because if he couldn't, then she would have to ask for some local help, a tactic she wanted to avoid at all costs.

Speaking of local help, there was a story in the sports section by Beau. Diana read it carefully, worrying her lower lip with her teeth as she went. It was about the bicycle and balloon races and poked gentle fun at the hoopla surrounding Derby Week. It was a good story—not up to the Elmo Stewart standard but sharp and witty all the same. Diana read it twice.

At 5:45, Alison had not shown up either in the press

room or at the Poolsider Bar. Assuming that she must have slipped by her into the elevators, Diana went up to the room. She decided she could use a long hot bath and a rest before going the next round with Derek Islington.

Alison was not in the room, either, but she had left a note, obviously quite a while before. "Dear Diana," it said, "I'm afraid you'll have to do your own reconnoitering and fortifying, if such is necessary. I've been invited out to dinner by the most dashing little jockey! He won't say where we're going, but I figure, how much trouble can I get into? Aren't they all in training or something? Anyway, I'll assume, rightly, that you're perfectly capable of taking care of yourself. See you later, probably."

Diana read the note, chuckling and shaking her head. "Way to go, Alison," she murmured. "And I do hope that jockey knows what he's in for!"

In fact, she was relieved to be able to spend a few hours alone. She drew a hot bath, filled it with some of Alison's lavender-scented bath oil and lay back against the slope of the tub, taking deep breaths with her eyes closed. The therapy never failed to work, and thirty minutes later, she stepped out of the bathroom in her white terry robe, her face glowing from the moist heat and her hair escaping in curly tendrils around her neck.

"Thanks, I needed that," she congratulated herself, and fell full-length across her bed. But it seemed to her she had scarcely settled on top of the chenille spread when someone knocked on her door.

"For God's sake!" Diana awoke at once and sat bolt upright, looking at the desk clock in a panic. Had she slept past nine? No, it was only just eight. She stared stupidly at the door for a second until the knock was repeated. Alison would have let herself in by now, and a hotel staff member would have called out to identify himself.

Checking herself briefly in the mirror as she passed by to see that she was decent, Diana went to the door with a puzzled expression. "Who is it?"

"A fellow member of your exalted profession, ma'am."

Beau. She unlatched the lock and opened the door.

"It's me, actually." He grinned disarmingly, but the grin dissolved when he took in her attire through the half-opened door. "Oh, lordy, did I catch you at a bad moment?"

Diana compressed her lips. It was a little late for prudery, she thought. Her bathrobe certainly revealed less than Beau had seen on other occasions. Diana clutched the doorknob tightly to chase away the memory of those other occasions.

"Actually, Beau, it *is* kind of an awkward time." She had less than an hour to get herself ready for dinner with Derek, and Beau's presence was not going to help, especially since she was not keen on telling him of her plans. "You see, well . . ." She glanced over her shoulder into the room and turned back to Beau, making what she hoped was a meaningful gesture with her eyes.

But Beau remained steadfastly expectant in the doorway, unable or unwilling to pick up her clues.

"I'm afraid it's not a good time, Beau," Diana said finally with a sigh. "You see, my roommate is—"

"In a pig's eye she is," said Beau cheerfully, and pushed past her into the room.

"Beau!"

"Alison Chase is having dinner with Arnold Sweeney, who rides Diana's Folly. That's someone you might be interested in talking to if you want to get yourself a good Derby story. I'm not making any puns on the name, you understand. I think it would be less of a folly than talking to old you-know-who. And a better story, to boot."

"Beau!"

"Anyway, from what I hear about Arnold, Alison Chase will be tied up all evening. Must be something to do with that filly he rides. He sure can handle women! Not that he'd be able to deal with you the same way, of course . . . you being—"

"Would you shut up already!" She shook her fist at him.

But Beau only winked and threw himself casually across Alison's bed, removing several pillows in order to prop his head up. "So, speaking of Diana's Folly, how'd it go?"

His expression was such a mixture of pleasure and triumph that Diana couldn't decide how to react. "How did you know about Alison and her jockey date?" she inquired, sitting primly on a chair in the far corner of the room. Mostly, she was embarrassed at having been caught in the lie about Alison.

"You forget," said Beau solemnly. "I'm at the hub of a scurrilous network of rumors and gossip. That's how I get my stories, you know."

"Cut it out, Beau." Diana got up impatiently and began pacing the room.

"I love the way you say that. 'Cut it out, Beau.'" He mimicked her accent perfectly, and Diana smiled in spite of herself. "And," he said, "I love it when you smile. Ladies in bathrobes should always smile."

Diana paused, shoving both hands into the deep side pockets. "You've seen many, I gather. Ladies in bathrobes, I mean."

"Nope. Where I come from, it's simply not done. Now, if you were wearing these . . ." From under the covers, he produced Alison's frothy lavender nightie. Diana had no idea how he had unearthed it, and she gasped. "Yours?" Beau inquired innocently. Then he shook his head. "No, not yours. How silly of me. *These* are yours." And before she could stop him, he lunged off Alison's bed and onto hers, grabbing the striped flanned pajamas that lay in a corner.

"You're impossible!" Diana made a lunge for them, but her robe began to fall open, and she sat back down, clutching at it. "You're a disgrace to your code of chivalry, that's what you are!"

Beau looked delighted. "I thought you'd never say anything so sweet, dear," he crooned. Then, noticing that she glanced at the clock, he turned serious. "But my mama did teach me something," he said, "and if you really want me to leave, I will."

He half rose from the bed, and Diana was sure that he would leave if she insisted. Trouble was, she didn't want him to go. He was a pain, to be sure, but he was so much fun. "Five minutes," she said with mock severity. "You have five minutes, then OUT."

Satisfied, Beau settled back against her headboard. "So?"

"So what?"

"So what happened?"

"None of your—" she started to say, and then thought better of it. "So, nothing," she went on glumly. "I came, I saw, but you could hardly say I conquered."

"Tough cookie, huh?" There wasn't a trace of "I told you so" in his voice.

"Tough cookie. He had that whole luncheon choreographed like the New York City Ballet corps in *Swan Lake*. I barely got a chance to ask any good questions."

"Barely?" The question was instant, and Diana saw why Beau was a good reporter. Not many people would have had the antenna to pick up on the implications of that little word.

She still wasn't sure how much she wanted him to know. "I did my best," she said guardedly. Then, seeing the look on Beau's face, she relented. "Not even. I mean, I tried. I asked all the general questions, but whenever I got onto something that seemed important, he evaded me. After a while, I decided we would just have to play pretty much by the book. His book.''

"Pretty much? What seemed important to you? What did he evade?''

Now Diana had to grant him a grudging smile. "You're relentless, aren't you?"

"They don't call me the word jockey for nothing.'' He looked at her, and she knew that he, too, was recalling the previous night at that very moment. She blushed at the memory of her own bold words, then gave a shrug to show that she was not flustered. "Really, Beau, there was nothing I could put my finger on. I mean, he never denied anything, but I never had the right questions to ask him. She threw him a sharp glance. "How could I? Nobody seems to want to let any information out around here."

"Touché. But you were the one who said, 'I want to do it myself.' "

Diana glared. Now was the time, she was thinking. Now was the time to lay aside her pride and ask him about those judges who had been appointed just before Islington's race-fixing conviction had been overturned. She was sure he knew more about that than he had let on. But she saw from his face that he was expecting her to do that—to ask for his help. And something stopped her. It was her story, damn it, and she was going to do her best to get by on her own before turning to Beau. She didn't want to be in his debt any more than she already was.

"I don't know," she said evasively. "I guess I just got the same feeling about him that you have. Nothing to go on—just a feeling." She let out her breath and shook her head.

"Trust it," he replied promptly.

"What?"

"Trust that feeling. It's right." Beau sat up. "Look. I know how you feel about tackling this, Diana. I felt the same way once. And you have my blessing—" He held up his hand to avert her tart remark. "I know, you don't need it. But you have it all the same. And you have my warning, too, remember? Trust that feeling and be careful."

"I do trust my feelings, Beau, and I think I can manage to be careful—with or without your patronage." Her green eyes flashed at him suddenly.

"Come on, Diana. I'm not putting you on a leash, you know."

"Thanks a bunch."

"But I do think I have a certain responsibility toward you."

"By what right?" she snapped.

Beau had gotten off the bed, and now he came over to her chair, leaning over her with his hands on either side of her head against the cushion. "Last night," he whispered. "I believe that gives a man some rights, don't you?"

She leaned back, pressing her neck uncomfortably into the chair. "Really, Beau," she said tightly, trying to make her voice sound light, "I hardly think that—"

"I *do* think that. I think it was special, and you're special, and you owe it to me to behave in a certain way."

Diana pushed both hands against his chest and shot up. "To behave in a certain way? In what certain way? Like your mistress? Like your chattel? Like a southern peach?"

"Like a woman who has made a commitment."

"I have *not* made a commitment!" She leaned her face close to his, her brows drawn tightly across jade eyes. "Do you know what I'm committed to, Beau?"

Beau sighed wearily. "To your job. To your story. To the truth."

Diana blinked. That was exactly what she was going to say.

"What I want to know," he went on softly, "is when

you are going to commit yourself to the other part of you. The woman. The lover."

He had not moved his face away despite her outburst, and the effect of his stillness was to make Diana hear her anger echoing out of proportion in the quiet room. She glared at him, trying to control her trembling jaw. He had hit a tender nerve in her, and she wanted to do the same to him.

"I'm seeing him again tonight," she said finally.

Beau flinched visibly. "Tonight? At his place again?"

Diana tried not to look smug and then hated herself for even feeling it. "No, he's picking me up for dinner. In about a half hour, as a matter of fact."

She could have kicked herself at the look of remorse that passed across his face. He looked uncomfortably around the room, as if he wished he could disappear right through the floor.

"So sorry, really," he mumbled, and made a beeline for the door. Diana watched him walking away, crossing her arms and tucking her hands into her armpits to prevent them from reaching out for him. They had left so much unsaid—*she* had left so much unsaid! Say it, a voice inside was ordering her. Tell him what you are feeling right now. Ask him not to leave you alone. . . .

But when he turned around, she only smiled weakly, for she did not trust herself to speak. "I'll leave you to get yourself done up in time, then," he said sheepishly.

"Thanks," she replied dryly. "I'll need all the time I can get."

His eyes traveled down the length of her terry robe. "That's debatable," he murmured. Then, with a half smile, he said, "Can I call you in the morning? If I promise not to patronize?"

Diana found herself smiling back. "I'd love it if you did. Call, I mean. Not patronize." She laughed. "And I'll try not to, either. Patronize, I mean."

He was halfway into the hall. "Diana . . ."

She held her finger to her lip. "Beau. Don't say it. I

really have to do this." She shook her head. "Back
where I come from," she said gently, "women do what
they have to do. What they *want* to do."

"If that were true," said Beau, one hand on the
doorknob, "you'd be in that bed with me right now."

With that, he shut the door.

Chapter 7

LE COQ D'OR WAS THE NAME OF THE RESTAURANT, AND Derek had been right! It was the closest one could come to Big Apple dining without crossing the Mason-Dixon Line. Geoff left Diana in the doorway shortly after 9:15, and she paused there for a moment to get her bearings.

She was beginning to enjoy being chauffered around in discreet silence and was not above enjoying the minor stir her entrance caused, especially when the maître d', with deferential speed, escorted her to one of two small, curtained alcoves in the rear of the room. She followed him in between the tables, keeping her eye on his pin-striped back, for she knew all eyes were on her rose-colored suede skirt and ivory satin blouse.

The restaurant was small and cozy, its intimate scale accented by deep plum walls and old, oriental rugs underfoot. The tables were small ovals and rectangles of polished wood, and Diana noticed that the place

settings were different from table to table, emphasizing
the quaint informality and charm. Well-chosen prints
adorned the walls, and Tiffany reproduction lamps,
hung low over the tables, lent a warm, golden ambience
to the room.

The maître d' lifted the edge of one curtain aside and
stepped back with a flourish. "Mr. Islington requests
that you wait here, Miss Jennings. He regrets that a
business phone call has delayed him for a moment, and
he begs your patience."

Nodding, Diana stepped inside. The tiny room was
lit only by candlelight, and Diana saw at once that this
particular table setting was considerably more elegant
than the provincial stoneware and old china in the outer
room. She also smelled the heady scent of freshly cut
lilacs and went to bury her face in the faience vase on
the sideboard that held the lovely blooms.

It was while she was standing there, breathing deeply
and marveling at the sight of lilacs that early in the
year, that she heard the voice. At first, she ignored it,
assuming it to be just the normal buzz of conversation
one always hears in the background in any restaurant.
Then she realized that the sound came from the
adjacent alcove and that it was just one man speaking.
Derek Islington.

It would have been ridiculous to attempt to ignore
the voice, to try and mask the clarity of the words so
that she would not overhear. Anyone—a reporter or
not—would have paused to listen to half a conversation
being conducted by an acquaintance through a thin
wall.

But not everyone would have immediately stooped
down to their handbag and slipped out the tiny tape
recorder that lay there, switching it on almost without
making a conscious decision to do so. That was the
reporter in her, and there was never any question in her
mind about it. Of course, she would never be able to
print information gotten in this way—it was a breach of

every moral and legal code in the book. But Diana's instinct told her that she would very much want to remember what she was hearing through that wall, and furthermore, that she might someday want someone else to hear it, too.

"I told you," Derek was saying, "I don't want him coming around at all again." His voice was well modulated and didn't sound at all tense. Diana craned her neck and held her breath to listen.

"That's what he says," Derek replied to the unknown speaker. "But he's going to have a hard time proving it, don't you think?" He laughed, that quiet, humorless laugh of his. "Those records have been destroyed for years. He couldn't even prove it if he were the judge! Hah, that's a laugh." He did not sound amused.

There was a longer pause. "Dammit, Ken, I don't care how you do it; just pay him and get rid of the evidence. You know where to leave the stubs and the other stuff. Just lock it in the usual place and I'll have Lou take care of it. And Ken? I don't want to have to bother with this sort of thing again, you understand? You keep him happy until Saturday and then see to it that he doesn't bother us again. I don't trust either of them anymore, the doc or his judge. They're acting too scared."

There were a few mumbled sentences of farewell and then a click. Diana, breathless and dazed, just barely managed to reach down and conceal her tiny Sony when Derek appeared at the entrance to the alcove. He was smiling pleasantly, without the slightest trace of suspicion.

"Diana! I'm so sorry you had to wait. Have I kept you long?"

"I didn't notice," she replied, her face muffled in the lilacs again. "I've been transported by these amazing blossoms." She raised her head, hoping that the contact with the flowers and the candlelight would explain the flush on her cheeks. "Where on earth did you get them to bloom so early?"

He approached the table and breathed in. "I have them grown at my greenhouse at Fleur D'Isle."

"I didn't get to see a greenhouse," she said, pouting.

He leaned over and kissed her hand. "That's because I was saving it for another visit."

Diana would have been delighted by this news, but as he said it, Derek bent down, and her heart stopped for an instant. She thought he might be reaching into her bag for the recorder. Instead, he opened one of the sideboard cabinets and produced a bottle of wine. "Shall we?"

Diana nearly laughed her relief. "Let's."

Derek opened the bottle, and Diana took the opportunity to move over to the table, taking her bag with her. She was beginning to breathe more easily now, although she had not yet begun to sort out the implications of what she had overheard.

"You seem to have made yourself quite at home here," she observed. "Your own wine, your own flowers. If I didn't know better, I would say you even had a hand in the design of this place." Derek smiled over the corkscrew. "Well, Derek, 'fess up. Did you play a part in the birth of the best restaurant south of the Mason-Dixon?"

"You might say," he replied, coming over and handing her a glass. "Actually, I own it."

"Are you serious?"

Derek arched his eyebrows. "Of course I am. I told you racing bored me. And I need something to tide me over between New York appearances."

"Do you come in and supervise the chef? Just like you supervise Street Fare's progress?"

"Who says I supervise Street Fare's progress?"

"Anybody who knows exactly where every one of his horses is at any given moment of the day is not completely bored by them," Diana said. "And if you're keeping him under wraps, I'm sure you're checking very carefully to make sure that he stays that way."

"Diana, you are a marvel." He raised his glass in salute.

"Besides, a good businessman protects all his investments, doesn't he?" She looked up at him from beneath her lashes. "I would think of it as a kind of protection—insurance against mistakes."

Derek chose to ignore this entirely and slipped into the chair beside her with an exaggerated sigh of relief. "Ah, what a pleasure to relax after a hard day."

"Is talking to reporters such a chore?"

He laughed and reached out for her hand. "I didn't mean you, of course. He paused and smiled. "But I am curious about one thing."

"What's that?"

"It just seems odd to me that someone like yourself would be . . . I don't know . . ."

Diana laughed. "You mean what's a nice girl like me doing in a place like the Kentucky Derby?"

"I suppose that's what I meant. Sportswriting in general. It just doesn't seem your style."

"That's funny. You don't look like the colonel type to me, either."

Now Derek threw back his head and laughed, and Diana settled back to enjoy the sight. She was feeling confident that night. Maybe it was because she knew she finally had a wedge into that netherworld of Derek's wheelings and dealings even though it did not yet make sense. But now she was certain of her ability to talk on an equal basis with this tough cookie no matter how carefully he choreographed their time together. She, too, had time in which to let things develop as they might. She knew that Derek was attracted to her because she was a woman and that she was being treated to a different, although equally contrived, part of his character than Beau had seen. For the first time, she was sure that her time and efforts

would pay off in the end even if she had to stay for
weeks after the Derby was over. Now it would pay to
be cautious, and she had learned long ago how to walk
slowly and carry a sharp pen. *That,* after all, was how a
nice girl like her got to be a sportswriter.

"But seriously," Derek was saying, "what made you
want to write about sports?"

Diana sipped her wine before answering. "It's what
I've always wanted to do," she said simply. "And I'm
good at it."

"That much is apparent. But tell me, do you always
get what you want?" His eyes gleamed with a new
interest, reflecting the candlelight in cool sparks.

"Generally. If I work at it hard enough." She had
caught the weight behind his words and wondered what
was going on behind that calculated gaze. "Why? Does
that surprise you, Derek?"

"Oh, no." He spoke with unusual emphasis. "I
couldn't agree with you more. I, too, am concerned
with getting what I want, at all costs."

"And what exactly is it that you want . . . at all
costs."

"Money. Success. Fame, or infamy, if necessary."
He smiled secretively and then shrugged. "The same
things as you want, I expect."

Diana pursed her lips. "I don't usually think of my
goals in such . . . bald terms, but I suppose you're
right, in a way."

"Of course I'm right."

"What about the Derby Cup? Do you want that,
too?"

Derek stared at her for a long moment before
replying. "That, too," he said softly, "because it means
all of the above."

"And what are the costs?" Diana continued, pressing
what she knew was an unheralded advantage with this
guarded man. "What are the costs you are willing to
pay for the Derby Cup, Derek?"

She saw his jaw set and knew she had gone too far. Instead of replying, he reached over and pulled a narrow silk tassel, probably to summon their waiter for the meal. Diana correctly interpreted this to mean that their impromptu interview was at an end for the time being. But she was not dismayed. She was now absolutely certain that what she had overheard on the phone was of great importance and that Derek had no idea she had heard him. Otherwise, he would never have hinted so broadly at his lack of scruples. Would a jewel thief hint at the fact that he possessed stolen gems? Absolutely, if he was confident he was not in danger of being caught. And Derek Islington was a confident man. Dangerously confident.

She was glad she had that tape recorder at her feet.

The meal was superb. Derek had ordered ahead of time—of course, thought Diana she could have predicted that—but there was no faulting his choice. The first course was a serving of exquisitely tender smoked fish, served on a bed of lettuce with a sauce of mayonnaise and capers. That was followed by a tiny serving of puréed red-pepper soup, a surprising blend of the sweet and the hot. The main course was a rack of lamb, grilled and encrusted with mustard and rosemary. Dessert was a flaky apple tart and crumbly Roquefort cheese.

Each course was accompanied by a superb bottle of wine, and Diana was not surprised to hear that two of them came from Derek's own vineyard. About halfway through the meal, on the pretext of extracting a hankie from her purse, Diana reached down and shut off the Sony. It was clear that no more illuminating information would be forthcoming that evening, and besides, she had had a little too much wine to want to deal with it even if it did. She settled herself back to enjoy the rest of the night in Derek's company and to put off any judgments she might want to make until the next day.

The truth was, she really liked Derek, in an odd, competitive way. They were kindred spirits, both intelligent, sophisticated and clearly focused on their respective goals. Diana now understood the source of his reputation for being coldhearted and calculating probably better than many people who had known him for years. But she was not about to hold that knowledge against him—yet. She, too, had been accused of being cold and hard. It all depended, she thought complacently, on what one did with it. As soon as she had proof that Derek used his skills to the detriment of others, she would go out of her way to see to it that he came to justice. Until then, she liked the way he was treating her, with respect as well as deference.

Of course, if she were being brutally honest with herself—and the wine made that a pleasanter task than usual—she would have to admit that there was a challenge involved in her relationship with Derek, a challenge that had more to do with Beau Gatling than with Derek himself. But her feelings about Beau were sufficiently complicated that she dared not examine her motives too closely. She only knew that his face, half smiling, half concerned, was never quite out of her consciousness as she traded clever small talk with Derek.

For the moment, she allowed herself to relax and enjoy the food, the wine and the good conversation. It had been several days since she had been able to discuss the stock market—another secret vice of hers—with any degree of intelligence, and she and Derek got into a long and pleasant argument about the merits of closed portfolios—Derek owned several, Diana none—versus open market trading—Diana did it; Derek didn't. In the end, Diana conceded that as she had never owned more than fifty-four shares of AT & T and seven shares of a defunct baseball team, Derek was probably right.

As coffee was being served, the maître d' came in and whispered in Derek's ear that he was wanted on the

phone again. A small frown of annoyance passed over
his face as he excused himself. Diana slipped over to
the sideboard to try and listen, but it was evident that
this conversation was taking place in a different room
or was so quiet that she couldn't hear. Diana took the
opportunity to visit the ladies' room. When she returned, Derek had not yet come back. She checked her
bag and saw that her tape recorder was still there, then
sat sipping her coffee and waiting.

"I'm sorry," he said when he at last appeared. He
was rubbing his hands together distractedly, and he
looked preoccupied. "It appears that the meeting I had
earlier this evening was not altogether successful. I'm
afraid I'll have to cut our lovely meal short, Diana."

Diana looked at her watch: it was eleven-thirty.
"You're going to a meeting? At this hour?"

He smiled. "Duty calls."

"Is it something to do with Street Fare?" She allowed
him to help her up and drape her shawl across her
shoulders.

"I thought you weren't interested in Street Fare."

"Everybody is interested in Street Fare, Derek."

"Yes," he replied dryly, "I think everybody is. But
this particular meeting is not directly concerned with
my horse, which, I trust, is safely bedded down for the
night. And that is where you must go now, much as I
would like to continue our . . . conversation." He allowed his hands to trail along the satin sleeve of her
blouse with practiced languor. "There's no telling
where the night might have ended for us."

Diana felt a chill running up her arm and down her
spine. "Maybe," she said slowly, "if I went with you to
your meeting, we could continue where we left off
later."

As soon as she said it, Diana sobered up. She
realized suddenly how much she wanted that story—
enough to play a dangerous game that she had never
played before in all her years as a sports reporter. And

she knew that her reasons for wanting that story were
not altogether pure; personal considerations were coming into play here, and they were obscuring her judgment even more than the wine. Much as she would
have liked to know what that meeting was about, she
hoped that Derek would not take her up on her offer.

But he was smiling at her in a way that told her he
had no intention of including her in his plans. "I think I
might like it," he said, "but I'm afraid your presence
would be a hindrance at this particular meeting." He
chuckled, as if at a private joke.

"Well," said Diana, shrugging it off as if she didn't
care, "I suppose I'll have to wait a while to uncover the
secret life of Derek Islington. But if it's not about
Street Fare, why all the secrecy? A clandestine rendez-
vous by the chefs of Le Coq D'Or? A sudden bull
market for your closed portfolio?"

Derek shook his head. "Haven't I told you? It's all
the same thing to me. Horses, chefs, stocks—business
is business, and when a decision has to be made, I make
it."

"Regardless of time or place or—"

"Or anything," he said firmly, and guided her out of
the alcove.

When they emerged from the restaurant, Derek
signaled to the valet to call for his car. Diana waited
with him, wondering whether she could get one more
clue out of him about his destination. She was sure it
had something to do with the phone conversation she
had overheard.

"I guess Geoff will just drop you off at your office,
since that's on the way to the Galt House," she mused.
"You do have an office downtown, don't you, Derek?"

He turned around and took her firmly by the shoulders. "No, I do not have an office downtown, and no,
Geoff will not drop me off on his way to the Galt House
with you." His expression was both serene and severe.
"Diana, I understand your curiosity, and I share your

regret that we cannot spend more time together tonight. But don't take me for a fool." His smile hardened perceptibly. "I haven't forgotten who you are."

"That's good, Derek." She smiled back. "Because I
haven't forgotten who you are, either."

For a moment, their eyes met, suspended in a mutual
challenge. Then Derek laughed. "Quite true. Of
course you haven't."

He leaned forward and kissed her on the lips. It was a
brief kiss, and cool, but with a measured undercurrent
of passion. Diana tried not to look surprised.

"Good night, Diana," he said, turning her lightly
around so that she faced Geoff and the opened door of
the Mercedes. "We'll get together again quite soon, I
hope."

"When?" Diana started to ask, but he shut the door
and took a step back, and Geoff pulled the car smoothly away from the curb.

"He probably *is* going to a secret bake-off in the
kitchen or something," she muttered angrily on the way
home. She was slightly disgruntled that she had not at
least gotten in the last word.

She was more than disgruntled when she got back to
her room and discovered that the tape had been
removed from her Sony.

Chapter 8

"DO YOU BELIEVE IT? GONE! AND I ACTUALLY DIDN'T even notice!"

Diana was still raving to Alison as they ate breakfast in the coffee shop the next morning. It was only 5:45, and Alison was on her way to watch Arnold Sweeney work out. But Diana had risen with her, far too riled to go back to sleep despite her exhaustion. The whole story of the previous night's events had poured forth while Alison dressed; Diana had told her about everything except Beau's involvement in the matter and her involvement with Beau.

Alison, realizing that Diana needed to let off steam somewhere and naturally interested in all the juicy details of the story, had empathically invited her to come along to Churchill Downs. In the nearly empty coffee shop, Diana had continued to dwell on what she saw as her defeat, her voice rising with barely controlled urgency.

"How could I have been so gullible, so thoughtless? I

looked at the tape recorder, and I didn't even bother to check and make sure the tape cassette was in it! I mean, most normal people would have thought to take it with them in the first place, right?"

Alison nodded over her coffee cup, knowing that no reply was necessary. Diana was, as Alison's mother would have decided, "on a tear."

"But not me! Oh, no, Diana Jennings doesn't need to check her lipstick or powder her nose. Oh, no, she's much too liberated and sure of herself for that sort of thing!" Diana curled her lip in a sneer, and Alison didn't bother to point out that the effect was ruined by a dusting of powdered sugar on her upper lips from the doughnut she was eating.

"And talk about gullible! Boy, did I take the prize last night! I spend my life in a city where you practically have to sew your valuables into your skin, and then, as soon as I leave town, I act like the rest of the world is bucking for sainthood! And after what I heard of that phone conversation, I should have been getting out a dime to call the police on that crook. How could I? How could I just leave it there and walk away?"

"Well . . ." Alison began tentatively, but Diana cut her off heedlessly.

"And how could *he?* I mean, race fixing is one thing, but this—it's outright theft! An outrage!"

Alison glanced around the room quickly. "Why don't you go to the police now, then?"

Diana stared. "Are you *kidding?* I don't want *anyone* to know about this yet!"

"Sorry. I don't know what made me think of it." Alison looked suitably contrite.

"Besides, now I don't have a shred of proof. I mean, how do I know who this guy is he wants to get rid of. 'The doc and the judge.' Hell, they could be two old horses of his. Or two old chefs!" She laughed bitterly. "Go to the police? That would be a laugh."

Alison smiled sweetly. "Then I suggest you lower

your voice, or the police station is where you're gonna end up, like it or not."

"Oh." Diana blinked, her mouth open. "Oh, no," she groaned, putting down her coffee cup to rub her temples with both hands. "I'm sorry, Alison. You're right. What's gotten into me? Any fool would know better than to act like I've been acting." She raised her head and glanced surreptitiously around the room. The only occupants other than herself and Alison seemed to be sleepy-eyed employees. "What's gotten into me?" she repeated plaintively.

"Relax," Alison advised promptly. "You aren't totally out of control, you know. And besides, there's no one here to hear you."

"I was out of control last night, damn it." Diana spoke between clenched teeth. "I blew it, that's all. I just blew it. Now he knows I'm trying to get something on him. I'll never get to talk to him again."

Alison watched her speculatively. "That's what really gripes you more than anything else, isn't it? That's what you hate most—losing control."

Diana started to bristle, then nodded ruefully. "You got it," she confessed, spreading her hands with a shrug. "You've got my number at last. The secret to my success. Control is all." Her voice ended on a bitter note.

"I'm not the only one who's got your number," Alison pointed out pragmatically.

Diana winced. "Right. I guess my act was never that tough, after all." She wasn't thinking about Derek as she said it but about Beau. Boy, talk about having her number . . .

"Look." Alison was being practical. "Let's lay out the facts. You snuck a tape recorder in there and caught Derek making incriminating comments to some guy Ken about some guys—probably a judge and a doctor. Nothing much to go on, except Derek pinches the tape, which means, a, he knew you had heard him, and b, he didn't *want* you to hear him."

"Right," Diana agreed glumly.

"Well, the way I see it, you two are about even. If you confront Derek with the theft, he'll just deny it. On the other hand, he's hardly likely to confront you about the eavesdropping because it proves he's a criminal."

"It proves nothing of the sort," Diana snapped.

"Well, you yourself said it was juicy stuff, right? Not the kind of thing he wants looked into. Anyway, it just seems to me like you're back where you started. Neither of you have a thing on the other."

"Except for one thing."

"What's that?"

"I don't have a story. Unless I can figure out who those two people are and positively connect them to Derek, I've got nothing to go on. And Derek is hardly likely to invite me back for a civilized afternoon tea after what happened, is he?"

"Well," Alison said carefully, "it sounds to me like you're better off out of it. He's not the type to mess with, Diana. And you're not the first to try, from what I've heard."

"What is it with everyone around here?" Diana griped. "Does Derek Islington have diplomatic immunity or something? Why is everybody so intent on talking me out of this story? I feel like I'm in the middle of a conspiracy of silence, for God's sake!" She motioned impatiently for the waitress to come with her check.

Alison did not appear to be phased by this outburst. She watched Diana for a moment, then observed, "This story really means a lot to you, doesn't it."

Diana turned to face her. "It really means a lot to me."

"Well, then," Alison said, commandeering the check from the waitress to sign it before Diana could do the same, "I suppose you're going to have to resort to further devious means to get it, aren't you?" She rummaged in her bag for the tip and flung it on the table with a triumphant flourish.

Diana stood up. "You know, Alison, you're quite a revelation. Are you sure you're not wasting your time in the feature department? You've got the devious mind of a top-notch news hound."

Alison surveyed her, hands on hips. "Are you sure you're not wasting your time in the sports department?" she retorted.

Diana laughed. "I think we're both wasting our time standing here arguing about it. Let's get going."

The morning sun was already firmly established in the eggshell-blue sky when Diana and Alison emerged from their taxi at Churchill Downs. Gray clouds could be seen scudding off to the east as if the breeze were riding them out of town. Diana unzipped her oatmeal wool cardigan and shook out her hair in the wind. This early, the only inhabitants of Churchill Downs were those who belonged there—the tourists and media mavens were still wrapped in their blankets and dreams.

But this was what Diana dreamed the Derby should be: crisp air, dappled sun and the brisk, snorting breaths of the horses as they leaned impatiently into their bits. On the far side of the course, the twin spires of the grandstand looked like flats on a stage set. The stables were backstage, where the real-life preparations for the Derby show went on. Diana much preferred backstage to the glamour of the show itself.

Alison, chattering brightly about Arnold Sweeney and his myriad charms, led Diana through the maze of holding stalls and narrow lanes, calling out cheerful greetings right and left. Diana was amazed at how many people she seemed to know. While she had been concentrating on one small, uncertain enigma, Alison seemed to have grasped the whole of the Derby in her tiny hands. Her initial affection for Alison Chase was growing into a deep respect.

The object of this rumination suddenly stopped short and gripped Diana's arm. "There he is," Alison whispered. "Isn't he a vision?"

It was, in fact, quite a sight that confronted them, although Diana did not concentrate solely on the sandy-haired man to whom Alison referred. Arnold Sweeney sat atop a lean roan filly, his body crunched into a small S shape in the saddle. He and the horse both wore the same look of fierce concentration as they moved forward between the stalls toward a small exercise paddock. The horse stepped high, her elegant hoofs dancing with anticipation. Her flanks looked like warm velvet, and her dark eyes rolled excitedly as she strained to reach the relative freedom of the paddock.

"There, honey chile, there," Arnold crooned softly in a surprising mixture of Irish brogue and southern drawl. "You'll get your lead soon, I promise. You'll soon be out there with the wind in your hair. Just let old Arnie show you the way, little girl."

One hand caressed the filly's mane, but even from where she stood, Diana could see the white knuckles that gripped the reins, giving the horse no chance to break loose from his iron guidance. His whole body, in fact, was like a tightly coiled spring, and Diana saw a striking resemblance between rider and mount in that respect.

"Quite a sight, eh?" prompted Alison, and Diana turned to give the required compliment on Alison's choice of men.

"And that's my namesake, huh?" she added, jutting her chin in the direction of the paddock where Arnold had just maneuvered the horse into a tight trot.

"Yup. Diana's Folly." Alison grinned. "Isn't she a beauty?"

"Aptly named, too," Diana remarked dryly. "In view of my recent exploits, that is."

"She had it first, though," Alison pointed out. "I guess you'll have to settle for Diana's Other Folly."

"Other Follies," Diana murmured under her breath. She was thinking of the other mistakes she had made in the past few days. "Definitely the plural form." She had not even begun to consider what she was going to say to Beau when she saw him again. She had even jumped at the chance to accompany Alison that morning to avoid that phone call from him. How could she tell him he had been right? How could she ask him for help after what she had said?

On the other hand, how could she not?

"Come on. Stand over here and we can watch without getting in Arnold's way. Maybe when he's done, you can interview him, get a little background info on that subject we were discussing earlier. He's been around the Downs for ages, you know." She did not take her eyes off Arnold as they moved closer.

Diana had already spoken to some jockeys and asked general questions about Derek Islington's reputation. But she had not had any specific questions to ask and, of course, had not gotten any specific replies. It might be interesting to ask someone like Arnold Sweeney if he thought there were any crooked judges or doctors involved in Street Fare's run that year.

"Don't you want to save him for yourself?" she inquired.

Alison flashed a big grin sideways. "I said you can interview him, that's all." She winked. "I have every intention of saving him for myself. Besides, I've got my girl jockey story just about wrapped."

For about half an hour, Arnold guided Diana's Folly around the paddock, carefully controlling her gait and stance every inch of the way. There was never a moment when he stopped his incessant crooning and never a moment when he let up on the pressure of the reins, knees and heels. Diana noticed that he didn't use a riding crop. He probably didn't need one.

The filly never got to run full out during the workout; Alison told Diana that this round was simply so that Arnold could reinforce his authority over the horse. Later on, in the afternoon, Diana's Folly would be taken to the race track and given her head, ridden by another jockey of equal weight but less importance than Arnold himself.

"That must be quite a sight," Diana murmured to Alison. "That beautiful horse, tearing around the track with nothing to hold her back . . ." There was a wistful edge to her voice.

"It's a sight, indeed," Arnold agreed, coming up to them on foot. He had dismounted and left Diana's Folly in the care of a stableboy. "And so are you." He leaned forward and planted a firm, proprietary kiss on Alison's lips. Diana noted with amusement that they were exactly the same height.

Alison pulled reluctantly away, her face glowing. "Arnold, this is Diana Jennings."

Arnold turned and looked up. "Ah, yes," he drawled with that uncanny Irish lilt. "The famous lady sportswriter. Welcome." He extended a small but well-muscled hand.

"Famous?" Diana lifted a skeptical brow.

"Alison told me all about you," he said, his misty blue eyes resting on Alison adoringly.

"It's always nice to get good press," Diana murmured, winking at Alison.

"So, Diana Jennings, how do you like your namesake?" Arnold asked, tearing his gaze from Alison at last.

"It might be the other way around," Diana pointed out wryly, "but I think she's terrific."

"That she is." Arnold's eyes, following Diana's Folly as she was led in a cooling walk around the paddock, held some of the same emotion Diana had noticed when he looked at Alison. She wondered if Alison was aware of her competition.

"The most glorious filly in the race," Alison chirped loyally. So she *did* recognize the competition.

"The most glorious horse in the race," Arnold corrected. "We don't draw any gender lines, do we, Diana?" He was speaking to the horse, but it was the woman who replied.

"Not if I can help it."

Arnold acknowledged the joke with a grin. "That's right. You and my Diana are in the same boat, aren't you? Fillies in a colt's race."

"What made you say that?" Diana asked sharply.

"It's okay," he said soothingly, not noticing her tone. "You're both good enough to win the race, aren't you?"

Diana realized she was basking in the reflected glow of his esteem for her equine counterpart. Nevertheless, she smiled graciously. "Thanks, Arnold. I hope you're right. But tell me, what chance does Diana's Folly really stand against a solid favorite such as, say, Street Fare?"

If Arnold saw that the question was not a casual one, he didn't seem to care. He pondered seriously for a moment before replying. "Well, now, that's hard to tell. I know my Diana can hold her own against any other horse that's running. But Street Fare, well, I just couldn't say." He paused. "Nobody can."

"Why not?" Diana persisted.

"You see the other mounts work every day," Arnold explained. "Street Fare—you never see him. You never hear how he's running. You don't know if he has any physical problems cropping up . . . you just don't know."

"Won't the prerace physical tell you if there's anything wrong with him?" Diana had flipped out her little notebook and was scribbling quickly.

"It's too late by then," he said glumly. "And besides,

with Gerald Murphy doing the examining, I wouldn't be too sure."

"Gerald Murphy?"

For the first time, Diana noticed a guarded look in Arnold's eyes. He seemed to be getting slightly uncomfortable. Alison took a protective step closer to him. "Yeah. He's the veterinarian assigned to do the medical work-up on Street Fare."

She watched his face closely as she spoke. "And wouldn't this Murphy fellow be able to tell if there was something wrong with Street Fare?"

"Oh, he could tell, all right," Arnold replied darkly. "He's the best vet in the area." He laughed bitterly. "Islington wouldn't let anything but the best near his horses, you can bet."

"But Islington has nothing to do with it, does he?" Diana asked, even though she already knew the answer. "Dr. Murphy is one of the vets appointed by the racing commission, isn't he?"

Arnold threw her a sharp look, but he didn't reply. On impulse, Diana continued. "Arnold, do you know of any possible connection between *the* Dr. Murphy and one of the state-appointed judges? A judge who might have had something to do with . . . with certain racing cases in the past few years?" She held her breath waiting for the reply.

"Hey, what is this with Murphy and Islington and Street Fare all of a sudden?" Arnold suddenly exploded. "For years, all you reporters keep away like Islington had the plague or something. Now everybody's snooping around, asking if there have been any new rumors, asking about Murphy again . . . and some judge. I don't know anything about a judge."

Diana's heart constricted. "Who else has been asking, Arnold?"

"First thing this morning, Beau Gatling comes sniffin' around—you'd think he learned his lesson after the threats he got from the Stewart thing." Arnold was clearly agitated, and Alison was stroking his arm to soothe him. "Damned fool reporters can't keep their hands off dynamite, that's what."

"Beau? Beau Gatling was here? This morning?" Diana's voice had an edge of hysteria.

"Yeah, Beau Gatling. You know him?"

It was Alison who answered for her, a dry smile on her face. "She never heard of him," she said. "Right, Diana?"

Diana ignored the irony. "When?" she demanded.

"Pardon, ma'am?"

"When was he here? Beau."

"Why he left right before you two showed up. He was standing right back there. Then I turned to see you, and when I looked back, he was—hey! There he is! Right there, walking between those two stableboys. Hey, Beau!"

Arnold had peered past them over Diana's shoulder as he was explaining Beau's mysterious disappearance. Now, as the jockey spoke, Diana was able to watch a parade of emotions cross his face in swift succession; perplexity, confusion, recognition, and surprise. By watching Arnold's face, she could easily imagine what was happening on Beau's face, even though he was behind her and facing in the opposite direction; stealth, relief, shock, embarrassment. I hope he stays good and embarrassed, she thought with grim satisfaction. The sneak.

Beau had no choice but to turn around and join them. Diana waited until he had come up beside her to turn and see his face. *Yup. Guilty as a fox in a henhouse,* she thought. *He's been trying to get a jump on my story.* She gritted her teeth and smiled.

"Why Beau. What a surprise!"

"Isn't it!" He didn't sound as embarrassed as he looked.

"You two know each other, I assume," Arnold surmised, a bit perplexed by their behavior.

"Mr. Gatling's reputation precedes him," Diana remarked.

"As does the lady's," Beau replied, sounding maniacally polite.

Alison, realizing that a storm was brewing, quickly made some excuse and dragged Arnold away, leaving the two of them alone.

"So." She faced him with her hands on her hips.

"Good morning," he said pleasantly, shoving his hands into the pockets of his corduroy chinos. "You look lovely in the morning. Do you know that?" He grinned disarmingly.

"Just what do you think you're doing?" she demanded.

"Paying you a compliment, I think."

"You know what I mean," she hissed.

"Your eyes are the most marvelous Nile green when you're mad. Know that?"

"Cut it out! I mean it, Beau." She lowered her brows sternly. "What were you doing snooping around here asking questions about Derek?"

"Derek, is it?" The hands clenched into fists briefly inside the pockets. "Gee, it's nice you two got to be friends!"

"And you can cut the innocent act, too," she commanded. "You aren't supposed to be involved in this, do you hear? I'm doing fine without your interference."

"Fine, huh?" Beau rocked back on his heels. "Went well last night, did it?"

Diana clamped her mouth shut. She had no intention of revealing how badly it had gone—not now. "It went fine."

"Oh, well, that's great. That's just great," he said enthusiastically. "Got a lot of good information, huh?"

Diana lifted her chin and faced him. "Could be."

"Aha! Could be!" He rubbed his hands together gleefully. "Well, that's good; that's very good. I'm really glad to hear you're getting somewhere. And hey,

if you have any questions—anything at all you need
cleared up—don't hesitate to ask, okay? I wouldn't
dream of offering it, of course, but if you should ask,
well"—he looked at her meaningfully—"*I'm* not
proud."

Now was the time, Diana thought. Now was the time
to lay aside her own pride and ask him what he knew
about Dr. Murphy and the mysterious judge. She had
already deduced that Cam would have no information
for her when he called back and that even if she went to
the state records herself, she would find them carefully
rearranged. The pieces of the puzzle she had inadvert-
ently picked up the night before were beginning to
make a little sense, but she needed proof. And to have
proof she needed names. If anyone had names, it was
Beau.

But she couldn't bring herself to do it. She just
couldn't give him that satisfaction. And Beau, who was
watching her carefully, seemed to sense it, because
when he spoke again, the sarcastic drawl was gone.
"It's okay, Diana," he said softly. "You've gotten this
far without any help, and you'll go on without it, too.
Right?"

Suddenly miserable, she could only nod.

"Right," he said with finality. "Then we won't
mention it again today, all right?" He smiled his gentle,
crooked smile.

"It's a deal." Not only did she not want to mention it,
she didn't even want to think about it for a while.
Whatever Beau knew, whatever he had overheard of
her questions to Arnold, whatever the truth was, it
would have to wait. Diana could not stand another
moment of tension. She would have loved to go back to
bed.

But Beau seemed to have other ideas. "Terrific," he
said, taking her elbow and setting off at a brisk pace,
"because we have a very busy schedule today, and we
can't afford to stand around here and argue."

"Busy schedule? I don't know, Beau." One thing she didn't want to be was busy. Sleep sounded a lot better than being busy.

"What's wrong? Aren't you free this afternoon?" There was a sudden hesitation in his voice that she found endearing.

She smiled. "Of course I'm free. It just depends on what you have in mind." *I can always sleep,* she was thinking.

"Nothing special," he replied nonchalantly. "Just a little visit to Bluefield Farms."

"Never heard of it."

"It's out in some mighty pretty bluegrass country," he offered.

"I've seen bluegrass." Her resistance was merely token.

"And it's got an actual Civil War Confederate marker on the property."

"I was on the other side, you may recall."

Beau lifted both arms deliberately and laid them on Diana's shoulders, drawing their heads together so that their brows almost touched. "They got a tough little old lady living there who makes a mean chicken dinner," he cajoled softly.

"Oh, yeah? And who is she?"

Beau landed two kisses on her nose and mouth before answering. "My mother," he said. "Who else?"

Chapter 9

BEAU GATLING DROVE AN OLD VOLVO THAT LOOKED AS IF it had been treated badly for much of its long life. But he drove it with style—she had to grant him that. As soon as they reached the outskirts of the city, heading south past the fairgrounds on Route 65, he shifted into fourth gear and leaned back against the headrest, both hands gripping the leather-thonged steering wheel.

"Is this the Indy 500?" she asked, watching the speedometer edge past sixty-five.

"No, no, that's over on the other side of the river. This is Kentucky, ma'am, and it's BLUEGRASS COUNTRY!" He let out a whoop and stuck his head out the window so that his dark curls vibrated in the stiff wind.

Diana chuckled. She wasn't the type to whoop, but if she had been, that's exactly what she would have done. Considering how miserable she had felt earlier about her inability to make headway on the Islington story, it was remarkable that she felt so good now. But the day was perfect, the scenery gorgeous and the man—well, except for his habit of trying to take care of her life for her, he was really quite a delight. Right now, Diana thought, he looked like a teenager, his mouth spread back in a huge grin over white teeth, his lean body draped in an aerodynamically impossible slouch against the seat. He had switched on the radio and was humming gaily to the infectious country twang on a bluegrass guitar. Diana wanted to eat him up, but she restrained herself.

"'My heart is shattered over youuuu!'" he crooned to her, "'but you left the pieces on the floor . . .'" His arm was hooked out the window so that his hand rested on the roof of the car, and he beat a metallic rhythm in time to the chorus. "'I never thought you'd be so cruuuel' . . ."

". . . and now I don't love you anymore!'" Diana raised her voice in a twangy contralto and joined him in finishing the refrain.

"Well, I'll be!" Beau looked at her in genuine surprise. "I never would have figured you for a country music fan."

"I'm not," she confessed. "But it's fairly easy to catch the drift, you know."

Beau nodded. "I know, I know. It's all pretty simple-minded. But that's me—I'll take the simple life every time." His voice oozed southern honey.

"Hah. Simple, maybe, but not simple-minded."

"Why, Dah-anna!" Beau deliberately shifted into a lower gear and wheeled over into the slow lane, his face incredulous. "I do believe you just paid me a compliment! Or do my ears deceive me?"

"Beau," she began, but he cut her off with a perfect imitation.

"'Beauu' . . . oh, I love it when you say my name. Say it again."

"Beauuu," she chanted. "Now you say mine."

"Diana."

"No. Say it the other way."

"What other way?"

"Beauuu!"

"Dah-anna!"

"That's it; that's the way! Beauuu." She was giggling so hard she could hardly get the word out.

"Dah-anna," he sang.

She had just started to drawl his name again when, with a heart-stopping squeal, the Volvo skidded to a halt on the side of the road. Both Diana and Beau lurched forward as far as their seatbelts would allow and then flew back against their headrests with a thud.

They turned to face each other—Beau, sheepish and Diana, incredulous. "What on earth was that?" she demanded.

"Sorry. Are you all right?" His eyes traced over her, full of concern. "Did you hurt your head?" He reached out and touched the back of her head tentatively, as if afraid of finding blood on his hand.

"I'm fine. A little breathless but fine. Now, do you mind explaining the reason for that little thrill session?"

He bit his lower lip, trying to suppress a grin. "I missed the turnoff," he said lightly, throwing the gear into reverse and spreading his arm across Diana's seat back in order to watch his progress behind his shoulder.

"You missed the turn?" Diana's eyes grew wider. "To your own house?"

"It's not my house," he said defensively. "At least, not anymore. It hasn't been my house for a while."

"Oh, really?" She folded her arms across her chest and watched him with amusement. "And how long has it been since you lived here?" she inquired.

"Oh, ages," Beau said, concentrating on finding the dirt turnoff he had missed.

"And how long did you live here before you left? Three days?"

"Ages." He winked. "But I was distracted," he explained. "By you." Two of the fingers resting on the seat crept forward and squeezed the back of Diana's neck. She shivered at the sudden sensation.

"Honestly," she said, clucking her tongue and rolling her eyes. "I cannot believe that you were acting like such a kid that you—" she caught sight of his grin and corrected herself with a giggle. "Okay, okay, so I cannot believe that *we* were acting like such kids that you missed the turn to your own house!"

Just then, Beau drove around a curve and into a clearing, and Diana gasped at the view that faced her. They were driving up a dirt road lined with willows and flooded on either side by clamorous red and yellow flowers. To the left, a wheat field, the color of toast, spread in the bright sunshine. To the right, the ubiquitous bluegrass took on a silvery sheen. The road swept gently around, and Diana glimpsed soft pools of deeper greenery where small stands of fir and elm nestled together in the folds of the gentle hills.

But the sight that really made her gape was the house itself. Standing gaunt and spare on a mild rise of land, it looked like something out of an American Gothic painting. It rose three stories to a steep gabled roof, and its richly weathered clapboards seemed held tightly against the sheer sides. Even the two trees that flanked it—a blue spruce and a spreading elm—stood at a respectful distance, while the house occupied its knoll with the mute grandeur of an old soldier.

Then Beau swung around to the front of the house, and the proud structure opened its arms into a wide and welcoming porch that ran around the far side. White pillars supported the wisteria-laced roof, and tall windows opened onto boxes filled with geraniums.

Diana leaned her head back against the seat and sighed. She closed her eyes and opened them twice to make sure the sight was not an illusion. Despite her weary posture, her heart was beating unnaturally fast. Bluefield Farms looked to her like home.

"Welcome home, Diana." The words were so unerringly accurate that Diana's eyes flew open. Beau was leaning across the seat, his face only inches from hers.

"What did you say?" The words came out sounding strangled.

Beau smiled into her wide green eyes. "I said, welcome home. It is my home, you know."

Diana shut her eyes tightly to clear her mind. On the surface, Beau's words were innocent enough. But given the shock of subliminal recognition she had just experienced, she was finding it difficult to comprehend. That house—his house—corresponded so exactly to her secret dream house that she felt goose bumps rising on her arms.

As a child, growing up in the city and loving it, she had nevertheless nurtured a deeply private fantasy. One day—after she had become a success and earned her Pulitzer, of course—she would find herself a house and settle down. She would have a family, perhaps, or perhaps not. But the house had always remained the same.

And it had looked very much like Bluefield.

Now, with Beau smiling tenderly at her, it was hard to believe that he had not somehow divined her secret. Diana searched his face for signs of complicity. Or was it, she wondered, only her own wishful heart?

"Beau," she began carefully, trying to recover her poise. Beau stopped her with a tender, lingering kiss. It was a gesture as soft and bittersweet as the afternoon, full of sunshine and unvoiced promises. But just as Diana was recovered enough to settle back and enjoy it, he lifted his lips from hers.

"This is a little embarrassing," he whispered, not looking at all embarrassed, "but I think my mama's watching us through the curtains."

Diana whipped her head around toward the house. Sure enough, she was just in time to see a starched curtain fall back against the pane. She looked back at Beau, her confusion now compounded by guilt. "Oh, Beau," she whispered, "maybe this wasn't such a good idea."

"I wouldn't worry," he reassured her, making no move to pull a respectable distance away from her lips. "She hasn't pulled out her shotgun in years."

His eyes twinkled, and Diana felt a flood of relief when she realized he had been kidding her. His droll sense of humor was doing wonders for her equilibrium. "I don't believe you," she told him. "I'll bet it was you who had the shotgun in your face, from all the angry papas in the neighborhood. Right?"

He affected a modest shrug. "Fortunately, my mama was a better shot than their papas, which is why I am a single man today." He rolled his eyes. "I can't tell you how many times she protected my endangered virtue!"

Diana hooted. "Oh, that's rich! That's really rich!" She put her hand on the door handle, ready now to face the house and Mrs. Gatling. But Beau covered her fingers before she could open the door.

"Not yet." His clear, dark eyes were suddenly serious. "I want your word first."

"What word?" In spite of herself, Diana cast another anxious glance toward the window.

"That we can continue where we left off later on." His eyes traveled longingly around the circumference of her mouth.

"When we're not so closely chaperoned, you mean?" She tried to make light of it, but Beau's expression made it impossible for her to smile.

"I meant what I said, Diana." The hand over hers tightened in a quick, intense gesture. "Welcome home."

He *had* to know what she had felt on first seeing the house. Why else would he say that? Diana could only nod and swallow, her throat inexplicably dry. It seemed easier to face the eerily familiar house and the eagle-eyed Mrs. Gatling than to remain in the car under the suffocating implication of Beau's knowing gaze. For another long moment, they sat perfectly still inside the car, until Diana felt her palms beginning to sweat beneath his imprisoning grasp. She hoped her expression was not betraying her discomfort, but from the way Beau's smile, dry and tender, spread across his face, she knew her mood had not escaped him.

"Okay, sports fans," he said, giving her hand a final pat. "Let's go in there and win one for the Gipper, shall we?"

His words did not exactly inspire confidence, Diana thought, clenching her jaw and breathing out heavily through her nose as she watched Beau bound athletically around the front of the car. She was quite shaken and glad, for once, to accept Beau's gallantly extended elbow as they went up the steps of the wide veranda. Her legs felt like wooden sticks. The odd sense of déjà vu she had experienced on seeing the house, Beau's abrupt kiss and enigmatic intensity, had all conspired to make a lovely afternoon seem complicated and portentous. And she doubted that Mrs. Beauregard Gatling, Sr., would do much to alleviate the problem.

She could not have been more wrong. Whether Beau had painted a picture of his mother as an irascible old bird on purpose or merely as a joke, Diana couldn't tell. In any case, the reality turned out to be a good deal more pleasant than Diana had imagined. Oh, she was tough, all right, and Diana could see that very little escaped her sharp eye. But the overriding impression she took away with her on the first afternoon was of a charming, intelligent and surprising woman whose warmth could not be disguised. Later on, Beau told her that Miss Emma, as he liked to call her, had taken an instant liking to Diana, which explained her unusually tractable manner. Diana did not tell him that she thought the mother was very much like the son, which explained the good feelings all around.

The inside of the house was a comfort, too, mostly because the uncanny resemblance to Diana's dream house ended when she stepped through the front door. The Gatling house was homey to the point of being run-down—neat as a pin and impossibly clean but with the patina of age and use that only good but well-worn furnishings can acquire. The large living room held a motley arrangement of overstuffed couches and occasional tables, covered with an eclectic assortment of old afghans and family mementos. The sunny dining room bore the unmistakable signs of innumerable family meals—Beau was the second oldest of five, she learned —and Emma presided over her own cooking as if her entire clan were still present and under her warm and watchful eye.

Emma herself was a reassurance. She was small and softly padded, and her gray curls had obviously once been the prototype for Beau's own dark halo. But except for the bright laughter in her eyes, the physical resemblance between mother and son was not overwhelming. She was gracious, yet casual, and not the least bit affected by the presence of a Yankee wolfing down fried chicken in her house.

"Beau tells me you're a sportswriter," she said during lunch. "What do you think of the Derby?" She had a fine, singsong drawl that reassured Diana about the sincerity of Beau's accent.

Diana cast Emma a grateful glance for not dwelling on her odd choice of careers. "I haven't seen the Derby yet," she said, smiling. "But the balloon, tricycle and steamboat races have been . . . well, interesting."

Emma snorted. "That's it. That's all the Derby is anymore. Balloons and baby bikes." She looked over at her son. "And hanging out with the boys, too. Right, Beauregard?"

Despite her severe tone of voice, Beau never broke stride with his chewing as he replied, "Right, Miss Emma." Then he winked at Diana. "When it comes to horse racing, Miss Emma is practically a Yankee herself."

"Well, I'm glad to see somebody around here is taking an intelligent view of the proceedings, if that's what you mean by Yankee," Diana observed innocently.

"I'll drink to that," Emma vowed, raising her glass of iced tea. "And if you didn't spend so much time partying with those vagrants you call reporters, maybe you'd write a piece pointing that out."

"What?" Beau pretended to choke on his chicken leg. "But Miss Emma! I couldn't ruin their party like that! It would be ungentlemanly."

Clearly, both mother and son were enjoying the repartee. Emma leaned across the table and said to Diana, "The original party boy sits before us, my dear. Kentucky's answer to Scarlett O'Hara."

Diana laughed. "Scarlett O'Hara couldn't write like Beau does."

"That's true, of course." Emma cast a fond look at her son. "But Scarlett was reckless, and so is he."

"I've heard Beau was a party boy," Diana said, shaking her head in mock sympathy. "But reckless, too? My, my."

"You heard? All the way from New York City?"

"No, he told me himself, of course. Said there was a real run on shotguns while he was growing up, what with all the irate papas and all."

Emma shrieked. "Hah! That's a hoot! He was so obnoxious that no self-respecting girl would go near him!" She pursed her lips above sparkling eyes.

Beau showed no sign of remorse. "It's the truth, Diana," he confessed cheerfully. "I was always one of the boys. Sports is all I ever had on my mind."

Diana grinned across the table. "Once an old boy, always an old boy, eh, Beau?"

"Once a chauvinist always a chauvinist—isn't that what you mean?" he replied promptly.

Emma watched this exchange shrewdly. "Do you know," she said to no one in particular, "I do believe all that might change."

Beau's reaction to this statement was strange. The impish grin faded and was replaced by a melancholy smile. He looked over at Diana, but she looked down at her plate quickly to avoid meeting his eyes. She knew full well that Emma had meant that Diana was to be the catalyst for the change, but she refused to think about what it might mean in terms of her own life.

After lunch, Emma rose to clear the table, and Diana automatically did the same. "You stay right where you are," Emma ordered her. "I don't know what they do up north, but where I come from, guests don't act like maids. It's not polite."

Diana sat back down, suitably contrite. "What about you?" she whispered across the table to Beau, who was slouched back in his chair, savoring the meal. "You're not a guest. Why shouldn't you give a lady a helping hand?"

"Because he's my son, that's why," Emma said over her shoulder, and left the room chuckling delightedly about her still-sharp ears.

Beau shrugged. "You heard the lady. And I never argue with a lady. Especially my mother."

Diana shook her head. "I don't believe she really lets you get away with that ridiculous double standard—a modern woman like that!"

"Are you kidding? She taught me that double standard!" Beau got up and reached his hand across the table. "Come on. Old southern tradition has it that now is the time for me to lead you on a breathtaking tour of my land, taking care to point out the vastness of my estate, the richness of my soil and the fertility of my mares." Raising her hand in a high arc above the table, Beau led her in a stately walk out to the porch.

"Sounds incredibly boring," she said. "And what happens after that, according to old southern tradition?"

"Once you're suitably impressed?" Beau levered his eyebrows wildly and twirled an imaginary mustache. "Why that's when I make my pass!" He grabbed Diana around the rib cage and began to tickle her, leading her down the path from the house in gales of laughter.

But she *was* suitably impressed. Bluefield Farms was not large by any standards; it did not stretch as far as the eye could see in any direction. As a matter of fact, Beau took pains to point out that the path they followed was the legal property of the neighboring farm. "But don't worry," he assured her generously. "Ever since I rescued his daughter from a burning southern city in Georgia, he's given me the run of the land."

"Hmph. I should think he would have given you his daughter."

"He tried," Beau deadpanned. "But I wouldn't have her. I've been saving myself for a prickly Yankee with moss-green eyes."

Once again, Diana was aware that his bantering smile had faded and had been replaced by an almost unwilling seriousness. It had been acceptable in Emma's dining room, which reeked of civility. But outside, on a path that was alternately sun drenched and dappled with gray-green light, Diana was constrained by his sudden change of mood. It was all right to think that Beau was greatly affected by her appearance in his life, but what about the changes he was wreaking in *her* heart and mind? That did not bear close scrutiny, and Diana was quick to steer the conversation back to a more conventional tone.

"I see horses. I thought Bluefield didn't own any

horses." She stepped up on a rocky incline to look out over a stand of high bushes at a group of mares and foals in the field beyond. It was, as always, an arresting sight. But Diana was acutely aware of Beau's dark, considering eyes watching her take in the scenery.

"We don't," he said, his voice close to her shoulder. "My grateful neighbor allows his mares to graze within sight of our land to impress our visitors. No prize stallions, you understand. But then, it's the thought that counts." His voice was thick with the usual irony, but somehow Diana understood that his heart wasn't in it. She didn't feel much like being witty herself.

"Beau," she asked cautiously, "what happened to you after you printed the Elmo Stewart story?"

She heard Beau sigh behind her, but she didn't turn around. "What do you mean? It was printed, people either liked it or didn't, and that was that. Why?"

"Arnold Sweeney said Islington threatened you. Is that why you stopped investigating him?"

He laughed a short, bitter laugh. "Yup. That's it. One quick phone call to Miss Emma and the whole thing was forgotten. Gentlemanly of him, wasn't it?"

Diana looked around, shocked. "You mean he threatened Miss Emma?"

"I mean he tried. But Miss Emma doesn't scare as easily as I do." His eyes narrowed. "And I don't think you do, either."

She ignored this potentially explosive remark. "I can't believe it. How can he get away with things like that?"

"You should know," Beau remarked.

"Well I don't. At least, not yet."

"Of course, maybe ol' Derek's changed. That was a while ago. He's pretty good at covering his tracks. He may have turned over a new leaf for all I know."

"He hasn't changed, and you know it," Diana said sharply. She knew he was fishing for information, just as she was, and she was sorry she had brought it up.

Beau watched her but didn't reply. "Underneath that cultivated, charming exterior is a man who has no compunctions about lying, stealing and cheating to get what he wants."

Beau smirked. "Sounds like dear old Derek to me," he said.

She had a sudden inspiration. "Do you know," she mused aloud. "I think there's another reason why you're so cagey about Derek Islington."

"Oh, really? It's not enough that he threatened my mother?"

"You're no chicken, and neither is she. You know what I think? I think there's a part of you that envies Derek Islington. Envies his money and his horses and his power. I think you're even jealous of his relationship with me!"

Beau moved so that his face was very close to hers, and his voice was so chilled that she blinked. "Should I be, Diana?"

She searched his face and swallowed before whispering her reply. "I'll tell you something, Beau. I want something from Derek Islington, and no one—not even you—is going to stop me from getting it. But he's not a human being to me, Beau. He is a story, a . . . a chance for me. Do you see? He is not . . . civilized." She ended more weakly than she had intended. "You are."

This speech surprised even her. She had started out hoping to goad Beau into telling her what he knew about Derek's court connections. But she had ended up trying—unsuccessfully—to tell him how she felt about him.

What surprised her even more was Beau's reaction. After a moment's pause, he stepped back on the path, threw back his head and laughed, long and loud, leaning against a tree trunk for support.

"What's so funny?" she demanded. Despite her

confusion, Beau's laughter was infectious and a tremendous relief of tension.

"Oh, nothing, nothing, really." Beau had some trouble recovering, and he threw his arm across Diana's shoulder for support. "It's just that I've spent most of my life being jealous of the Derek Islingtons of this world, and now you just pop out with it as if it was as simple as the nose on your face." He leaned forward and kissed it for emphasis. "I thought I was doing such a great job of hiding it, too. And now, after all those years, this incredible woman comes along and tells me I have something the Derek Islingtons don't have!" He tightened his hold around her neck, pulling her head onto his shoulder in an impulsive squeeze. He was chortling from sheer relief. "I may be a chivalrous, chauvinist pig, and I may spend my days hanging out in a bar with the boys, but my God, my soul has come out of the stable. Do you hear that? I'm civilized!"

He shouted this last statement so loudly that the horses in the far field looked up, startled. Diana, pressed against Beau's side, felt a great rush of elation. Suddenly, everything was right. The day, blowsy and sunny, Miss Emma, the meal, the odd sensation of being home at last on that gentle acreage, all conspired to make her feel as if she had reached a goal in her life, a goal she hadn't known she was striving for until she reached it. She could feel Beau's pleasure and warmth bubbling up along her flank as he pressed her close, and despite all that she had taught herself about there being more important things in life than this, Diana Jennings could not think of a single one at that moment. She was glad she had spoken, however awkwardly.

Then Beau stopped laughing, and using both hands, pushed her an arm's length away from him to gaze at her. He held her there for a long time, his dark eyes probing hers in complete comprehension. The laughter was still in his eyes, but something else was there as well—something as warm and comfortable as the day itself.

Diana met this new expression with a smile. She had never felt less pressured in her life, never felt more willing to share the moment with a man, for whatever it might bring.

"Is there someplace where we can . . . be alone?" she asked him bluntly.

Beau's smile deepened, revealing a hidden dimple in his left cheek that she had never noticed before. Diana stared at it, feeling as if all her senses had been heightened. "I do declare, Scarlett," Beau murmured, "must you always do the asking? I mean, a guy's entitled to lead once in a while, isn't he?"

Diana squinted one eye shut and traced the shadow of Beau's curls along his forehead with one finger. "I thought you were supposed to be Scarlett."

He winked. "Wanna bet? In this scene, I get to play Rhett. I've got the right credentials."

She smiled. "I guess I can't argue with that, can I?"

"You could try, I'm sure." He took a step closer. "Wanna try?"

She shook her head. "I just want to find someplace with some soft grass. Now."

"Now? How about right here?" Before she could protest, he had flung himself down on the springy earth beneath the tree and pulled Diana heavily on top of him.

"Beau!" Diana was laughing and protesting at the same time. "We're right in the middle of the path! Someone will see us!"

"Just a bunch of horses," he replied. "And they won't tell. I have them trained, you see." Nevertheless, wrapping his arms tightly around her back, he began rolling over and over, supporting his weight on his elbows to avoid crushing Diana into the coal-black dirt. After several rolls, with Diana shrieking hysterically, they came to a halt under an arching, wild primrose bush. The ground sloped softly down toward the field, and the earth, covered with still-tender grass shoots, made a natural pillow for their heads. The bush was not yet in bloom, but the shiny leaves made a delicate canopy over them, leaving a network of fragrant sunlight to filter through.

Diana stared up into Beau's eyes, aware of the dappling of light through his black curls. Her sense of exhilaration was still acute, but she was also aware of a breathless suspension, as if she and Beau were poised on the edge of a tremendous step into the unknown. Neither knew if the other was ready to make the first move, and they remained perfectly still, face to face, for what seemed like hours.

Then Beau began moving his lips toward hers, slowly, tentatively, as if hesitant to rush headlong into this uncharted emotional territory. He would move a few inches closer, and his lips would begin to purse, and then he would stop, draw back slightly and search the corners of Diana's waiting face for signs that he should stop or go. For her part, Diana seemed to have lost the ability to initiate any action on her own. Having made the first move with her usual bravado, she wanted to do nothing more than await the inevitable, ecstatic first contact of lips on lips. While she waited, she could already taste Beau's mouth on hers and feel the tangy insistence of his tongue inside her mouth.

When it came, when he covered those last few inches between their lips with a soft groan, the reality far exceeded the anticipation. The first contact was softer than velvet—it was like a cushiony pillow of warm silk. And when his tongue curled upward inside her eager mouth, it was with a lapidary edge, cutting sharp diamonds of desire wherever it traveled.

Soon her whole body was a necklace of that desire. Beau's hands and lips wove a jeweled trail along the

wide bone of her jaw, and heralded by the tender
explorations of his fingertips, strung strands of delight
down the long slope of her neck and between the lapels
of her chamois shirt to the declivity between her
breasts. Diana struggled to be free of the pale green
material. She longed to be clothed only in the gemlike
sparkle of Beau's ebony eyes and to wear only the
diamond heat of his touch.

Beau watched her fumble with the buttons, his half
smile blown into a full-pouting shape by his passion.
When she had undone them all, he cradled her neck in
the crook of his elbow and lifted her head back so that
she could slip out of the sleeves. Diana's head fell back
heavily against his strong forearm, leaving her nipples
exposed to the sudden rush of cool air. They felt hard
and brittle, and it wasn't until Beau applied the expert
pressure of his tongue that they became warm and
pliant, rising to peaks of alert sensitivity.

The warm, pungent smell of the soil and the sweet
promise of primrose on the air soon mingled with the
sharper scent of Beau's bare torso as he slipped out of
his shirt and pressed his body along Diana's. She could
feel her own flesh giving off the fragrant heat of passion
as she wrapped her arms underneath the slim curve of
his waist to press him closer. They moved quickly, yet
without urgency, two practiced lovers discovering uncharted land for the first time. And no matter where
their hands, lips and legs wandered, they always returned to the locked embrace of their eyes.

Beau rolled over so that he was lying beside her,
reaching around her to brush off the accumulation of
soft soil and leaves that had clung to her back, pressed
beneath his weight. Not it was she who lay on top of
him, brushing back the forest of curls on his forehead
while she foraged into the heat of his neck and the
angular plate of his chest with deep, hungry kisses. He
tried to hold up her hair in a cool knot at the nape of

her neck, but his hands were too busy exploring the breadth of her hips and the rise of her buttocks beneath her corduroy slacks, and she shook off his cautious gesture.

Diana had never had a particular affinity with nature, had never felt the lure of the great outdoors. Her sexual experience, in particular, had always been confined to the safe civility of the bedroom. But now, mesmerized by the depth of her own response to the man poised beneath her, she found herself involved in an intricate dance of nature, with the earth, the leaves and the sky all becoming entangled in the same choreographed passion. Beau's eyes were half closed as his mouth traveled along the private path between her breasts and, as she moved upward, across the furrowed span of her hips and loins. His hands were doing practiced maneuvers to bring her thighs between his, and despite all that Diana had taught herself about propriety and control, all that she had experienced in other, paler situations, she never once doubted her ability to perform all the steps or her desire to do the dance with Beau.

Beau was hard beneath her when he raised her up so that he could remove his jeans. It seemed like it would take forever; he kept taking time out to cover her mouth and eyes with hungry, anticipatory kisses. Diana moved her hands down from around his neck to help, but their fingers got tangled in their rush to be free of the constricting cloth.

"Dah-anna," he whispered into her ear, sending a chorus of tingling sensations all down her side. "I can hardly believe what's happening to us today. Say my name and tell me it's really true, hmm?"

She turned her head and whispered, but it came out like a ragged croak. "Beauuu. There. Now can we stop talking and make it come true?"

He chuckled hoarsely into her ear. "I always knew

you were a woman of action beneath that professional veneer. All of a sudden, it doesn't seem important, does it? The horses, the story, the cassette . . ."

Diana froze, her hands still splayed around Beau's slim waist. "What did you say?"

Beau, who had already begun to move on top of her, paused in some surprise. "Come on. I thought you didn't want any more talking."

She moved her hands around to his chest and pushed hard. "I asked you what you said, Beau." She closed her eyes against the sudden nauseous turn in her stomach.

"Dah-anna," he pleaded, but she only tightened her strong fingers against his chest.

"How did you know about the stolen cassette, Beau? I never told you about it."

"No, that's right. You didn't." She could feel the release of pressure as he finally stopped trying to lie back down across her bare breasts. Now he rolled off with a muffled oath. "You didn't tell me anything, did you?"

Diana lay inert under the primrose bush, her eyes staring sightlessly through the lacy greenery. "So you took it upon yourself to find out, right? A few questions asked in the right places—Who told you? Lou? Are they laughing about it down at the Downs?"

"No one's laughing at you, Diana, for God's sake!"

"You don't seem to have any problem getting information, do you? Everybody's anxious to help Beau, the original party boy. You haven't had any trouble keeping an eye on me, have you?" She snapped her head around to face his. "Have you, Beau?"

He closed his eyes and took a deep breath, trying to bring his body and mind under control. "Diana. I've tried to tell you. You don't know how serious this could be. You know what kind of a man he is. Why do you persist in refusing any help?"

She sat up so quickly that dirt sprinkled across Beau's

chest. When she spoke, her voice was as icy as her sea-green eyes. "You're wrong, Beau. You're not trying to help. Spying on me and doing nothing constructive is not trying to help. You're trying to take it out of my hands. Out of some archaic, misguided notion that I can't run my own life, you are trying to do it for me."

"That's not true."

"It's all right for me to take the initiative with sex but not with work, is that it?" She was shivering, and the hand that reached out to pull on her clothing trembled almost uncontrollably. For the first time with Beau, she felt ashamed.

"Diana, stop raving and listen." Beau sat up and faced her, still almost nude but not flinching from her hostile gaze. "I've fallen in love with you. Doesn't that account for anything in your life? Doesn't that entitle me to some proprietary feeling for you? I love you! I want to protect you!"

"No!" A moment before, she had felt only anger. Now Diana felt a rising tide of panic, and it lent a hysterical edge to her voice as she stood up. "I don't want protection. If that's what love means to you, then I don't want that, either! I want to live my own life, you understand? I want to do it by myself!"

She had already started to stumble away when his voice followed sadly after her. "You can't be in love by yourself, Diana. You need me for that, at least."

The tears stung her eyes, but she forced them back before flinging the last words over her shoulder. "All I need from you is a ride home!"

Chapter 10

DIANA DRESSED WITH A VENGEANCE.

The Louisville Press Club was holding what it euphemistically described as a dinner dance (black tie optional). The invitation lay where she had tossed it derisively an hour before. Since most of the locals seemed to find it difficult to knot a tie, she had thought bitterly, it would probably not be a formal event.

But she was determined to go dressed to the teeth. The disastrous events of the afternoon and the knowledge that not only Beau but most likely several of his colleagues knew about the cassette fiasco were all the ammunition she needed to fuel her fierce temper. In the course of arming herself in a navy blue straight skirt and a flaming red silk blouse, Diana snagged a pair of stockings, ripped the back off an earring and snapped her eyebrow pencil clear in half.

"Take care of me . . . protect me . . . that's not love, damn him. That's ownership!" She jabbed the stub of the pencil on her tongue to wet it, scowling at

190

the black mark it left in her mouth. Her fingers were trembling so that it was hard to trace an even line across her lids. It was a good thing Alison wasn't around to witness her preparation for battle—she would have surely locked Diana in her room for her own protection.

Twenty minutes later, she stepped out into the hallway, a smile painted in deep crimson across her mouth. She intended to go down to that dinner and show them all that she was in control of the Derek Islington story. She didn't need the damn cassette, anyway. Beau and his friends might know it had been stolen, but only she knew what was on it. Only *she* had those precious leads to go on. Unless . . .

She stopped still in front of the elevator. Unless Beau *did* know what was on those tapes because he had heard it. Unless it was not Derek but one of Beau's many associates who had taken the tape. Unless Beau had taken it himself!

It seemed perfectly feasible. Diana stood still while the elevator, on its way down to the lobby, stopped and opened in front of her. She didn't seem to notice, not even when two puzzled people inside called out, "Going down?" She was thinking of the questions Beau had asked Arnold before she got there that morning. He had mentioned the doctor and the judge to Arnold. How else could he have known about it unless he heard the tape?

She jammed her finger on the "up" button before she even realized that she had made a conscious decision. Beau would most likely be down at the party—it had started almost an hour before, and he was not one to miss a chance to socialize. She would go up to his room and search it, see if the tape was there. If he wanted to play dirty pool, she thought grimly, so would she.

Diana was well beyond making the usual arguments of caution or conscience as she rode the car up to Beau's floor. It was even useless to remind herself that the tape cassette meant very little to her story anymore, now that she had developed a pretty clear hunch about where more incriminating evidence could be found. Her mind seemed filled by one certainty: Beau had gotten his hands on her cassette, and she was going to get it back.

The hallway was deserted, but Diana instinctively kept her footsteps light and peeked around each corner before traversing the stretch of patterned carpet to Beau's door. While she walked, her hand fumbled in her pocketbook for a credit card. It was already secreted in her palm when she reached his room. She took a moment to listen carefully and look back down the hallway; no one in the room and no one in the hall. Then, with practiced ease, she inserted the stiff plastic card in between the jamb and the bolt.

The door swung open even more easily than she expected it to. Not a Manhattan hotel room, she reflected wryly, stepping quickly inside to the darkened interior. Or a Manhattan occupant. Any native New Yorker would have thrown the double bolt before leaving the room as a matter of course. It gave her some small satisfaction to think that Beau's surprising worldliness didn't carry that far. You can take the boy out of the country, she thought, but you can't—

"Yesss?"

The soft drawl, coming at exactly the same moment as she threw on the light switch, had the effect of an electric shock. Diana nearly jumped out of her skin and swore loudly.

"Is that what you came up here to say?" Beau demanded mildly. "Because if that's all, you could just as easily have used the phone."

"What are you doing here?" Her first response was anger, and she spoke through clenched teeth.

Beau shrugged. "The room's paid for," he said placidly. "Might as well use it, right?" He was lying stretched out on his bed, his fingers locked behind his head. Now, with elaborate casualness, he uncrossed his feet at the ankles and recrossed them the other way. Diana found the gesture infuriating.

"You're supposed to be downstairs," she snapped. He was wearing a tuxedo that fit beautifully, and only his loafers, scuffed and shapeless, belied his dapper image.

"Ah," he said, nodding as if he hadn't known.

Diana had been leaning against the door for support. Now she moved away and began pacing the room, frantically grasping for some way to handle this unexpected development. "I thought you were out," she added accusingly.

"Really?" His brows made perfect half moons above his sparkling dark grin. "Then why the visit? Did you leave your panties here the other night or something?"

If anything throwable had been in range, Diana would have thrown it. As it was, she looked around wildly, her jaw working. Beau, having guessed the extent of her anger, moved hastily to a sitting position, his hands in front of his head.

"I'm sorry. I'm sorry; that was unkind." He peeked out from between his fingers. "Truce?"

"Never." She was still looking for something good and hard.

Beau stood up. "All right. Battle, then. What are you doing trespassing in my room?" He placed his hand meaningfully on the telephone.

"What do *you* think?" she demanded.

"I think you'd better give me an answer, Diana." There was no more humor in his voice, and she knew it.

"It's you who have some answering to do, Beau Gatling." Some of her anger had abated as the extent of her predicament sunk in, but Diana was not about to back down.

Beau pursed his lips consideringly and then nodded. "Fair enough. You came for answers. Well, ask away." His eyes glinted. "Ladies first, after all."

Diana scowled. "How did you find out about the missing cassette?"

"Arnold Sweeney."

"Arnold? He and Alison were at the restaurant last night?" She couldn't believe that she could have missed them or that Alison would not have told her.

"No. But Arnold's brother is a waiter at the Coq D'Or. And he knows enough about his boss's . . . shall we say, proclivities? . . . to keep a sharp eye out whenever he comes in." He smiled thinly. After all, his brother is a jockey. He has a vested interest in keeping the other side informed—and healthy.

"How did he know about it?"

"He saw it. There's a one-way mirror in the room you were in, apparently, and he saw you bend down to switch it on while Islington was in the next room."

Diana groaned. "So how did he know it was taken?"

Beau's face was grim. "Saw that, too. While you were out of the room, Derek motioned to the maître d', who slipped in and liberated the cassette. Apparently, there's more than one one-way mirror in that joint."

Diana recalled the walls lined with lovely antique mirrors and groaned again. So Derek had the cassette, and he knew that she knew he was up to something. The chances of her getting a story had just slipped out of her reach. She felt utterly deflated and slightly dazed.

"But you knew about Dr. Murphy and the judge. How did you know that if you didn't hear the tape?"

He shook his head. "I've known about Dr. Murphy and Judge Taupin for years," he said wearily. "It's just that no one has been able to prove a connection. Murphy is perfectly legal, and Islington had every right to hire him, once the regulations were changed in 1977. What no one can prove is the connection between Islington and Judge Taupin. It's fairly obvious that Taupin was responsible for getting Islington's race-fixing conviction overturned and for passing the new exam regulations, too. But no record exists of Taupin and Islington ever meeting face to face, let alone being in cahoots. No records of cash payments, no laundered deals, nothing. He even wrote his decision to overturn the 1974 conviction while Islington was out of the country." He spread his hands. "The guy looks pure as the driven snow."

"What about Murphy? Couldn't he be the liaison?"

Beau shook his head. "He could be. But he wasn't even on the scene until 1978. And he's never done anything questionable, at least not the way the law reads now."

Diana was distracted; she was thinking so fast that she had to sit down. What they were looking for was actual proof of a connection between the three men. Obviously, Derek had taken pains to ensure that no one could prove a connection between him and the judge. But if there were such a connection—payoff, bribes, anything—it would have to come through a third party. Who else but Dr. Murphy?

"We need proof," she said, almost to herself.

"We've looked for proof before," Beau said. "No dice."

She looked up at him. "When was the last time Derek had a Derby contender?"

"Dark Star was the last one. Why?"

"So he hasn't had that much at stake since then, right?"

"Wrong. He's run the Belmont and the Preakness—those aren't exactly penny ante stakes, you know."

"But this is the first race he's run in Kentucky since then? The first major race, I mean?"

"Diana. What are you getting at?"

Her expression was grave, but Diana's eyes had begun to sparkle. She was beginning to realize that she might have a chance at the story, after all. But she would have to play her cards very carefully. And it was important that Beau know nothing more about what was on her mind. He would never let her get away with such a wild scheme as she was beginning to hatch. Never in a million years.

"Getting at?" She kept her face still. "Nothing, really. I was wondering if they had pulled anything off since Dark Star, but apparently they haven't." Beau was looking at her strangely, so she hurried on. "Listen, Beau, I'm really sorry about barging in here like this. I really don't know what came over me."

"I do. You were livid because I was trying to control your life."

His calm candor made her blink. "Oh, that. Look, I probably overreacted this afternoon, too." She giggled lamely. "I don't know what came over me then, either."

"Maybe too much. Too much for you to handle." He was watching her closely.

Diana bristled. "Perhaps," she said coldly. "Maybe I'm just too cold for your warm southern nature. Maybe you're just too much for me to handle."

"Maybe." He hadn't even blinked.

"Well." Diana got up abruptly. She was getting very uncomfortable, and Beau wasn't doing much to alleviate it. "I had better get out of here before you call hotel security or something." She started for the door. "I'm sorry, Beau, and thanks for letting me know about Taupin and Murphy. Not that it'll do me any good."

She had almost reached the door when he shot past her, flinging out his arm to keep her from opening it.

"Not so fast," he said, and she realized how angry he really was.

"Why? Why not?" She felt her panic beginning to rise. She wanted to get out of there fast, before Beau guessed what she had in mind.

"Because I haven't gotten to ask my questions yet, that's why."

She looked at his hand splayed across the white door.

"I take it this is an invitation to stay?" she inquired dryly.

"I didn't think people who broke into hotel rooms needed an invitation," he retorted.

"I've already answered your question. I came to find the cassette. You don't have it; I'm leaving." She considered dodging past him but saw it was useless.

"Not yet, I said." He took a step closer to her without moving his hand off the door. She could feel his breath on her neck, rippling the thin silk collar.

"Beau, I mean it. Let me out." She put out her hands to push against him but immediately pulled them away. The feel of his torso under the cotton tuxedo shirt was too much to bear.

"Why? You have no problems with barging in here and taking what you came for. Why shouldn't I do the same?"

For a moment, Diana felt a stab of pure fear. What was he talking about? "I . . . I just came for some honest answers," she mumbled halfheartedly.

"You came for honest answers? You want honest answers? Well, so do I." He took another step forward, and this time his hand came off the door, but Diana was so alarmed at the look on his face that she took a step backward. "I want an honest answer from you, Diana Jennings. What's it gonna be?"

He took two more steps; Diana did the same. "I don't know what you're talking about, Beau," she whispered.

"You don't? Oh, but I think you do. I think you're afraid of what I'm talking about, but you know. You want the truth from me? I said it before, but you were afraid to listen. I'm in love with you, Diana Jennings." And he wrapped his arms around her, tipping them both together onto the bed. Their lips met harshly, eagerly, and then there was no sound.

It seemed so simple after that. For a moment, Diana

tried to summon outrage. But all she could feel was
relief—relief that he had not guessed her plan. Then,
when that first recognizable tingle of desire hit, she
realized that she felt relief of another sort altogether.
Beau loved her! By any definition, he loved her. She
settled deeply into his arms. There was no need to
pretend here—she was home.

It wasn't that she had lost sight of her immediate
goals in the face of this sensual assault. Rather, she had
just discovered what her goals really were. Her perspective had never seemed clearer then when she
reached up and with a throaty chuckle, murmured,
"Well, why didn't you say so?" She twined her fingers
around his neck and thrust them up into his hair.
Competition and revenge seemed as foolish and remote
as a balloon race. The real race was taking place inside
her heart.

And in her body. What had begun with such promise
earlier in the day showed every sign of coming to
fruition, but that night there was something else happening as well. Perhaps it was the fact that her adrena-
line had been so well primed. Maybe it was the fact that
Beau's kisses along the underside of her chin and
behind the tight curl of her earlobe were particularly
ferocious. Although the hotel room lacked the natural
spontaneity of the primrose bush, Diana knew that
tonight there would be no interruptions and no holds
barred.

She was right. There was none of their usual banter.
Even when Diana opened her mouth to whisper his
name, Beau covered it with his so completely that she
felt her breath exhaling into his lungs. When she moved
her arms farther down his back, kneading the stirrup of
muscles that banked his spine, he quickly slipped down
lower on the bed so that the serpentine action of his
tongue along her neck and throat left her paralyzed
with delight in midcaress.

This time, there was no ritual to their undressing.

Silk, satin, pressed trousers, fell like leaves of wheat in
a high wind of passion. Diana had grown comfortable
with Beau again, and she could afford to relax, confident that he would take her to places she wanted to be.
She closed her eyes and let her head roll lazily from side
to side, her lips curved in a gentle smile. He removed
the last piece of clothing—the scarlet silk blouse—and
now he was drawing the thin material slowly over her
bare breasts. It was such an exotic sensation—cool and
exciting—that she had to open her eyes and watch.

Beau was staring at her, as if to drink in the
abandoned sensuality of her expression. "That feels
delicious," she murmured.

"Don't talk."

"But I want . . ."

"Don't talk."

Diana gave in and only smiled, watching the grave
furrow between his thick brows. He seemed to be
taking it all very seriously.

"Now close your eyes."

"But . . ."

"Diana. Close them." The look on his face was
intense, and Diana obeyed. For the first time since they
had fallen into their embrace, Diana had the idea that
all was not going to be comfortable. Beau was not going
to be content merely to lead the dance they had danced
before. He apparently had some new steps in mind.

Eyes shut, she waited, her heart beating thickly
against her chest. She heard the liquid rustle of her silk
shirt falling to the floor, and then Beau laid siege to her
breasts again—this time with his tongue. He traced
damp circles skillfully around her nipples and down
into the tender crook of her arm until Diana could
barely stand to lie still on the bed. Just when a thin
bead of sweat appeared on her forehead, Beau bent his
head lower and brushed her aching breasts with the soft
brush of his hair.

The variety of sensations was endless. Beau turned

her over on her stomach and began working on the taut
muscles of her back, taking extra care with the knot of
nerves at the base of her spine. Every once in a while,
he would lean down and breathe softly against the
damp hairs at the nape of her neck, and Diana would
arch upward toward him like a live wire.

In all this time, neither of them spoke a word. Beau
had been right; they had entered a whole new dimen-
sion of feeling, and for once, words were totally out of
order. For someone who had made her living with
words, it was a unique experience for Diana. Not only
was she not speaking, but she wasn't thinking in the
same way as she usually did. When she had been with
Beau before, in this bed and at Bluefield Farms, she
had been aware of her loss of control and of the
magnitude of the physical experience she had shared
with him. But this was different. Diana had no way of
gauging how far she had gone or how close she was
coming to the edge of that chasm. She merely existed,
in every nerve ending and with every inch of her being,
for the pleasure of Beau's touch.

He had slid down to the foot of the bed, turning her
body over once again. Diana watched with heavy-
lidded eyes as he knelt before her, his features thick
with desire. Beginning with the pale crevice of skin
behind her knees, he began working his way up her
legs, kissing, nibbling, caressing and licking first one
thigh, then the other. Diana grabbed the material of
the bedspread and twisted it between her fists. Of its
own volition, her body seemed to arch and snake
toward that encroaching ecstasy. She ached to get her
hands on Beau's body but at the same time was
unwilling to abandon his concentration on hers.

Finally, as he reached the gentle, olive-skinned pasture at the top of her legs, he repositioned his body on
the bed. Diana understood that the time had finally
come for her to pay tribute to Beau's desire. Eagerly,
but without losing contact with his body, she rolled

over so that Beau lay beneath her. Then, propping herself up on her elbows, she raised her torso until their bodies met only at the waist and below. Beau arched forward to catch her breasts in his lips, but she nuzzled him away and bent to her own work.

She covered the top half of his body with kisses, taking exquisite care to leave no patch of skin unloved. Her mouth roved hungrily across the soft hair on his broad chest and down to the ridged marble of his ribs and waist, traveling back up the inside of his arms. All the while, her loins were caressing his in gentle arcs of motion; then she felt him harden and quicken beneath her, and their rhythm accelerated like a ship hitting a sudden current.

Beau was careful not to groan out loud, but she could see his lips compressed against the growing need to cry out. The silence in the room was becoming unbearable, and Diana felt her own breath pounding through her like an unleashed flame. When he could no longer bear to have her body detached from his, Beau heaved her tightly against him, and she buried her face in his steamy dark curls, her hands clinging to his shoulders as if he were a life preserver.

Beau rolled over once again. Although her eyes were tightly shut against the strain, Diana knew they had truly hit uncharted seas and that now was the time they must work together. She parted her thighs and guided him within. Rather than rising up above her, Beau molded his body to hers, and together they swung around so that they lay face to face on their sides. Still touching at every possible point of reference, they began to climb together with infinite patience, neither of them missing the chance to let the other savor a particularly dazzling instant of sensation. Locked inside her tight capsule of pleasure, Diana had never been aware of another body as she was of Beau's, lying beside her and yet enveloping her completely so that she had no need, no desire, to orient herself in the dim room. The walls of her universe were Beau, and as they led each other slowly toward the outer limits of that sea of passion, Diana felt limitless power and boundless love. This was not the loss of control that she had always feared love would be; this was a perfect sharing, a spinning wheel of give-and-take unlike any experience she had ever known.

Their climax, when it came, was one single, stormy explosion. Locked tight against Beau's chest, Diana felt, rather than heard, him cry out, for the sound was indecipherable from her own. There was a moment in which she felt that the bed, the room, the world had slipped away and that the starry darkness she saw behind her eyes was, in fact, the only reality. Then those stars were set in motion and began spiraling upward and outward, falling finally in a shower of light like slow-motion fireworks.

They lay together in that shower of stars, feeling the aftershocks of heat touching their skin with random brilliance. Gradually, the heat and light faded to a warmer, steady glow. When Diana's senses settled so that she once again felt the bed beneath her and Beau's body was separate from hers, only then did she dare to open her eyes.

Beau opened his at exactly the same moment. For a while, they just lay there, blinking in the harsh light of the bedside lamp. Then a smile crept upward onto their lips, a smile that erupted into a tender chuckle when they could find their voices at last. They lay there, laughing quietly, knowing that no words, no spoken endearments, could follow where they had just been together.

It took a long time for the mood to leave them, but Diana understood that nothing could happen until it did. For the first time in her life, she had no desire to analyze her feelings. It was enough to remain perfectly still on the bed until they could talk on a more mundane level. Everything that could possibly be said about their feelings for each other had, she thought, already been said.

Beau recovered first, clearing his throat and starting over several times before he could get his mouth to form the word. "Diana," he said carefully, stroking her hand, which lay across his waist. "Can you do me a favor?"

"What?" she whispered. She hoped it would be something very undemanding—anything to allow time for that incredible experience to sink into her soul.

"Can you reach over to that table and get me the glass of water sitting there?"

Diana hooted with laughter and relief. That was mundane, all right, and she was only too glad to comply. They sat cross-legged on the bed, sharing the tepid water between them.

"I've never tasted anything so good in my life," Beau vowed.

"It's perfect water," she agreed solemnly.

"Like nectar."

"Ambrosia."

"I'm in love with you."

Diana paused with the glass halfway to her lips. She still wasn't ready to deal with this.

Beau apparently was. "I meant it when I said it before," he said in a low voice. "I mean it still."

She took a big swallow and tried to laugh. "You mean what just happened didn't change your mind?"

Beau winced. "Don't. Don't be clever. What just happened between us doesn't deserve that treatment."

"You're right." She bit her lip.

"I don't need to hear a response," he went on. "I just think it's only fair to warn you."

"Now who's being clever?" she asked.

"No, I mean it. You obviously don't know what I mean when I say I love you, or you don't take it

seriously, or . . . or I don't know what. But I think it's
time I stated my case. No more misunderstandings for
this old boy."

Diana shimmied up to the head of the bed and
snuggled against the pillows, shivering a little now that
her body had begun to cool. Beau saw it and immediately jumped up and pulled down the bedspread,
covering her carefully up to her chin. Then he sat on
the edge of the bed, one hand resting meditatively
between her breasts, as if that was where it belonged.

"Thank you," she said demurely.

He raised one finger and tapped her breastbone
lightly. "See? That's what I mean. I do something for
you, and immediately you make fun of it."

"I wasn't making fun—" she began, but he cut her
off.

"You know what I mean. It's happened before, when
I hold the door or help you into the car or cover you up
in bed . . ." His eyes traveled down the length of her
body under the covers, and Diana shivered automatically. "Even when we make love," he added in a softer
voice. "You can't seem to accept what it means to me to
love you and to take care of you."

"They're not interchangeable terms, Beau," she
pointed out.

"That's exactly it. They are! To me, they are!" He
stood up, agitated, and began pulling on his pants.
Then, as if that act afforded him some protection
against Diana's arguments, he sat down again on the
bed. "They are to me," he said more calmly, "and
that's my point. The things I do for you I do because I
love you."

"Like keeping tabs on me—and on my cassette?"

"I didn't ask. I was told." Beau's eyes narrowed, and
for the first time, Diana felt uneasy, lying there smug
and certain in his bed. She had been so ready to
disregard what he was saying about love and protection, so eager to ignore its implications, that it hadn't

really occurred to her how deeply he believed it to be true. Somehow, the knowledge of his sincerity made her feel sad. After the union they had just shared, it represented a fairly wide gap between them. And, by bringing up the tape, she had just widened the gap considerably.

"You were told because your friends knew you were out to take care of me."

"My friends know how far I'll go for them. It stands to reason they know what I would do for you."

"Would you do the same thing for them that you're doing for me, Beau?"

He seemed to be getting more and more morose as the conversation went on. "It's not the same with you—you know that."

Diana leaned back heavily against the pillows. "But don't you understand? That's just it. I *want* it to be the same!"

"What you want has nothing to do with it," he snapped, and Diana felt a curious, queasy drop in the pit of her stomach at those words. They were slipping away from each other, and neither one of them could stop it.

"You promised not to get involved, Beau," she said with a heavy sigh.

"That was before I *got* involved—with you. I have a commitment to you, Diana, and that's what I have to honor. Not some vague promise to ensure your fight for equality. The reality is the way I feel for you. Protecting the woman I love is more important than protecting her professional integrity."

Had Diana been less relaxed, less enveloped in the afterglow of physical satiety, those would have been fighting words. That Beau was so serious and so dead wrong would have brought out her most scathing, argumentative instincts. But she was still wrapped in that cocoon of pleasure. And she had begun to understand that Beau—however wrong—was sincere in the way he felt about her. Her own feelings about him had also mellowed her point of view, though not to the point that he would have considered to be reasonable.

"I find that idea a little hard to swallow, Beau," she said. She smiled wanly and rolled her eyes, trying to make light of her opinion.

But Beau only muttered gloomily. "Try a little harder, then." If Diana was emotionally lethargic as a result of their tumultuous lovemaking, Beau seemed to be feeling everything all the more acutely. Instead of caressing her, he was rubbing the palms of his hands abstractedly along his thighs. Diana watched, unable to keep a smile off her face despite her uneasiness.

"I'd be glad to try again," she murmured, putting her hand over his on the inside of his thigh.

"You're missing the point. We can make love from now until doomsday and it would always make everything else between us seem all right. But you still don't understand that part of loving you is taking care of you—not just in bed but everywhere."

She was beginning to be angry again. "Come off it, Beau. You can't sit there and tell me that loving me gives you the automatic right to assume control of my life!"

"I can, and I am."

"But that's not fair!"

"I didn't say it was fair, Diana. I said it was love."

"That's right, Beau. *You* said it was love. That's not what I call it." Diana glared at him and pulled her hand away from where it lay unregarded on his leg. Beau acknowledged the angry gesture with a little sigh.

"Tell me something, Diana," he said in a more reasonable tone. "If it was reversed, if you loved me—no, no, don't say *anything,* just listen—if you loved me, would you want to protect me, to take care of me and assume my burdens?" His eyes lit up with the challenge. "You're big on equality—would you feel the same way about me?"

Diana was nonplused. The question raised so many issues that she could not begin to answer. Most of all, she didn't trust herself on the subject of love. Beau knew it and drove straight to the heart of the issue. "That's *if* you loved me. A hypothetical situation, perhaps."

Now it was Diana who longed for the protective anonymity of her clothing. How could she face Beau, face her real feelings about him, lying naked and exposed as she was? Beau's dark eyes were steady and open, and she knew that he wanted to hear only one thing.

But she could not bring herself to admit it. Too much lay between them, unresolved and potentially damaging to the independence she had worked so hard and long for. Now, with all those unanswered questions before them, she couldn't bring herself to tread the most dangerous ground of all, to admit the depth of her commitment to him.

"No, Beau," she said in sad, measured phrases, aware of her own self-betrayal. She was unable to meet his eyes as she spoke. "I don't think I would. I think I would respect your need to live your own life, to make your own decisions, no matter what mistakes those decisions involved. I think that's what I want for you—and I want the same thing in return."

The use of the present tense was telling—Diana hadn't meant for it to come out in quite that way. But having made the slip, she was glad of it. Without the uncertainty of those last few words, the speech would have sounded impossibly pompous and false. Even as she said it, Diana wondered if perhaps it was.

Beau stood up slowly. His face and body were very still, and as he turned to look back down at her, Diana got the impression of carefully controlled rage. "You really believe that," he said in a low voice. "You truly do." He shook his head in a minute gesture of disbelief.

Diana had the urge to pull the covers protectively

over herself to escape his probing stare, but she didn't move. "I really believe it. And I think you do, too, Beau. There's no double standard anymore. Don't you see? If you can go out and hustle a story, place yourself in danger, why shouldn't I let you? And why can't I do the same thing?"

"Because that's not love!"

The rage finally exploded, and this time Diana flinched at the force of his words. He was no longer still, but trembling; shivering, really, although he had managed to reach down and sweep up his shirt and shoes in one fierce motion.

"That's not love, and you know it! Don't lie there with your damned condescending attitude and preach to me about how you would love me. You don't know the first thing about love, and you don't know the first thing about yourself if you believe that crap! You know what your trouble is, Ms. Jennings? You're so busy trying to even up the odds that you can't even tell when the race is over! It's over; don't you know that? Don't you *want* to give your heart away to the winner?"

He was pulling on his shirt as he shouted, but Diana was too shocked to notice anything but his eyes, which burned into hers like vengeful coals. Now she was trembling, too, and a nameless fear had gripped her heart with icy hands.

When he spoke again, Beau was less violent, but the sadness in his voice was equally wrenching. "No," he said, "I don't believe you really do. I think you're so wrapped up in keeping control over those so-called feminine weaknesses that you don't even have time to examine your strengths. It's not your gender that stands in your way, honey; it's your damned hardheaded inability to care about anything but your story—your damned story, and yourself!"

Without bothering to put on his shoes, Beau swung around and slammed out of the room.

Diana watched him go. When the reverberations of

the door crashing behind him had finally died into silence, she lifted one hand and smiled weakly.

"But Beau," she called out softly, "you can't run out like that. This is your room!"

She was actually able to laugh ruefully at her own humor for an instant. Then she collapsed into tears.

Chapter 11

"THESE MORNING CONFESSIONS ARE KILLING ME!"

Diana rolled over in her bed and reached for another tissue. Alison, her legs crossed in an attitude of attentive sympathy, held out the entire box.

"I hadn't realized you'd been making such a habit of it," she observed, watching another sodden white ball hit the wastebasket by Diana's bed. The basket was filling up fast, but Diana's red-rimmed eyes gave no indication that the waterworks were abating.

"That's just it," she said, pouting. "It's no use confessing to yourself. You never get anywhere that way. I should have called in a consultant sooner." A ragged hiccup escaped.

"Well, don't look at me, my child," Alison warned. "I'll listen, but you won't get any advice from this counselor."

"Advice—hah! That's the last thing I need," muttered Diana. "I got all the advice I'll ever want last night." Her swollen lip vibrated, and another series of sobs broke out.

"Oh, honey!" Alison scooted off her bed and knelt by Diana's. "It's okay."

"No, it's not!"

"Okay, it's not." Alison knew better than to argue.

"It's not, because Beau was right! Completely and utterly right!" Diana scrunched up into a miserable ball, unable to accept the comfort of Alison's maternal caress.

"Hmmm," Alison murmured, half to herself. "Since when is *that* such a tragedy?"

Diana peeped out from beneath her hands. "What?"

"I said, since when was it such a tragedy for someone other than you to be right?" Her face was solemn, but there was a quiet twinkle in her eyes.

Diana ignored it and scowled through her tears. "Oh, I know what you're thinking," she accused. "You think I'm upset because he's right and I'm not! You think it's only my pride that's hurt. You believe all those ugly rumors about me back at the *Chronicle!*"

Alison cocked her head. "That's funny. I could have sworn it was *you* who believed them, not me. Well, then, why don't you clue me in on the real tragedy?"

Diana stared at her for a few seconds before crumpling into another fit of tears. "I'm upset because I love him!" she wailed.

"Ahhhh! Hallelujah! Praise the day and pass the Kleenex!" Alison jumped to her feet and began parading around Diana's bed.

"Are you nuts?" Diana demanded, tears abruptly stanched by this amazing sight.

"No, darling, you are!" Alison faced the red eyes and baggy pajamas with her hands on her hips. "Since when, I repeat, is that such a tragedy?"

Diana seemed to consider this for the first time. She hiccupped thoughtfully several times before speaking.

"But . . . but what good does it do me? My definition
of the word and his are worlds apart! Besides, I've
already ruined everything by making him think that I
don't love him. And anyway," she continued ruefully,
"what good would it do even if he did know? It would
never, never work out. He's got these ridiculous no-
tions about locking me up in the bedroom and never
letting me do anything on my own!"

Alison came over to the side of the bed and leaned
her face close to Diana's. "Honey, when you stumbled
into this room last night, all hysterical and everything,
it was quite clear to me that no one had ever made love
to you like that before in your life." She stood up.
"Anyway, what's so bad about the bedroom? There
are some cases in which I wouldn't mind in the
least!"

Diana stared at her and shook her head. "You're
unbelievable, you know that?"

Alison's eyes shone. "That's what Arnold says. You
think I can have him talk to Beau on the subject of
bedrooms?"

Diana knew when she was licked. She blew her nose
hard and swung her legs over the side of the bed. "I
give up," she declared to her rumpled reflection in the
mirror. "I try and get some female support, and this
wild woman tells me to crawl back between the sheets."
She clicked her tongue against her teeth. "Shameless
hussy."

"Who, me?" Alison feigned innocence.

"Yes, you." Diana turned on her and grinned severely. "Just because you got me out of that bed—for
which, I admit, you deserve a Pulitzer—doesn't mean
you're gonna get me back into *his* bed so easily."

"Oh, yeah? Then where are you planning to go all
dressed up like that at seven-thirty on a Friday morning?"

Diana drew herself up to her full height, sniffling

only slightly, and clutched her flannel pajamas around her like an ermine stole. "I," she announced haughtily, "am going to finish what I started."

"You *are* going back to his bed!"

"Not that, silly. I'm going to finish up the story on Derek Islington." She stalked regally to the closet and flung the door open.

"Oh, really? And how do you intend to do that, Sherlock?"

"Quite simple. I now have a pretty clear idea of what I need to prove a connection between Islington, Murphy and Judge Taupin. I think I know what I'm looking for, and I *think* I know where to look for it." She turned and met Alison's incredulous stare with a shrug. "I also intend to get that cassette back, but that's purely a personal matter."

Alison gasped. "You know, you really are crazy! What about Beau?"

"I haven't forgotten," Diana said over her shoulder. "He's involved in this, too."

Alison appeared to be praying for divine guidance. "I wasn't thinking about the story, Diana. I was thinking about you and Beau. Don't you have a little unfinished business to discuss with him?"

"That will have to wait. I can't deal with that until I deal with this."

"Can't or won't?" Alison inquired sharply. "For God's sake, Diana, you waited so long for this! What are you waiting for?"

Diana flashed her a warning look, then made a funny face to dispel the tense mood. "First things first, dear," she said. "A girl's got to protect her future. Know what I mean?" She dove into the closet and emerged holding a pale pink sheath of Alison's. "What do you think the chances are of my squeezing into this little number," she inquired.

Alison threw up her hands in defeat. "About as good

as the chances of your ever unscrambling your priorities," she muttered.

The dress did fit, actually, although Diana would never have managed to pour herself into it without Alison's expert assistance. Alison, recovering quickly from what she termed her friend's "tragic resistance to her own hormones," was not one to hold a grudge. Once it appeared that she could not dissuade Diana from her madness, she went all out to help her achieve the desired effect.

The desired effect was a knockout. Thanks to the wonders of fashion technology, Diana was encased smoothly in a pair of support pantyhose that, in turn, enabled the dress to flow over her angular hips like ice water. The waist was a little short, but Alison rectified that with a wide cummerbund of gray-green lizard, which she swore brought out the unusually reptilian cast to Diana's eyes that morning.

"Like a viper" was what she said, and Diana was satisfied. Her hair, swept up in a simple knot at the top of her long neck, provided a sharp contrast to the plunging vee of the bodice, which exposed just enough skin to be shocking but not enough to be illegal.

"Actually, it might be illegal, anyway," Alison pointed out. "Especially at this hour of the morning. This isn't Manhattan, Diana."

Diana looked up from strapping her bone sandals with the three-inch heels. "Are you kidding? I wouldn't be caught dead in this getup in the city!"

"Thanks."

Diana started to apologize for the implied insult to Alison's taste, but Alison stopped her. "Never mind. On me it looks great. On you it looks dangerous. Who's your prey, anyway?"

Diana arched her brows coolly. "Never reveal a source," she said, and opened the door to leave.

"But how will I know where to look for the bodies of your victims," Alison called after her.

"That's the whole idea!" She shut the door.

Her trail, Diana thought a short while later, would have been easy enough to follow. The sleepy bellboy in the hotel lobby had practically walked into a post when he saw her, and the clerk at the car rental agency had refused to let her take the economy model, insisting that she take a sporty coupe, as his guest.

Smiling as she drove the car out of the city, Diana caught sight of her reflection in the rear-view mirror. Neither the bellboy nor the rental clerk had noticed the lines of tension around her eyes, and neither of them could have known the effort it had taken for her not to run straight to Beau Gatling's room and throw herself into his protective embrace.

That was assuming he had returned to his room. The night before, Diana, lying there in his bed and blubbering like a baby, had felt foolish. She made several desperate attempts to control her tears as she waited for him to come back. But when, after an hour, there was no indication that he would return and no appearance from the hotel security staff to usher her out of his room, she had slipped out of his room and down to her own. She both dreaded running into him in the hall and passionately desired to find him waiting for her in her room.

Neither had happened. Alison had been there instead, and Diana had collapsed into an endless stream of tears and incomprehensible complaints. She had fallen asleep that way, washed out by her own emotions, and then, as soon as she woke up, the tears began again.

Thank God for Alison, Diana thought now. She would probably still be lying there, drowning in salt-water pity, if Alison hadn't kidded and cajoled her into action. And if her actions didn't quite meet Alison's expectations—well, Diana was not the type to change her stripes overnight. Alison had made some good points. So, for that matter, had Beau; damn him! But a job was a job. There was still a story to be written, and Diana Jennings was going to write it.

Fleur D'Isle was magically silent in the early-morning sunlight. Diana was sure that some of the stable hands were up with the horses, but she saw no signs of life around the main house and the small outbuilding in front of it. She parked her car a safe distance from the pillared entrance to the private drive that led up to the brick courtyard and walked slowly toward the house, keeping close to the tree-lined verge. She had taken the precaution of removing the distributor cap from the car and hiding it behind a nearby tree. If anyone found her, she would have an irrefutable, albeit tired, excuse for being there on foot.

But no one was around to find her. Except for the harmonics of a family of whippoorwills overhead, Diana heard nothing but the beating of her own heart. And that, she thought, was loud enough to wake the dead in the immediate vicinity. Was she scared? she asked herself curiously. She was petrified. Only the image of Beau Gatling, who would probably do this kind of thing without giving it a second thought, kept her feet moving in the right direction. *If he can do it, so can I,* she kept reminding herself.

Diana went immediately to the small square outbuilding to the side of the courtyard. It had taken her a while to recall the nature of the odd expression she remembered crossing Derek's face when she asked him what it was. Only when she realized that there had to be some physical evidence of illegal race fixing *some-where* did the memory surface. The trophy room, he had called it, and she was sure that if there had been nothing but trophies in it, he wouldn't have hesitated to show them off to her. She wasn't sure what she was looking for in the way of good, hard evidence, but she was certain it would be in that windowless cell of a room.

The problem was how to get in. The door was secured with a heavy bolt and padlock, and Diana's credit-card trick was of no use at all. The four walls of whitewashed cement were sheer and impenetrable. Diana began to wonder if she had made the right decision in coming out to the farm with so little planning. Diana's Folly, indeed, she thought with a grim little chuckle.

Well, she might as well try the house. It was highly unlikely, but perhaps there would be a key hanging around somewhere within easy reach clearly marked "Trophy Room." Failing that, she could always have a look around for her cassette. Cursing her bull headed decision to wear high heels and a tight dress, Diana approached the brick portico. Her costume had other emergency purposes, but comfortable snooping wasn't one of them.

The French shades on the first floor were all pulled down and the windows shut. But tiptoeing around the back of the house, Diana saw the double doors of the parlor, where she had first sat with Derek. Looking over her shoulder, she saw the same postcard vista of rolling hills and gracefully sloping trees. It seemed even more unreal in the pale wash of early-morning mist. Diana shivered involuntarily as she approached the veranda. She tried the double door in the middle of the room. It was shut but not locked. It seemed to take hours to twist the brass handle downward until the bolt was thrown. Then, holding her breath at her own audacity, Diana entered the room.

The first thing she noticed was the smell; a combination of rich wood, cigars and a lemony air freshener. People had been in the parlor the previous night—men had been there. There was, of course, no reason why Derek should not entertain in his own parlor, but in her

heightened state of expectation, Diana thought she
sensed the residue of another odor—the odor of male
excitement and the pungent tang of dangerous secrets.
It was useless to try and describe it logically, but Diana
was sure she was right, and whatever doubts she had
had about Derek's complicity ended at that moment.

"Take that, 007," she whispered jauntily, and the
sound of her own voice gave her comfort. Beau would
have liked that touch—her being sure on account of a
smell. As a matter of fact, Beau would have probably
enjoyed this entire escapade. And Diana could not
deny that she would have enjoyed having him along
with her, if only for the sheer camaraderie of it. And
yes, she had to admit, she would have felt a lot safer
having someone else with her on general principles as
well.

Other than the smell, the room was pretty much as
she remembered it. Treading as if on glass, Diana made
her way cautiously around the edge of the huge Persian
carpet, running her eyes along the bookshelves that
lined the walls between the French doors. Everything
was still and clean, like a movie set. Diana wondered if
any of those books had ever been read. Some of them
were collectors'. editions, she knew. But there was
culture, and then there was *culture*. A man who
collected rare classics and then did not read them was
not civilized.

In the far corner of the room, situated at an angle
facing outward, was a narrow French provincial desk.
The slender, fluted legs seemed too frail to support the
elaborately carved top. Diana ran her finger idly across
the elegant fruit-and-vine pattern beveled into the
edge.

And there it was.

A key; a long, old-fashioned skeleton key. It did not
have "Trophy Room" written on it, but it didn't need
it. Diana looked at it stupidly for a moment, wondering
whether her imagination had managed to produce the

exact object she had been thinking of. Then she
swallowed hard and reached out her hand quickly to
cover it, half expecting it to evaporate beneath her
fingers.

It was quite real, though, cold and heavy in her hand.
It lay in the middle of the desk, which had nothing else
on it, almost as if it had been placed there. Perhaps
Derek had intended to put it away and had forgotten.
Perhaps he had planned to use it that day and had left it
out to remind himself.

Whatever the explanation, Diana was not about to
wait around and find out. Her palms had begun to
tickle, a sure sign of an imminent attack of nerves.
Diana wanted to be out of that house and in the
comparative safety of the trophy room before it struck.

She slipped the key into her cummerbund and headed back to the French doors. But just as her fingers fell
on the handle, she saw something outside that turned
her knees to water.

Around to the left of the house, half hidden by a
well-tended privet hedge, a man was crouching. He
appeared to be headed out toward the expanse of land
at the rear of the house, but his head was twisted back
over his shoulder toward the brick driveway. He was
making his way along the hedge toward the open spaces
between the house and the pasture land, creeping with
astonishing speed, considering that he didn't look
where he was headed. His powerful legs, in navy sweat
pants and white sneakers, moved with confidence and
even grace, obviously not burdened in the least by the
extra weight of a Sony tape recorder that was protrud-
ing from under the crook of one arm. And even from
the distance at which she stood, Diana could see the
sparkle of pure excitement lighting up Beau Gatling's
eyes.

"Why, he's even gone and stolen Derek's Sony!" she
exclaimed, shocked out of her caution. She was torn
between a surge of rage at his disregard for her

concerns and an irrepressible desire to giggle at the sight he made. There he was, doing exactly what she had asked him not to do, after all the arguments they had had on the subject! He was clearly the most arrogant, pigheaded man she had ever come across.

But he looked so damn funny, skittering along under the hedge so skillfully, his curls bobbing and his face so obviously full of absorption in his game. Because it was a game for Beau—he was Robin Hood, and Derek was the wealthy landowner, and the whole affair was just a great deal of fun to him.

Either he was supremely confident, or he was a fool. Diana watched, wondering which of her reactions was the proper one to have under the circumstances and which was merely triggered by the insane rush of desire she had for the man at that moment.

But it was not a game for her. And, in another moment, she realized that it didn't matter either way. Even before she heard the parlor door being opened behind her, Diana knew she had been caught.

From the silent ease with which Derek slipped into the long room, she knew her presence was not a surprise. But as she stood immobile with her back to him, her mind was not on her own problems. She was wondering whether Derek knew of the other intruder as well. And if he didn't, whether she was going to tell him.

She liked to tell herself, when reflecting back on that morning days later, that she actually did consider spilling the beans about Beau. No matter what had transpired since then, Diana still liked to think of herself as a self-contained woman, one who considered reality in its proper perspective—saving her own skin. But even in her most coldly rational moments, she knew that there was never much of a contest between telling Derek of Beau's presence or remaining silent and buying those moments for Beau.

"Good morning, Diana."

"Good morning to you, Derek." She replied without turning her head to show that she, too, could remain cool under pressure. Only when it was perfectly clear that his entrance had not taken her by surprise any more than hers did him did she turn with a pleasant smile to face him. Despite an urgent desire to draw his attention away from the double doors, Diana was careful not to move too quickly. "I was just looking for you," she added.

"Ah, were you?" His brows were carved, it seemed, in a permanent arch of irony.

"Well, the doors were opened, you know." She smiled sweetly. "So I thought . . ."

In the split second it took for Diana to turn back to the doors and gesture toward the handle, she realized two things. One was that Beau was not yet safely out of sight. If Derek had approached her at that moment, he would have been able to see exactly what Diana saw.

And the second thing she realized was that Beau had seen her.

He had frozen, clearly outlined against a slight gap in the hedge, his mouth opened in a narrow "o" of disbelief. For that suspended instant, their eyes met across the dewy green expanse of lawn, and she could read the shock there as clearly as if he had been only inches away. Diana wondered what Beau was seeing in her eyes; she was concentrating so hard on concealing her panic from Derek that she had no idea what, if anything, she was communicating to Beau. She saw his thick brows knot together, and then his mouth clamped shut so firmly that Diana was sure she should have heard the sound. In another moment, he was gone.

"I do think it's rather foolish to leave doors unlocked around here, don't you?"

The entire episode with Beau had not taken much more than a second, yet as Diana resumed speaking, she was aware of Derek's eyes narrowing against her as she crossed the room toward him. Behind her, as she retreated from it, the glazed windows of the French doors seemed to throb with the evidence, but Diana forced herself to move with steady allure. *Time,* her muffled footsteps seemed to warn her; *buy time for Beau to get away.*

Derek leaned against the doorway and watched her, his arms crossed over a smoky gray cashmere vest. Diana caught his sardonic look and held it with a clear green gaze until she saw an unwilling admiration creep into his eyes.

"We usually don't have to worry about criminal activity around the farm," he observed.

Diana stopped less than two feet away from him, well aware that he was having difficulty in keeping his eyes off her tawny cleavage. The dress was paying off, after all. "I don't imagine you have to worry about that," she agreed dryly. She was recovering her poise.

Derek recrossed his arms, and the eyebrows shot even higher. "Of course, there's always a first time, isn't there, Diana?"

She considered prolonging their verbal battle but decided on a new tack. After all, she had her own escape to think of, didn't she? Widening her eyes, she placed her palm squarely across her breasts. "But you don't think *I* was doing anything out of the—why, Derek, that's ridiculous!" If the surprised look came across as false, surely he could not fault the deep-throated chuckle that followed it.

He sighed and shifted against the door frame. "Naturally not," he murmured. "I'm sure you have a perfectly sound explanation for your presence, enticing as it is." Now his eyes rested on her pink dress with a touch of insolence.

Diana nodded demurely. "Naturally."

Derek's lips turned slightly upward in what was

either a smile or a sneer. "I'm all ears, darling," he drawled.

"Well, I was returning home from a rather late visit—an unexpected overnight stay if you must know—and the damned car just died on me, right there in front of your place. Lucky, wouldn't you say?" She finished off with a challenging smile.

He met the smile and the challenge with one of his own. "I'm not sure it was quite that lucky," he said, straightening up and taking one step closer to her, "but you do make quite a vision on a Sunday morning."

"Thank you, Derek! Now, I'm sure you wouldn't mind if I borrowed your phone," Diana went on, realizing that her throat was beginning to constrict. "I was hoping I wouldn't have to wake you, but now I'll just call a garage and be on my merry way."

"Oh, we get up quite early here on the farm," he said, not even bothering to look at her face while his eyes grazed her bare arms. "There's always so much to do, you know, especially with Derby only one day away."

"I can just imagine," she said precisely, and his eyes shot up to meet hers. She met them without blinking, but she was thinking of Beau. Unless he was clumsier than she thought, he was safely out of danger by now, and Derek's Sony with him. And she was thinking that if Beau excelled in the breaking-and-entering competition, she was surely the winner at verbal jousting. She was beginning to understand the look she had seen on his face when she first caught sight of him—there was danger mingled with a certain thrill, and yes, even pleasure. At that precise moment, Diana would have been lying if she had not admitted that she was enjoying herself.

"I'll bet you can imagine," Derek was saying, and all of a sudden she was no longer having anything resembling a good time. Derek's arm shot out and encircled hers. "All right, Diana, where are they? I left two things conveniently on my desk for you to find, and now they're both gone. I'd like them back."

Her mouth had gone instantly dry at the moment she felt the contact of his fingers. "I . . . I don't know what you're talking about." she stammered.

He uttered an ugly laugh. "For a lady who has so many answers, that's a pretty lame reply, don't you agree?" His other hand moved to rest briefly, intimately across her hips. "I can't say I wouldn't like to search you," he murmured, "but I don't imagine you would enjoy it. Where's the cassette?"

"The cassette?" In spite of her fear, which was now quite real, Diana had to laugh. "You think I have the cassette hidden on me? For God's sake, where?"

They both looked down at the sheer, taut, pink material stretched over her torso. Derek gave a rueful chuckle. "It is rather impossible, isn't it?" But he snatched her small shoulder purse and rifled through it with one hand, flinging it away when he found nothing. "However," he went on, slate eyes glittering, "I'm not averse to giving it the old college try."

Diana repressed the urge to scream for Beau as Derek's hands began to fumble with her clothing. She began to struggle, but just as she was about to pull away, he produced the key she had hidden in her cummerbund.

"Well, well, what have we here?" He lifted it out and turned it slowly around before her face. "I must say, Diana, if you knew enough to take this key, then you're even more clever than I had given you credit for."

Diana said nothing. *So I was right,* she was thinking. *It is the key to the trophy room. And there are some trophies in there Derek wants kept out of sight.* Fat lot of good it did her now to be right.

"As far as the cassette goes, I'm sure it will turn up somewhere," Derek said calmly. "Anyone who's clever enough to hide a distributor cap is clever enough to hide a cassette as well. I'm sure it can't have gotten far, can it?"

Diana's heart sunk at the mention of the distributor cap. If he knew about that, then he was clever, too. But at least he was wrong about the cassette. Not that it made her predicament any easier to bear, but it was some small comfort to know that at that very moment, Beau might be listening to the tape and putting two and two together just as she had. "You're quite right," she said firmly to Derek, and shook a little to get out of his grasp.

"Oh, not so fast, my dear," he said, tightening his hold. "I think we have a little more visiting to do first, don't we?"

"Oh, really? What for, Derek? Planning to call the police?" She spoke out of sheer bravado.

His gray eyes were hard, although he smiled. "Oh, no, I don't think so. I don't like the idea of accusing my dear friends of breaking and entering. Do you know what I mean? Besides, I really don't want them here right now."

"I can imagine not."

"No, I thought that we might pay a visit to my trophy room." He held up the key and dangled it close to her face. "After all, that is what you wanted to see, isn't it?"

Diana swallowed hard. "I changed my mind," she croaked.

"A gentlewoman never goes back on her word," Derek reminded her gently, leading her out of the room. "Besides, I'm sure you'll be interested in what my little trophy display has to offer."

"I'm sure the district attorney's office would be interested too, wouldn't they, Derek?"

"Perhaps. But they are not going to get the rare opportunity to examine my prizes that you are, my dear. As a matter of fact, you are going to be able to go through my hall of fame with a fine-toothed comb."

Diana allowed herself one last, longing glance out the French doors before Derek maneuvered her out of sight. "Fine-toothed comb?" she repeated politely. *Pay attention,* she told herself. *This could be important.*

"As a matter of fact, I'm afraid your research is going to last so long that you will have to miss the Derby tomorrow." He clicked his teeth and shook his head. "What a pity. You won't get to see Diana's Folly."

Diana stopped short and yanked her arm back. "What are you talking about?"

He took the arm back and tucked it tenderly inside his elbow, but Diana could feel the increased pressure to hold it there. "It's simple. You see, even if I *have* done something wrong, you and I both know you can't possibly prove it without hard evidence." He flashed her a tight smile. "On the other hand, we can't have you running around asking foolish questions and making a lot of trouble for us on the day before the Derby, now, can we?"

"Why not, Derek? If you're so innocent, what harm could it do?"

They had come through the entryway and stepped out onto the bright sunshine of the front portico. Diana looked around wildly.

"Come on, Diana. Let's cut the ping-pong game. I'm not about to let you leave here until the Derby is safely ensconced in the annals of sports history—without the benefit of your reporting, I'm afraid."

She smiled bitterly. "Then I'll just assume Street Fare is going to be the winner. Good guess?"

He ducked his head modestly. "An excellent guess. Why else would I bother to run the race?"

They were crossing the courtyard to the small white building. "And what happens to me after the race?" she inquired. "You know, reporters don't just disappear into thin air back where I come from." Thank God Beau had seen her, she was thinking. But just at that

moment, Diana understood the meaning of the
shocked expression she had seen on Beau's face *after* he
saw her. He thought she was there *with* Derek. He had
no idea of her danger. After the fight they had had the
night before, he would just assume that she had gone
there of her own accord—which she had—and that
Derek expected her—which he most certainly had not.
Beau must have thought *he* had been betrayed!

The knowledge struck her with such force that she
could barely hear Derek speaking. "The civilized
world?" he was saying with a sardonic laugh. "Of
course they do. They disappear all the time! Anything
can be arranged, you see, with enough money." He
noticed the tide of panic clouding her eyes and assumed
it was because of what he was saying. "Don't be silly,
Diana. Of course you're not going to disappear. Once
the Derby's over, what possible harm could you do me?
I'll find the tape, and you can be sure that whatever
evidence you find in the trophy room will be long gone.
I'm only keeping it for purposes of persuasion. Do you
understand? Once the race is run and everyone does
the job they've been paid to do, then the evidence will
be destroyed, and you won't have a leg to stand on, as
they say in the stables."

"You miserable low-life, you . . ." Desolation made
her furious.

"Now, now, don't be nasty. This is just a little visit, I
promise." He smiled again, almost pleasantly. "A
gentleman never goes back on his word, so you don't
have to worry."

He took the key and inserted it in the heavy door,
which swung open with a protesting groan. Inside,
Diana could see nothing but stale gloom, and the musty
odor made her flinch. "If I have no hard evidence," she
said, trying to sound brave, "why don't you just let me
go on my merry way now?"

Derek looked at her without a glimmer of humor or

pity despite her desperate attempt at a swagger. His face was now a hard mask. "Don't be silly," he snapped. "I'm not a gambling man like some of these fools around here, Diana, and you know it. I've always stacked the odds in my favor. You're just another point on my side of the card."

And he slammed the door.

Chapter 12

"NO DEAD BODIES. WELL, THAT'S SOMETHING, I SUP-
pose."

She sat on a dusty bench with her chin in her hands,
blinking while her eyes adjusted to the blackness. Her
grim bravado was like a whistle in the dark; it didn't
remove the horror, but it helped her attitude about it.

Fortunately, the danger was not acute. She had
realized that much almost at once, with a rush of relief
so palpable that she had had to sit down. The room,
about fourteen feet square with a pitched roof filled
with cobwebbed beams, hid no lowering pendulum or
paid assassin as far as she could see. It was dirty, but
there was some ventilation from a slatted window near
the crux of the roof. When her heart had stopped
racing, she could hear faint sounds from outside—low
voices, muffled footsteps and finally the deep purr of a
car engine proceeding down the drive. Some light,
some sound, some air—the room had not been

built as a death chamber.

Ah, but it was still a prison. All the gruff humor in the world could not alter the damp chill of claustrophobia that settled along Diana's spine, making her shiver uncontrollably. "And what about food?" she inquired through chattering teeth. "Doesn't he realize I gave up breakfast in order to pour myself into this outfit?" She snorted in the direction of the heavy door. *"That* was a great idea. By the time I get out of here, this dress will be four sizes too big. Oh, whatever happened to the age of chivalry?"

As soon as she said it, she burst into tears. The age of chivalry—wasn't that what she had gone to such great lengths to deny? Wasn't that her main objection, her only objection, to Beauregard Gatling?

"Great, Diana. Not only did you manage to alienate the man you love, you big idiot, but you've ended up compromising your precious principles as well. Now you've got no principles and no man!" She pouted derisively and brushed away her tears with her fist. "And where did it get you? Into an abandoned garage for a two-day fast!" She grimaced and shook her head. "And we're not talking about La Costa here, either," she added dryly, her eyes scaling the dim, blank walls.

Somehow, though, her soliloquy was helping. It didn't make her feel any better about her immediate situation, but it did lift some weight off her mind to admit, out loud and without rancor, that she had made a mistake. What felt even better was to admit that she loved Beau.

She loved Beau. When she had said it that morning to Alison, it had been a lament. Now the words had a positive effect on her psyche. She loved someone. Despite the stress of her current situation, it was all falling into place with amazing ease. She *loved* him, pure and simple. The problems were still there, not the least of which was getting free, but the basic fact remained. She loved him, and she had to let him know, so he wouldn't think she had betrayed him with Derek Islington.

"I love Beauregard Gatling! Hah! I really love the guy!" She must sound like a fool, sitting there chuckling delightedly in the darkness. But then, there wasn't anyone around to hear her. Diana raised her voice to the rafters. "I love him! Do you understand what that means?" She lifted her hands into the dimness above her and clasped them victoriously together over her head. "That may be Diana's Folly," she yelled, "but there you have it!"

Then, as the echoes of her voice filtered back down around her ears, she drew both hands down and held them, palms up, in front of her. "His house is my house," she added in a reverent whisper, staring at her long fingers as if she had never seen them before. "And my heart is his."

Of course, that didn't solve the more practical aspects of Diana's folly. There was still the evidence to find and then the small matter of escape. After wasting several more hours in alternate states of fear, anger and sensuous reverie about Beau, Diana finally began to apply herself with her usual hardheaded determination.

The room was essentially empty. Several old benches lined the walls, and shelves ran around the length of the room high above them. Diana had to stand up on the rickety benches to grope around on the shelves, grimacing as her hands thrust into thick spider webs and age-encrusted jars and bottles.

It was between two of those bottles, about half way through her search, that Diana came across the scrawled receipts. They were written on index cards, all dated during the past three months. They all said the same thing: "I hereby declare that the monies I have paid to Judge B. K. Taupin in exchange for his special consideration were paid solely out of my own pocket and for my own purposes." Dr. Jeremiah Murphy's signature was barely visible at the bottom of each one.

"Talk about insurance," Diana breathed. She was sure that Dr. Murphy had similar blackmailing material hidden away somewhere on his own premises. Judge Taupin had probably taken care to do the same thing. Most likely all three men would agree to destroy the incriminating material once they had completed their job, just as they probably had when the new medical exam laws were made, when Islington's race-fixing conviction was overturned, and when Dark Star fell on the track. Derek Islington was right; he did stack the odds in his favor.

But the next thing she found was even more incriminating. Wedged behind two tall glass bottles, green with age, so that only the most determined fingers would detect their slim shapes, lay two syringes. They were long and blunted, rusty with age, but Diana had no doubt that they had once been used to inject medication into one of Derek's winners—maybe even Dark Star. Diana wondered if Derek even knew they were there. Perhaps one of his staff—Lou Belvedere?—had hidden them there as his own form of insurance, should the occasion ever arise.

The receipts were good enough, but Diana took the needles, too, just in case. Now that she had the proof she had wanted so badly, the need to escape intensified. The idea that Derek might get away with his scheme to fix the Derby was unthinkable to her. But how could she possibly get out? No windows, no ladders, and the benches would never support her weight to climb up to the slatted ventilation hole. Diana paced the floor for several more hours, jamming her fingers together in a frenzy of frustration.

The dim light was already fading to black when she began another exhaustive search for a means of escape.

So far, the only thing she had produced in the way of escape aids had been two lengths of leather bridle cord and a half-empty can of shellac. The bridle cord snapped into dusty shreds at the first tug, and she threw it on the ground in disgust. The shellac presented no possibilities at all.

"Oh," she moaned, rattling the door for the millionth time, "where are my trusty credit cards when I need them?" Suddenly, she stopped rattling, hit her forehead once against the door to berate her stupidity and set to work.

She broke four fingernails trying to pry it open and ruined Alison's expensive lizard belt by using it as a paintbrush. But in the end she managed to paint several of the index cards with enough layers of shellac to make them as hard as plastic, as hard as plastic credit cards. As she worked, Diana sent up a little prayer of thanks to the light-fingered Red Sox rookie who had taught her everything she knew about crime. "You've done me proud twice this week, Bobby," she muttered. "And I swear, when I get out of here, I'll give you a free course in the finer points of breaking and entering, not to mention getting back out again."

The worst part was waiting for the coats of shellac to dry. Diana blew on the cards until she was dizzy and nauseous, and the combination of shellac fumes, hunger and impatience led her to tears more than once. As far as she could judge the time, it was early evening by the time the cards were dry enough for use, and Diana stood for what seemed like hours at the door before she was confident that her escape would not be witnessed.

"This would never have happened in Manhattan." She grinned as she jimmied the bolt backward with the stiff card. The last time she had tried this trick, it had worked, but with mixed results. This time, there was a lot more to lose—and a lot more to gain, as well.

It worked. Easily, in fact. So easily that Diana stood in the doorway for several moments, convinced she was walking into a trap. Surely someone as clever as Derek Islington wouldn't be foolish enough to leave her unguarded in such a minimum-security situation. But then, Derek had searched her. And he didn't know about the shellac trick. "Not as clever as you think, eh, Mr. Islington?" Diana muttered to herself with great satisfaction as the door gave way. "Well, what do you expect from a two-bit hick?"

And she walked out of the deserted courtyard.

Chapter 13

THERE WAS ONLY ONE THING WRONG WITH HER COCKY plans, and when she discovered it, Diana could have kicked herself. The car was there, just as she had left it early that morning, but the distributor cap had been removed from its hiding place behind a tree. Even if Derek had been thoughtful enough to replace it after discovering it there, which of course he had not, Diana had neither her purse nor the car key.

She looked at the stiff index cards she held in her hand. "Is that all you're good for?" she said to them accusingly. "Opening doors? What about starting cars?"

It was a subject the light-fingered Bobby hadn't covered. Sadly, her own criminal ingenuity didn't cover it, either. Peering gloomily under the hood, Diana wasn't even sure she would have remembered where to replace the distributor cap even if she had had one.

"Jennings, you've got a lot to learn," she muttered, and set off on foot down the road to Louisville.

She had one more thing to learn: it was not early evening, as she had thought, but the middle of the night. As a matter of fact, by the time she got a sympathetic—and, mercifully, nonlecherous—milkman to deliver her to the Galt House on his way to work, it was close to three A.M.

For a moment, she stood in the lobby by the elevators, swaying slightly from tension and fatigue and toying with the idea of slipping straight up to her room and the peaceful blankness of sleep. But she sternly reminded herself that she had a story to write and that it was unlikely she would get any sleep, anyway, until she had seen Beau.

The question was would Beau see her? After his abrupt exit from the room the night before and the shock of seeing her at Derek's that morning, Diana had her doubts. Even if he did agree to talk to her, she wasn't sure she would know where to begin or what to say. Somehow, the explanations she was planning on giving and getting had seemed a lot clearer back in her little jail cell.

"Now, now," she cautioned herself, "if you're brave enough to escape from the clutches of one man, surely you're brave enough to throw yourself into the arms of another, aren't you? Well, aren't you?"

She stepped out of the elevator on Beau's floor and caught sight of her reflection in the mirror. It was not an encouraging sight. Not only did she not look brave, she looked downright disheveled. Her hair was half loose and covered with cobwebs, and her dress had faded to a nondescript pink from the dust and looked more smashed than smashing. Her eyes were dull with hunger and fatigue, and she reeked of shellac.

"Perfect," she said grimly, and knocked on his door.

He answered it so quickly that she jumped. He was fully dressed despite the hour, and the room was hung with overhead light and cigarette smoke. A faint swirl of bourbon was in the air.

"You're here!" she exclaimed loudly, suppressing a wild urge to turn and run. The confusion caused by his abrupt appearance sent her carefully planned speech flying out of her brain.

Beau's expression, on the other hand, expressed no surprise at Diana's appearance. Instead, he arched his brows and pursed his lips, looking beyond her to see if her voice had carried down the sleeping hallway. Then, when she looked suitably guilty for her outburst, he shook his head and shrugged.

"That's what you said the last time you appeared at my door," he observed. "Where else did you expect me to be at three A.M.?"

Diana shifted uncomfortably. The hall was drafty, but she didn't know if she was going to be invited in. "Well," she said lamely, "you did leave the room rather abruptly last night."

He shrugged again but didn't smile. "Yes, I did, but I came back after I had cooled off a little bit. You, on the other hand, did not. As a matter of fact, you don't look like you've been home in quite a while." He sniffed the air. "What's that funny smell?"

"You know damn well where I've been all day," she said insolently. "Or, rather, you think you do. But you don't know the half of it."

"I'll bet I don't." He leaned against the doorway, framed by cigarette smoke and bright light, staring at her as if she were a stranger. Diana once again considered turning around and walking away. She was dying to tell him what she had found out, but maybe it wasn't worth it if he wasn't even going to listen. She would just write the story herself and *then* let him see how he felt! All her emotions were once again in turmoil. What had seemed so clear and simple at Fleur D'Isle had become, in the space of a few seconds, a seemingly insurmountable problem. How could they have a relationship if they were always worlds apart?

She had, in fact, started to turn away without being

aware of it. But Beau reached out and yanked her into
the room with such force that she stumbled. He stead-
ied her with a firm grip on both shoulders and slammed
the door shut with his foot.

"Oh, no you don't," he hissed furiously. "I've been
sitting in this room for twelve hours going crazy with
worry over you, not even sure if I should bother and
trying to make sense of this mess you've gotten us
into."

"*I've* gotten us into!"

He ignored her. "And you're not leaving this room
until I get a full explanation. I deserve that much at
least after what I've been through for you."

"What *you've* been—"

"What were you doing in his house at eight A.M.,
dressed to kill? Tell me!"

He gave her a little shake before releasing her.

His violence stripped Diana of her last vestige of
control. Instead of explaining in the rational fashion
she had planned, instead of confessing her love to Beau
and appealing to his humor and understanding, she
began to shriek like a madwoman in his face.

"What *you've* been through for *me*? What *I've* gotten
you into? And who the hell are you? Who told you to
go traipsing around like some two-bit snoop, rescuing
that damned cassette like it was a damsel in distress? I
didn't see you hanging around to rescue *me* when you
saw me in Derek's living room. All that talk about how
dangerous he was, and you take off like a scared rabbit!
Why didn't you help me?"

"I didn't think you wanted my help—or needed it, at
that point," he snapped.

"Oh, you didn't, did you? Some chivalry! You didn't
wait around to see what was really going on, did you?
No, you were too busy saving your own skin! And
that's another thing! Do you realize how stupid, how
completely *insane*, it was for you to be snooping around
there like that? At least I had some semblance of an

excuse. He doesn't hate my guts—or he didn't then.
But you! You scurry over there like Robin Hood, like
you're out on a morning lark. Do you realize how close
you came to getting caught? Do you think Derek would
have just tipped his hat and let you go? My God, he
would have *killed* you!"

"Diana . . ."

"Do you have any idea how serious the situation is
with that man? Do you know what sort of games he's
playing? Are you *crazy?*"

She stopped only because she had run out of breath.
The sheer irrelevance of what she was saying didn't
bother her in the least. She was unleashing a stream of
pure emotion at that point, and the fact that it was
coming out all garbled made no difference in the world.

Her face was only inches from his, and she could feel
the heat of her own rapid breathing reflected off it.
Beau blinked several times, and the pupils of his eyes
dilated into invisible pinpoints in the dark depths of his
irises. Diana could see her own reflection mirrored in
them, grossly distorted, but, she thought, clearly mad.

If she was mad, however, what Beau did next was
certifiable. He stared at her for a moment, opened his
mouth and laughed and laughed.

"Beau!" She took a step backward involuntarily and
put her hands on her hips. "Beau, stop it!" Diana
wondered if he had really snapped; fleetingly, she
looked at the bottle of bourbon on his desk to see if he
was drunk. No, only an inch or two was gone from the
bottle. He *had* snapped, then.

He stood between her and the door, so there was no
chance of escape. As he continued laughing, slapping
his hands together and letting tears run down his
cheeks, something strange began to happen to her. Her
hysterical anger and worry became infected by his
merriment, and she found herself unable to suppress a
grin of her own. She didn't know why, but soon she was
smiling, too.

Beau, catching sight of her face, managed to croak out, "Diana! Don't you realize what you just said? What it means?"

She didn't realize what she had said, not yet, but somehow she knew that it meant everything was going to work out, after all. There was still a lot of explaining to do, a story to write and possibly even a call to the authorities to be made. For the moment, it was enough to be standing there at three A.M. on the morning of the Kentucky Derby, laughing like maniacs from sheer relief.

By the time the telephone jangled, they were laughing so hard that they didn't hear it until at least the twelfth ring. Beau picked it up, but he couldn't even manage to say hello. They both listened in, doubled up with giggles, as a severe voice from the front desk told them to keep it down.

There was only one way to stop it, and they both hit on it at the same time. Without a word, they were suddenly locked in an embrace that made laughter impossible. It was all Diana could do to catch her breath as they fell onto the bed with a simultaneous moan of relief.

A moment before, Diana had been tired, confused and even irrational. Now, as Beau's lips met hers in an electric flash, she felt energized, clearheaded and, without a doubt, ready to declare her love. Their bodies had always been accurate barometers of their passion. Now they would be instruments for communicating their commitment as well. Diana was glad that words had failed her. What better way to express herself than with her new-found body english?

She had no idea that the vocabulary could be so varied within the limited range of a kiss. But now she found herself exploring the infinite ways in which she could press her mouth to his, all of them providing a new sensation and a new insight for them both. Following the aftershock of their first kiss, which had molded their mouths together so closely that Diana could feel the convex imprint of each of Beau's teeth against her own, the pressure decreased. Now their lips met as lightly as possible, so that only a minimum of contact was made. But that touch was excruciatingly stirring. Diana felt every nerve in her body focused on a narrow pinpoint of feeling in the center of her lower lip, sending complicated impressions of heat and light all the way down her body. Even her fingers tingled and ached to lace into Beau's ragged curls. But she forced herself to keep her hands still at her side, pressed under the weight of Beau's body beside her. There would be a time for fingers, arms, legs, bodies, later on. Part of the pleasure was in the waiting.

When it seemed that the single spot on her mouth was swollen beyond endurance by Beau's laserlike touch, Diana began to move her mouth in minute increments around the surface of his. Each kiss was small and singular, and each one told a different story of her love for him and his for her. One was short and ticklish, reminding her of the delicious laughter they had shared. The next was lingering and faintly bittersweet, saying that the pain they had been through was worth the trouble. Then, on the outermost corners of his mouth, she placed a firm, hungry cry for more and nibbled her way eagerly back to the center.

Now it was Beau's turn, and Diana felt the subtle switch in their energies with a surge of joy. *This* was what loving was all about, not the hungry acquisition of satisfaction, and being lonely, without companionship or understanding. Not the competitive jockeying for identity, the frustration without sympathy. For the first time in her life, Diana was able to reap the benefits of her own strengths by sharing them equally with a man of different strengths.

Beau's lips wandered from her mouth and across the broad planes of her cheeks and brow, decorating her with sensation and leaving a trail of colored lights along

the slope of her chin and onto her neck. He had begun
to use his fingers now, but lightly, playing them like soft
rain across her forehead and darting with sweet hunger
into the forest of her hair. Tremulously, Diana raised
her arms and began brushing the tips of her fingers
across Beau's shoulders. Even through his flannel shirt,
she could feel the ripples of his muscles as they
quivered with anticipation.

The time had come to remove the encumbrances of
their clothing. Beau stood up and held out his hand to
help Diana rise as well. Standing only inches apart,
their eyes blazing beams of desire across the narrow
separation, they began to undress without touching one
another, for they knew it was not yet time. Working
slowly, they moved like mirror images, lifting their
arms to their shoulders and then to their hips without
looking at what they were doing and using only one
another's eyes as guides. It was an exercise in concentration and self-control.

Once they stood naked together, the urge to fling
herself against his shining body was almost too much
for Diana to bear, and she saw that Beau was struggling
with the same desire. But still it was not time. At the
same moment, they each took a step apart. In the
bright glare of the overhead light, Beau's body stood
out in sharp relief. The crevices of muscle and the
shadows of soft body hair were dark and velvety, while
the surface of his skin glowed with perspiration. He
stood very still, but she noticed a faint twitch in the
sculpted curve of his left breastbone. His arms seemed
to be straining to stay at his side.

With infinite patience and luxury, Diana was able to
chronicle the movements of her lover's body. The
strong lights did not detract from his allure. As her eyes
devoured every inch of his flesh, she could feel her
nipples hardening, aching for his touch. A sharp, liquid
rush flashed across her loins and down her thighs,
making her legs weak. Beau's groin trembled as well,

and as he grew before her, she saw the smallest tremor escape his smoky gaze.

Then Beau spoke. At first, Diana's instinct was to spring forward and silence him with her mouth on his. But then she realized that part of the pleasure was in prolonging the moment until nothing else remained to be seen or said. They had made their vows with their lips and eyes. Now they might try words. For Diana, who had finally begun to examine the limits of her own needs and found Beau waiting there, words had become merely another source of sensation.

"It's not time yet," he murmured, his eyes narrowed in an effort to contain himself while he spoke.

"But soon?"

"Soon." A lazy grin appeared, a little lopsided but disarming. "Can you wait?"

Diana couldn't trust herself to smile, but her eyes lit up. "Why not? We've got all the time in the world, haven't we?"

"At the very least," Beau replied, but she could see him digging his nails deeply into the palm of his hand to hold himself back.

Diana didn't even bother to mention the other pressing issue they had to attend to—that of Derek Islington. For once, her priorities were firmly in place, and she planned to let them stay that way. There was too much to think about right here. "It's . . . it's like it's the first time, you know?" she said, clearing her throat nervously. She wasn't used to talking about her innermost feelings that way. "I mean, the first time . . . for us." She was only mildly surprised that she was having more trouble expressing herself in words than in gestures.

He nodded slightly. "It is, in a way. It's the first time we're sure—both of us." A faint whisper of uncertainty muted his smile. "You are sure, aren't you, Diana?"

Her lips parted, and she stared at him blankly before shaking her head. "Look at me," she pleaded. "Look at you. Can you doubt my desire?'' As if to underscore her urgent words, her body gave an involuntary shudder.

Beau smiled. ''I never doubted that. But you know what we are, you and I. Love can change the way you look at the world, but it can't change the world. It can't change us, Diana. We are what we always have been, perhaps what we always will be. Can you accept that?''

''We're more than that,'' she insisted hoarsely. A line of sweat was traveling down Beau's chest, getting tangled in the soft hairs of his belly and loins. Diana couldn't take her eyes off it, and her mouth was thick and dry. ''We are what we can learn from each other—about ourselves, I mean. Love can change the way you look at yourself. And you've opened up a whole new world of possibilities for me. I can live with that—and with you.''

Beau's eyes looked suddenly misty; whether from tension or emotion, she couldn't tell. But his voice was clear and gentle. ''You don't know how I've waited and hoped to hear that, Diana. For a while this morning, I never thought I would.''

Diana swallowed and waited to see if he was going to say anything more. She had run out of words, and her physical desire had become a blinding need. When Beau didn't continue, she drew in her breath with a quick hiss. ''So why don't we just shut up and love each other?'' she demanded through clenched teeth.

She could see Beau's throat tighten. ''Dah-anna,'' he muttered, scooping her against him fiercely. ''I was just being liberated and waiting for you to make the first move.''

''Very funny. Beau, oh, God, you feel so good!'' They fell back onto the bed with dizzying abandon.

''You feel so right,'' Beau whispered; then he bent his head and laid his mouth hungrily over her mound. Diana curled around him until her face was buried in the throbbing warmth of his loins. She began to trace swift circles against the grain of the hairs on his belly with her tongue but soon found that she was unable to do anything but concentrate on the flame that Beau was building inside her with his mouth and hands. Even breathing was difficult, and when she finally pulled him up and wrapped her legs around his back, they were both drenched in sweat.

The carefully measured portions of arousal had gotten out of control and become a deluge of need. Beads of water flicked off Beau's forehead and shone like crystals in the damp curls as he swung above her. He bent now and then to lick salty pools from between Diana's breasts, but Diana barely noticed. She was unable to separate the parts of her body from his and had no idea what their individual limbs and lips were doing, nor did it matter to her. All that mattered was clinging together and letting the moment go beyond any imaginable limits. Nothing either of them did made any difference now. They raced toward a mutual climax, unable to direct or slow the action. All their skill and caution were forgotten. They were two bodies with one thought and one thought only—to reach the peak together.

It seemed like hours afterward that they remained locked into their contorted embrace—Diana wrapped crablike around Beau's torso and his body pressed around hers like a cup. They still rocked slightly with the remembered rhythm of their ascent, and the bed beneath them seemed to be vibrating from the storm.

Finally, with one toe, Beau reached out and hooked a runaway blanket, pulling it over both of them so that they lay cloistered in a pool of woolly blue light. Groaning slightly, they adjusted themselves reluctantly and opened their eyes to confront one another.

"You," mumbled Beau between sleepy kisses, "are incredible. Do you know that?"

Diana chuckled, delighted at the way Beau's head

bobbed slightly on the warm pillow of her breasts. "I sure do now."

"I never imagined a prickly northern pear could be so full of warm, ripe loving."

"Imagine *my* surprise," she reminded him.

He looked up, and she ran her fingers lightly along the narrow plane of his nose. "Are you really surprised?" he inquired. "Didn't you know what tremendous potential you had?"

Diana gave the question serious thought, insofar as she was capable of that process in her current state of nirvana. "I guess I always knew deep down how great I could be," she admitted at last.

"And the very soul of modesty to boot." Beau tweaked one nipple playfully between his lips.

"Well, you asked, didn't you?" She gave his nose a gentle pinch. "Of course, I did need a little old-fashioned honest-to-goodness southern charm to bring out the best in me."

"Why, thank you, ma'am," he drawled. "It weren't nothin', believe you me." He laughed. "Like pulling teeth, that's all."

"Beauuu!"

"Dah-aannna!"

Chanting their now-familiar litany of names in sing-song harmony, they wrestled intimately beneath the blanket for a while until the air became hot and steamy. Then, just as Beau was beginning to look ready for another passion play, Diana yanked the blanket off and exposed them both to the glare of the overhead light and chilly air.

"Hey!" Beau yelped, and huddled on top of her for warmth. "What's the big idea? It's my turn to lead!"

"Nope." She shook her head and wriggled out from beneath him, sliding over to the edge of the bed and fumbling among their discarded clothes on the floor.

Beau looked down at himself with a rueful sigh.

"Nope is right," he muttered. "Not after that sudden exposure. What's the big idea, anyway?" he complained.

Diana lay back against him, hiding something against her chest. "I have something else in mind," she purred. "Something much more romantic and intimate."

He grinned and snuggled closer. "Really? Terrific! Tell me what." He gave a delicious wriggle of anticipation.

Diana flipped the index cards and the two needles out in front of him. "This!" she said triumphantly.

Beau's eyes widened as he reached around her shoulders to pull the cards into view. He took them from her, and she laid the syringes carefully on the bedside table. "Lady," he whispered, "this is about the sexiest thing I've seen in a long time."

"You know what they are?"

He nodded. "Where on earth did you get them? And how?"

Diana snatched them out of his grip and held them away. "You're the super sleuth," she teased. "You guess."

Beau leaned back against the headboard and pretended to ponder, although Diana knew he was only flaunting his fabulous body full-length before her. She deliberately averted her gaze. "Well?" she prompted.

"Well, I know where you got them. That key I left on the table, right? Boy, it was a good thing I didn't take it, huh?"

She shook her head. "Well, it was good, and it was bad. But you still haven't guessed how I got the proof."

"I don't have to. I'm sure Derek Islington took one look at you in that illegal pink dress and confessed all."

"Illegal? Boy, that dress makes the same impression on everyone, doesn't it?"

"It made quite an impression on me, that's for sure. If you could have seen the picture you made, silhouetted against those fancy French windows—like you belonged there, you know?''

"You should have seen the picture *you* made! But Beau, did you really think I was there as Derek's . . . guest?''

"I didn't know what to think. I don't even know why I insisted on going out there to get that damn cassette, if you want to know the truth. I guess just to prove to you that I meant what I said. Anyway, when I saw you, I tried to tell myself that it didn't matter, that I didn't care about what happened to either of you.'' He laughed ruefully, reaching out to smooth her tangled hair. "Spent the better part of the day trying to convince myself of that.''

"Poor baby.'' She reached up to stroke his hair, dropping a kiss on his extended arm.

"But what happened? What did the key lead to? What doors did it open?''

She chuckled. "The door to trouble, that's what.''

Beau sat up. "Did her hurt you? Because if he did—''

"Beau, relax. I'm here now, right?''

"What did he do to you?'' Beau demanded.

"Really, it wasn't anything . . .'' Diana sighed and corrected herself. "Yes, yes it was. It was awful. He locked me in that guard room outside the main house. He was going to keep me in there until the Derby was over. Then he was going to destroy those receipts, and . . . let me go.''

Beau listened in silence. Then he slammed his head back against the headboard with such violence that Diana winced and let out a stream of obscenities.

"Beau, Beau . . . stop it! Please!''

He brought himself under control with an effort. "I can't believe I let you go through that alone. I ought to go out there and strangle the bastard right now.''

"Not so fast. I escaped, and I'd rather he didn't know it just yet. Besides, you and I have a story to write. We have it all, now—the receipts, the syringes, the cassette."

"I still don't understand," said Beau, looking not at all convinced that he should not be out stalking Derek with a hunting gun. "How did you know what to look for? How did you know where to look? How did Derek find you? And how in the hell did you get out?"

Diana grinned. "Didn't they ever teach you to ask questions one at a time in journalism school?"

He made a face. "I flunked out of journalism school. Now tell me everything. Don't leave out one detail, do you hear?"

So she told him the whole story—from her initial decision to pursue an interview with Derek right up to her ingenious use of shellac for the escape. She left out nothing, not even the feelings of anger and frustration she had felt toward Beau when he had attempted to interfere. It was important to her that he know all that, important to their future together.

Whenever Diana reached a point in the story where she had jumped to a conclusion without facts, Beau was able to supply what she needed. He had gotten out his old files on the Islington case, and they were strewn around the room. Together, as the night grew to a close, they managed to flesh out the bones of an amazing tale, implicating Islington, Taupin and Murphy in a race-fixing scheme involving Street Fare.

"I'm sure you have enough here to pull Street Fare from the race this afternoon, not to mention putting old Derek in the hot seat," said Beau. It was almost dawn, and Diana, wrapped toga style in a bed sheet, was sitting at Beau's desk typing the last few paragraphs of the story. Beau had changed to a bath towel, and he was pacing the room, thinking aloud. "Once the police get these receipts and the needles, they won't have any trouble convincing Taupin and Murphy to spill the beans." He came and stood over her while she worked, and she could still detect his warm, smoky body scent. "I'll call my friends downtown while you finish your story."

"Correction," she said, craning her neck to smile up at him. "Our story."

"What do you mean?"

"I said, our story. Joint by-line in both papers. It *is* our story, Beau."

Beau stood up, put both hands on Diana's bare shoulders and swiveled her around in the chair. "Diana, listen to me. He knelt down in front of her. "I made you a promise once. And I don't break promises" —He wrinkled his nose at her quick look—"unless my beloved's safety is at stake, that is."

"I didn't notice you charging into Derek's living room when your beloved's safety was really in jeopardy," she pointed out cheerfully.

"For which I will never forgive myself," he rejoined promptly. "But by then I had managed to convince myself that your story was more important to you than your skin—and certainly more important than me."

"Well, you were wrong then, and you're wrong now." She stood up, pulling him up with her, and wrapped both arms around his neck. "We've both learned our lessons, don't you think? I learned about trusting you, and you learned about believing in me." She kissed the tip of his chin, and he inclined his head to drop a kiss on the bridge of her nose. "And that," she said, leaning back to look into his smiling eyes, "is why I'm absolutely sure it should be our story, in answer to your question. It's a way of declaring my commitment to you and to the whole world. I want everybody to know Diana Jennings doesn't work alone anymore. We're a team now, right?"

He pulled her back against him. "Are you kidding? Half the press corps in America must know it by now. We've been holed up in here together so many times

I'm surprised they haven't switched the Kentucky Derby to room 919!"

Diana rested against him and smiled dreamily out at the silvery sky. "They could," she pointed out. "They've got Diana's Folly right out there in front, don't they?" She chuckled and heard the answering rumble from within his chest. "Well, let them talk. I don't care. You and I are the hottest duet since Woodward and Bernstein."

"Honey," Beau drawled, lifting her up slightly so that her bare feet grazed the floor as he walked them over to the bed, "Woodward and Bernstein had nothing on us."

She looked down in feigned surprise as he unwrapped her sheet and let his towel fall to the floor. "Well, they certainly didn't have our fashion flair for working attire, that's for sure."

"They didn't have another flair, either," he growled demonically, pulling her on top of him.

"Beau, what about our deadline? Don't you want to call your friends downtown? They'll probably want to make some arrests or something."

"They probably would," said Beau, nuzzling her, "but I don't want to be arrested."

"Not us. Islington!"

"Who's that?"

"This is gonna shoot our deadline all to hell." Diana chuckled, giving in without much of a fight. "But then, when you're a media star, who cares?"

"Who cares, anyway?" His eyes were closed as he stroked the cool skin of her buttocks with his warm hands. "The next race is about to begin." He opened his eyes and smiled. "Wanna try for another tie?"

Get 6 new Silhouette Special Editions every month for a 15-day FREE trial!

Free Home Delivery, Free Previews, Free Bonus Books.
Silhouette Special Editions are a new kind of romance novel. These are big, powerful stories that will capture your imagination. They're longer, with fully developed characters and intricate plots that will hold you spell-bound from the first page to the very last.

Each month we will send you six exciting *new* Silhouette Special Editions, just as soon as they are published. If you enjoy them as much as we think you will, pay the invoice enclosed with your shipment. **They're delivered right to your door with never a charge for postage or handling, and there's no obligation to buy anything at any time.** To start receiving Silhouette Special Editions regularly, mail the coupon below today.

Silhouette Special Edition

Silhouette
Intimate Moments

more romance, more excitement
—— $2.25 each ——

- \# 1 ☐ DREAMS OF EVENING
  Kristin James
- \# 2 ☐ ONCE MORE WITH FEELING
  Nora Roberts
- \# 3 ☐ EMERALDS IN THE DARK
  Beverly Bird
- \# 4 ☐ SWEETHEART CONTRACT
  Pat Wallace
- \# 5 ☐ WIND SONG
  Parris Afton Bonds
- \# 6 ☐ ISLAND HERITAGE
  Monica Barrie
- \# 7 ☐ A DISTANT CASTLE
  Sue Ellen Cole
- \# 8 ☐ LOVE EVERLASTING
  Moëth Allison
- \# 9 ☐ SERPENT IN PARADISE
  Stephanie James
- \#10 ☐ A SEASON OF RAINBOWS
  Jennifer West
- \#11 ☐ UNTIL THE END OF TIME
  June Trevor
- \#12 ☐ TONIGHT AND ALWAYS
  Nora Roberts

- \#13 ☐ EDGE OF LOVE
  Anna James
- \#14 ☐ RECKLESS SURRENDER
  Jeanne Stephens
- \#15 ☐ SHADOW DANCE
  Lorraine Sellers
- \#16 ☐ THE PROMISE OF SUMMER
  Barbara Faith
- \#17 ☐ THE AMBER SKY
  Kristin James
- \#18 ☐ THE DANVERS TOUCH
  Elizabeth Lowell
- \#19 ☐ ANOTHER KIND OF LOVE
  Mary Lynn Baxter
- \#20 ☐ THE GENTLE WINDS
  Monica Barrie
- \#21 ☐ RAVEN'S PREY
  Stephanie James
- \#22 ☐ AGAINST THE RULES
  Linda Howard
- \#23 ☐ THE FIRES OF WINTER
  Beverly Bird
- \#24 ☐ FANTASIES
  Pamela Wallace

Silhouette Intimate Moments

more romance, more excitement

#25 ☐ THIS MAGIC MOMENT
Nora Roberts

#26 ☐ OLD LOVE, NEW LOVE
Jane Clare

#27 ☐ DIANA'S FOLLY
Jillian Blake

#28 ☐ WALTZ IN SCARLET
Muriel Bradley

**LOOK FOR *ENDINGS AND BEGINNINGS*
BY NORA ROBERTS
AVAILABLE IN JANUARY AND
INTERESTED PARTIES BY BROOKE HASTINGS
IN FEBRUARY.**

Silhouette Intimate Moments

Coming Next Month

A Secret Splendor by Erin St. Claire

Arden Lowery knew that the mystery of birth could be surrounded by half-truths, secrets and unspeakable lies. With that knowledge, she set out to find the man who had fathered her baby and the love that had been too long denied her.

Race Against The Wind by Sue Ellen Cole

It had been hard enough for Sabina to gain respect as a female jockey in a race run by men, but now the man who was her lover off the track was her fiercest competitor on it.

Star Spangled Days by Jennifer West

Leigh Farrar was an opera singer, yet her own husband, Laszlo Koltai, seemed determined to resist her song and follow the call of his own tormented past—a past that only her love could lay to rest.

Dangerous Paradise by Joanna Kenyon

When Stephanie was sent to interview a reclusive writer, it seemed to be just another assignment, though perhaps more interesting than most. But the moment she met David Harding, she found herself in danger—danger which threatened her life and her heart.

Enjoy love and passion, larger than life!

Now that you know Silhouette Intimate Moments, let them take you into the world of your dreams... and beyond... each month.

Start with a 15-day free trial!

Once you've read Silhouette Intimate Moments, we think you'll agree that they're so full of love and excitement, it's hard to put one down! We've developed these books for a special kind of reader—one who isn't afraid to be swept away by passion and adventure.

The characters in all the Silhouette Intimate Moments novels lead thrilling lives—and their feelings are as real and intimate as yours. So you'll share all the joys and sorrows of each heroine.

Enjoy the convenience of free home delivery...

First, we'll send you 4 books to look over for 15 days. If you're not delighted, simply return them and owe nothing. But if you enjoy them as much as you enjoyed this book, just pay the invoice and we'll send 4 Silhouette Intimate Moments novels right to your door every month. There's never a charge for this extra service—we pay all postage and handling costs.

Mail the coupon below today. And soon you'll receive romance novels that capture your imagination and carry you away to the world you've always dreamed of!